He saw the glow ...

The old tank was bathed in a cold, blue light, growing stronger and pulsating almost in rhythm with his pounding heart. He took a few staggering steps backward, still not believing his eyes. Then, he saw it move.

The ancient gun tube rose slightly, shaking off the last of its woodland crypt, and swung a few degrees to the left. Murphy screamed as the muzzle blast knocked him down. Searing pain shot through his head. He could see the M-60 burning. Tongues of orange flame boiled from the naked turret ring and engine bay. Someone was screaming. Jackson was a charred, blackened skeleton, with hollow holes where his eyes had been and bony arms upraised, frozen in death halfway out of the driver's hatch.

* * *

PANZER
SPIRIT

PANZER SPIRIT

TOM TOWNSEND

PAGEANT BOOKS

PAGEANT BOOKS
225 Park Avenue South
New York, New York 10003

Excerpts from *The Fellowship of the Ring*,
by J.R.R. Tolkien,
copyright © 1965 by J.R.R. Tolkien. Reprinted
by permission of Houghton Mifflin Company.

PAGEANT and colophon are trademarks of the publisher

Cover artwork by Franco Accornero

Printed in the U.S.A.

First Pageant Books printing: December, 1988

10 9 8 7 6 5 4 3 2 1

FOR CHUCK . . .
Through all the little wars; a dangerous adversary and friend.

And for Esther, who kept the faith.

ACKNOWLEDGMENTS

My special thanks go to the American–Scandinavian Foundation for their permission to use parts of Mr. Henry Adams Bellows fine English translation of the *Elder Edda*.

And to Houghton Mifflin Company for their permission to use lines from J. R. R. Tolkien's *The Fellowship of the Ring*.

Prologue

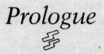

THE LAST COW was still somewhere downrange when the old German decided that it was too dark to keep looking. Cold twilight hung over the valley like a damp sponge, and although the first snow had yet to fall, it could not be far away. Karl Leiter walked tiredly up the path toward home. He would miss this little valley where his cows had grazed since the last war. It was as if history had turned a full circle in the forty years since he had come home from the internment camps and begun to regather the remnants of his life.

The panzers had fought in this forest at the war's end; a horrible battle of which he knew little. He remembered the valley when it was littered with rusting, burned-out hulks; when broken, splintered trees had just begun to sprout new leaves, and the spring rains tried to erase the ruts of steel treads.

The stale stench of death had faded then to a subtle, sickening sweet odor; an invisible fog in spring and summer.

Four decades of changing seasons had reduced all but the deepest craters to shallow depressions. The tank tracks were gone and the odor of death was only an eternal memory. Once again, the pines had grown tall and strong. One by one, the wrecked panzers had been dragged away to be cut up for scrap or used as targets on the American Army's firing ranges at nearby Grafenwöhr.

All except one.

Now the U.S. Army had leased Karl Leiter's land to extend their training area. Once again the forest would be shot to pieces, the fields bombarded and plowed with the tracks of armored vehicles. Again, it would look as it had when he came home from the war. He was glad that he would not be here to see it. But the price had been right and Karl was getting old, too old to chase wandering cows about the forest at twilight. He smiled. Some things are eternal. The panzers had fought here. Nature healed her wounds, and now new panzers would come. What, he wondered, would become of that last old tank?

Around a bend in the trail, he paused and looked into the darkening woods for a long minute. Then he nodded and stepped into the trees.

He would say good-bye.

Reverently, he picked his way through the trees as if he were approaching the temple of some sleeping god of old. The forest had grown up around the tank, laying it to rest beneath a burial mound of dead limbs and pine needles. In the twilight, beneath the mantle of brush, it was a gray, vague shadow of what it had once been. Perhaps that was why the Americans had never found it.

Karl thought this tank had been called a *Jagd-panther*, a tank built especially to hunt other tanks; sleek and turretless, heavily armored and fast. Like their namesake, the panthers had killed from ambush and faded into the forests to kill again and again.

Its gun barrel drooped beneath the funeral shroud. Karl brushed away a few pine needles and patted one steel fender. Mustard-yellow battle paint had faded to a color of dirt. The hatches had always been closed and Karl had never tried to open them. He had seen enough death during the war. Whatever was inside, he did not want to explore. There could be few ways to die any worse than inside a tank. Searing flames would instantly consume the oxygen. Hydraulic oil would ignite. Then the ammunition, always stored with the warheads pointed menacingly at the crew, would explode. To see inside held no interest for him. Perhaps it was the grave of German soldiers; perhaps it had simply been abandoned. It mattered not.

Karl stood in silence before the old hulk; then suddenly, he wanted to see the crest one last time. With nervous fingers, he pushed away some dirt from the sloping bow. His pulse quickened as the painted face on the red shield smiled wickedly up at him. He had never been sure whether it was a dwarf or an elf, or some other ancient forest spirit. The ears were pointed and its smile leered with sharp teeth and curling lips. The eyes were red and wolflike behind heavy brows, and below the face were the twin lightning bolts of the SS. It was odd that the paint had never faded.

"Well, Old Panzer. Once again the Americans are coming," Karl whispered. "I would guess you gave them hell the last time, but I think now there is not much fight left in you." The painted face smiled back at him and for one millisecond seemed to sneer, "Wrong, old man, wrong."

He reburied the crest, patted the dented fender one last time, and turned away. *"Auf Wiedersehen,"* he said, and started for home. When he reached the trail, he looked back once. The darkness was complete now. In the trees he fancied there was a dim glow, bluish and barely discernible. He blinked once and it remained. "Witch lights," he whispered to reassure himself; only the phosphorus glow of decaying wood and plants, nothing more. He turned away and started up the path for home. "Farewell," he whispered and began to hum the drumming notes of *"Panzer Lied,"* a stirring old march of the German armored divisions that had not crossed his lips in forty years.

Chapter One

⚡⚡

"DRIVER, HALT," Sergeant Hank Murphy yelled into his tank's intercom. Beneath him, 106,000 pounds of M-60A3 main battle tank rocked on its hydraulic suspension and came to a sudden stop.

"Where the hell are we, Sarge?" Private Jackson, the driver, called back sarcastically over the earphones.

"What do you think I'm tryin' to figure out? This damned map was made in 1945," Murphy answered as he banged open the cupola hatch. Snowflakes drifted onto his face and melted in little wet spots on the acetate cover of his old map. Ahead of him was a trail junction which did not show on the map. The right fork continued along the low ridge west of Tank Table Six on the Grafenwöhr Range. The left fork dropped into a little wooded valley.

"Lieutenant's gonna be pissed as hell if we don't

catch up with the platoon pretty soon," the driver said.

"Fuck the chickenshit lieutenant and fuck you, too. If you'd checked the goddamned end connectors, we wouldn't have spent half the morning freezing our asses off putting a tread back on this beast."

The loader's hatch came open beside him and Private Sanchez appeared without his helmet on. "I think we go to the right, Sergeant."

"How would you know, greaseball?"

Sanchez shrugged. "I don't know. I jus' think it's right."

Murphy glared at the loader. It seemed like there was everything but real Americans in the U.S. Army now. If they weren't black, they were Mexican or Puerto Rican, and half of them couldn't even speak English. They didn't know shit, they didn't want to know shit, and if you tried to pound some sense into them, they went running to the judge advocate screaming "racial discrimination," which were the only English words that they all could pronounce without an accent. Fuck the army.

"Move it out, Jackson, left turn," he said.

"It's the other way, Sarge," the driver argued in his ear.

"Shut up and move out." The tank lurched forward, dug in the left tread, and headed down into the valley.

The forest was a black silhouette against a sky of slate gray. Snow covered a trail which showed no sign of use in many years. Secretly, Murphy had almost believed that the other trail was the correct way to go. But he chose the left by applying his own proven rule of military logic: "Anything a private says has to be wrong."

Towering pines rose higher above him and the trail narrowed. The sky dwindled to only a narrow strip of snowflake-dotted gray above the jagged, toothlike treetops. The M-60 ground slowly through the falling snow, leaving a pair of dark, ugly tracks in its wake.

Sergeant Murphy had been in the army for seven years. Too late for Vietnam, he had never seen combat and sometimes it bothered him. Life was one training exercise after another, interrupted by the dull, endless routine of tank maintenance. He supposed he should be thankful that he was not getting shot at. Duty in West Germany might be dull and the pay terrible, but it was relatively safe.

"Sarge?" the driver again. "Wouldn't it have been the shits to hunt Kraut armor down a road like this back in World War II? Man, this is an ambush valley if I ever saw it."

"I imagine some GIs did just that. And in a goddamned old Sherman with beer-can armor and a BB gun." The driver locked one tread and eased the M-60 around a narrow turn, plowing up a half-dozen small trees in the process. Murphy was bitching at him for scratching the paint when a glow in the woods caught his eye. "Hey, stop the tank," he ordered.

Within the black curtain of forest, there was a bluish glow, pulsating softly in the winter gloom. Murphy squinted his eyes and decided he was seeing things. There was something there, a mound, maybe a bunker, but whatever it was, it had to be old to be so overgrown. "Jackson, you see that?"

"See what, Sarge?"

"In the woods. Looks like a bunker or maybe an old tank."

"Great," Jackson answered sarcastically. "If it's

an old tank, it's probably a target and that means we've wandered off downrange and may be fixin' to get our asses blown off."

"Naw, this ain't no impact area. Shut it down. I want to have a look." Murphy was already on the ground when the big diesel went silent. Jackson's head was out of the driver's hatch. "You want to come?" Murphy asked.

"Not me, Sarge, just wake me up when you get through," Jackson replied, and his head disappeared into the tank's hull.

Murphy walked toward the trees. New snow had filtered down through the pines to cover the forest floor. His spit-polished boots crunched ominously, disturbing the heavy silence. Ahead was a strange mound, unnatural and speckled with white in the eternal twilight of the forest. A feeling of foreboding swept over him and suddenly he wanted to turn back. Unseen eyes seemed to watch his every step, coaxing him onward, closer and closer, until there was no longer any doubt that the dim outline beneath the forest debris was a tank.

He began pulling at the larger limbs. They broke away in his hands. Dead pine boughs disintegrated to the touch as he exposed first the muzzle brake and then the gun tube. In another few seconds he had cleared the sloping, frontal armor. He backed away in awe.

"Holy shit," he whispered. "A goddamned Kraut tank. The son of a bitch must've been sittin' here ever since '45."

Visions of war souvenirs danced in his head. Luger pistols worth an easy five hundred bucks, medals and uniform parts, Zeiss binoculars, and who knows what other goodies might be inside, just waiting to be picked up and sold to dumb-ass GIs who liked that shit. With new interest he pulled away more brush looking for hatches. The goodies would of course be inside, if there were any. If it had already been stripped, then the hatches would probably be open and there would be nothing left but scrap metal.

There was no driver's hatch, so he began climbing the frontal armor. He put one hand onto the gun tube to help himself up and, for a second, he thought he could feel it move, just as if someone had touched the traverse crank inside. Instinctively, he jerked his hand away and almost fell. "Shit," he muttered. "Must have been my weight moved the gears." On top of the old tank Murphy at last saw a hatch. He climbed to it and was elated to find it still closed. Brushing away some pine needles, he hooked his fingers under the edge and pulled with all his might. Nothing happened. He applied more pressure, straining until he realized that a cold sweat was dripping on his forehead.

"A crowbar—I'll get the one off the tank." He grunted and slid back down the sloping bow.

It was then that he saw the glow. No longer far away or indistinct but all around him. The old tank was bathed in a cold, blue light, growing stronger and pulsating almost in rhythm with his pounding heart. He took a few staggering steps backward, still not believing his eyes. Then, he saw it move.

The ancient gun tube rose slightly, shaking off the last of its woodland crypt, and swung a few degrees to the left. "Oh, no!" Murphy whispered suddenly. As impossible as it was, he knew what was going to happen. He turned to see the M-60 with crystal, unreal clarity, parked on the trail no more than thirty yards away. Sanchez was sitting on the turret, smoking a cigarette. The hatches were all open. Inside, Jackson would be napping in his driver's seat and Moore, the gunner, would be reading one of those dirty magazines he kept in the binocular rack. Murphy tried to yell a warning. His mouth opened, but he could will no sound to leave his lips. He felt detached, not truly part of it all, as if he were viewing the whole, horrible scene on a small TV. From inside the Panther came a chilling, dull clunk of metal against metal. The breech was closing.

"It's going to happen, it's going to happen and I can't stop it!" Murphy screamed, and then the muzzle blast knocked him down. White light blotted out the M-60. Searing pain shot through his head— dulling his senses to all but the pain itself. The world spun in uneven circles. When it slowed for a second, he could see the M-60 burning. The turret had been blown completely off and was lying upside down by the trail. Tongues of orange flame boiled from the naked turret ring and engine bay. Already the snow around it was melting. Inky black smoke rose in the still air. Someone was screaming. It sounded like Sanchez. Jackson was a charred, blackened skeleton, with hollow holes where his eyes had been and bony arms upraised, frozen in death halfway out of the driver's hatch. His helmet was still on, and Murphy watched the 1st Armored Division crest melt away in the flame. The world spun faster and his vision faded into a small circle of light which passed quickly away down a long black corridor.

Chapter Two

𝖲𝖲

COLONEL MICHAEL O'LEARY laid the fat file on his desk and shook his graying head. He was a tall man, thin and raw-boned, pushing forty, but still with a twinkle in his Irish blue eyes. Retrieving a half cup of cold coffee, he took one sip, cursed quietly, and set it down on a thick book titled *German Armor: 1939 to 1945*. His watch read eleven A.M. as he rose and walked toward the window. General Walker would be expecting his decision within the hour.

O'Leary's office at the U.S. Army Tank Museum in Ansbach looked down over a wide avenue bordered with preserved examples of armored fighting vehicles through the ages. With winter sunlight on the snow, they sat like squatty gargoyles passively guarding the approach. There was the massive, dinosaurlike Mark VII, which had reached the unprecedented speed of 6.5 miles per hour in 1916 and struck terror into the hearts of Imperial German troops at the battle of Somme. Beside it was an early Stuart, which spearheaded the 1st Armored Division drive into Tunisia in 1942. An M-3 Grant looked like something out of an old Disney cartoon, with turrets stacked on top of turrets and guns of various sizes pointing everywhere. Actually, high silhouette and all, it had been the first decent tank the British Eighth Army had had to face Rommel with. It had done well.

Of course there was a Sherman, that marvel of mass production that had spelled the demise of Hitler's Panzer divisions, not because of superior design, construction, or armament, but simply be-

cause U.S. industry pumped 52,000 of them into
the European theater.

He shot a guilty glance at the file.

The Jagdpanther was a rare find. The museum
did not have one and he knew of only two others
left in the whole world. There was one at Aberdeen
Proving Grounds and another at the Royal Tank
Museum at Bovington, England. Even with all the
related problems, he could not turn down division's
offer to give the museum one. The restoration
would be long, difficult, and expensive. Funds
would have to be diverted from some other project.
If, as the army suspected, there were still bodies
inside, then there would be the damned political
niceties to the Bundesrepublik government—military funerals and all that. Also, there could be more
booby traps.

The phone rang and he jumped. He pushed the
intercom button, and a secretary told him that
General Walker was on the line. He took a deep
breath, sat down in his padded chair, and picked
up the phone. "Good morning, sir," he began.

"Mike." The general's voice was gruff. "It's
nearly noon. Are you going to get that booby-
trapped relic off my training area and preserve it
for posterity, or do I blow it up?"

"The museum graciously accepts your offer, and
we will remove the old relic for restoration."

"Good. How soon?"

Colonel O'Leary coughed and almost stuttered.
"Very soon, General, very soon. I plan to bring in a
vehicle expert for this one—"

The general cut him off: "I thought you were the
tank expert around here. That's why I appointed
you to that plush curator's job."

O'Leary laughed nervously, moved the coffee

cup, and wiped away the brown ring it had left on the cover of *German Armor*. "Yes, General, that's true, but the Jagdpanther is such a rarity that I want to bring in the world's leading authority." He smiled at the empty office. "The man who wrote the book, so to speak."

"Who the hell is that?"

"His name is Fafner, James Fafner. An old colleague of mine, used to be with Fourth Army. He's Civil Service now, a GS-Twelve I think; lectures at the Knox Combat Simulation Center. I used him once before on the Sherman we pulled out at Juno Beach."

"Fafner . . ." Walker's voice sounded suspicious. "Isn't he the screwball that the Pentagon's been investigating? They think he's been fighting for the Israelis, commanded a company of old super-Shermans on the Golan Heights or something?"

O'Leary winced and then said without the slightest trace of falsehood, "Totally unfounded rumor, sir. Nothing was ever proven."

The general grunted doubtfully.

"Of course, sir," O'Leary probed cautiously, "the Israelis are on our side, and if one of our people had been there, we might have gained some valuable insight into the capabilities of the Russian armor being doled out to Third World nations."

There was an unnaturally long silence while O'Leary sweated. "All right," General Walker growled at last. "Get his ass over here and get that damned bucket of Nazi bolts off my tank range."

O'Leary said good-bye, put down the phone, and let out a long-held breath. Now, if he could just find Jim and if Jim wasn't in some sort of trouble and if he could get him over here, then maybe the two of them could make some sense out of all this.

Michael O'Leary and Jim Fafner had gone to grade school together at Fort Bragg. Their fathers had both been captains then, so they lived on the same block, in identical houses befitting their fathers' military rank and social standing.

Throughout boyhood they had supported Revell and Monogram by building every plastic tank model kit that appeared in the PX hobby shop. The two boys differed only in that Michael built American models while Jim's interest was in German ones. When their collections outgrew their bedrooms, they culled out the old and broken every Fourth of July by blowing them to bits with firecrackers.

They had learned tactics from Avalon/Hill board games. From Tactics II, all the way through Panzer Blitz, Fire Fight, and Squad Leader, they played and learned and acquired a better background in tank warfare by the age of twelve than most regular-army majors ever got.

They had joined the army together, just two weeks after they graduated from high school. They both went to armor school. They both applied for officer candidate school and were both accepted. Fort Knox and then a couple of bad tours in Vietnam had followed.

Afterward, the two had lost contact for several years. Michael had heard Jim was married and then divorced. He had also heard Jim had left the service for several years and worked as a civilian instructor at the Fort Knox Combat Simulation Center, a sort of expensive war-game school the army used to teach tactics. Michael had managed to get the curator's position at the army's tank museum, and figured he would try to stay there until he retired.

During this time, Jim had written *German Armor*. Michael had been impressed. It was undoubtedly the best technical work on the subject to date. Several other technical books followed, as well as numerous articles in historical and military magazines. By now Jim Fafner had pretty much become the accepted authority on German armored fighting vehicles.

The two boyhood friends had been reunited a few years ago when the museum needed help with the restoration of a Sherman tank pulled up out of the ocean at Juno Beach. The project had lasted six months. Michael and Jim had been two schoolboys again, playing with a new toy tank. Except this time the tank was real and there was a $100,000 budget for the restoration, along with all of the U.S. Army's facilities. It had been refreshingly obvious that neither of them had ever quite grown up.

The project had been a turning point for Jim. Since then he had taught only part-time at Knox. More and more often he was turning up in far corners of the world. Michael was not positive about the Golan Heights incident, but he suspected there was some truth in it. Perhaps Jim had been working for some intelligence-gathering agency. Perhaps he just wanted to see how good a Sherman really was in combat, and the Israelis had the only operational ones left. Either way, a Jagdpanther, apparently intact, should spark his interest.

Michael pushed the intercom button. "Ingrid?"

"Sir?"

"Place a call to Combat Simulation at Knox. I want to talk to Mr. James Fafner."

Chapter Three

THE ONLY AMERICAN to board the British Air flight in Johannesburg looked like a cross between a college professor and a safari guide. His hair was sandy brown and sun-bleached; his face was tanned, and a pair of military sunglasses hung from a pocket flap of his tan bush jacket. But there, the white hunter image ended. He carried three cameras, all 35mm Nikons. His pockets were stuffed with pencils and notepads. Two travel-worn briefcases and a leather camera bag filled his arms as he struggled down the aisle and dropped into a window seat. Long before the 747 was airborne, he was oblivious to everything around him.

From one briefcase he removed a laptop computer, which he placed on the fold-down tray. Into it he began transcribing page after page of notes from a heavy, official-looking file stamped CONFIDENTIAL. As the hours passed, he became more and more deeply involved. Somewhere over the Mediterranean, a stewardess asked about coffee or tea and was answered with a detached, "They're all lying. It couldn't possibly happen that way."

"I beg your pardon?" she managed coolly before the man finally realized she was there.

He looked startled for a second and then removed the small-framed reading glasses from his nose and answered as if nothing unusual had happened. "Tea, please, with lemon," he said, and returned to his notes.

Jim Fafner considered the army's official report to be just that much bullshit. He leaned back in his seat and shook his head as he thumbed through it once again. Just over eight hundred pages had been used to say that a German tank, apparently abandoned at the end of World War II, had sat with a round in the chamber of its 88mm gun for over forty years.

Two theories were offered as to why the round would have discharged. First, and considered most likely, was the theory that the commander of the unfortunate M-60 the antique round had blown to smithereens had either entered the tank and fired it accidentally or had tripped some booby-trap device, which fired the weapon.

A second theory suggested that ground vibration from the approaching M-60 could have caused the unstable propellant charge in the 88mm round to ignite and fire the weapon.

"The army is covering up something." Jim mumbled to himself. It all made about as much sense as the Rodriguez incident a few years ago. Sergeant Rodriguez had been a tank commander with 1st Armored who found out that Sergeant Garcia, another tank commander, was sleeping with his wife. Rodriguez decided to eliminate the home-wrecker and, during a live-fire exercise, put a 105mm SABO round through the back of Garcia's turret, then claimed the round had "cooked off," or fired accidentally. But fate was unkind. The army did not buy the story and Garcia had been the only survivor. Now, Rodriguez was doing twenty-to-life and Garcia was still sleeping with his wife.

By the time his plane landed at Frankfurt, Jim had filled a microdisk with notes and theories of his own, but the whole thing still made no sense.

He waved his passport at a disinterested in-

spector and passed through customs without opening a bag. At the currency-exchange booth he
changed a few hundred South African rands into
deutsche marks and headed for the U.S. Army's
information booth.

The airport was a sea of humanity: GIs and their
families, college students, Arabs, and even a few
Germans. He smiled as he passed a new McDon-
ald's along a row of airport restaurants. The Mc-
Donald's was crowded. An Arab sheik and two
Japanese businessmen gobbled Big Macs, Quarter-
Pounders with Cheese and golden fries at a stand-
ing-room counter beside a French mountain
climber and four nuns. There was an obvious absence of Americans.

At the information booth, he was surprised to be
told that a helicopter was waiting for him. He had
expected a five-year-old Dodge staff car for the 180-
klick ride to Ansbach. On the helipad, he finally
thought about the cold and remembered it was
December in Germany. There was snow on the
ground, and he did not own anything warmer than
the cotton bush jacket he was wearing.

Michael was waiting for him when the chopper
touched down on the snow-covered museum lawn.
The two shook hands warmly as Jim started to get
out.

"Stay in," Michael said. "We're flying on to the
training area right now. Give you a look at the new
toy." Jim nodded, and shifted uncomfortably in the
seat as Michael strapped in. "General Walker's in
kind of a hurry about this one, wants it off his tank
range right away."

"Have they cleared the booby traps yet?" Jim
asked, pulling up the collar of the flight jacket he
had just borrowed from the pilot.

Michael looked a little embarrassed. "They can't get the hatches open."

"Really?"

"Maybe they haven't tried too hard," Michael had to admit. "They're all pretty squirrelly since the accident."

Jim changed the subject. "So how're Betty and the kids?"

"Fine. Jimmy is eight and Becky's twelve. Betty plays golf three times a week."

Jim's eyes wandered off. He had almost forgotten that some people did go home at five o'clock to a wife and family, Little League baseball, and piano recitals. Then again, perhaps he wanted to forget. "This time yesterday I was teaching Russian gunnery to South Africans."

"Why you?"

He smiled mischievously. "One of their little off-the-record raids into Angola netted a dozen Russian T-34s built in 1945. I scrapped four and got eight of them running. We adapted a ballistics computer from their Saladin armored cars, and I had to stay around long enough to be sure they worked right."

"So that's why it took four days to find you."

The chopper came in low over the trees and circled an ugly black splotch on the snow where the M-60 had been hit. Near it were a couple of jeeps and a small truck. Several figures in army green could be seen watching as they descended. Both men stared in quiet horror at the blackened remains of the M-60. "Damn," Jim said to no one in particular, "haven't they moved it yet?"

"They want to let it cool some more."

As they stepped out into the snow, Jim turned suddenly back to the pilot. "Can I keep this a while?" he asked, indicating the flight jacket. The pilot nodded and lifted the chopper up into the afternoon sky. He seemed to be in a hurry to be somewhere else.

Michael had a few quick words with one of the military policemen and then turned to find that Jim had already walked to the edge of the woods and was staring at the Jagdpanther's shadowy silhouette. A yellow tape, with RESTRICTED AREA stenciled in black, sealed off the approach.

"Bomb-disposal team is here. Where do you want them to check first?" O'Leary asked.

There was a strange, hard look in Jim's eyes and he did not answer at once. The old tank seemed to hypnotize him. At last he turned and said distantly, "Get them about half a mile down the road. I'll check it alone."

Michael shook his head and hoped he was kidding. "Come on, now, we don't pay you that well." After another long moment, he sighed and said, "Okay, just you and me, partner, just like—"

"Not you and me, just me," Jim corrected, and then added somewhat softer, "Let me do this alone. It's the best way."

Michael was not at all sure it was the best way, but he let out a deep breath, nodded his skeptical approval, and backed away to the trail.

Jim walked into the silent forest. Afternoon sunlight filtered down through the trees and painted the old tank with an eerie camouflage of moving light and shadow. Most of the limbs and brush had been removed—whether by the army or from the gun's muzzle blast, he was not sure.

He was a little surprised to see that it actually was a Jagdpanther. Past experience had taught him to doubt all reports and believe only half of what he saw himself. Technically, the Jagdpanther was not a tank but a tank destroyer. Jagdpanther translated to "hunting panther" or "hunting cat."

The name fit.

It was a turretless version of the Panther medium tank developed by the Germans early in 1943. Most experts, himself included, considered it to be the finest tank killer of the war. A grim smile crossed his face. "If they had made a few more of these babies, history might remember the European campaign a little differently."

He marveled at its size. The massive frontal armor sloped back from a knife-edged bow at a rakish, sinister angle that seemed to say, "If I can't blow you away, I will cut you in half and grind the pieces into the earth." The gun tube was almost as long as the tank itself. Shielded by a steel mantlet, it protruded from the frontal armor and poked between trees that must have been only seedlings when it was parked here. Vines had grown up over the suspension and road wheels, but in some places they were pulled away and he could see the treads. Jagged with short, clawlike teeth, they seemed poised to rip and tear—a cat waiting in the trees—silent, unmoving, but crouched and ready to strike.

A sudden, cold wind sent a chill up his spine. For one fleeting second, he thought the forest dissolved into an avenue of blood-red banners with black swastikas blowing in the wind. And for that one microsecond of time, the Jagdpanther was new. The treads clanked on cobblestone and its Maybach engine purred like a fifty-ton pussycat. Standing in the commander's hatch was a figure dressed in a black tunic with silver epaulets and the death-head insignia of the SS Panzer divisions on his peaked cap. His hand was raised in salute, perhaps to the crimson banners, perhaps to an unseen Führer. But as Jim watched, the specter lowered his salute slowly and pointed at him where he stood on the ground. At first he could see the face clearly: a young man with thin blond hair and piercing, blue eyes who wore his cap cocked at a jaunty angle. But the face changed, dissolving slowly into a hollow-eyed skull with bits of leathery skin still clinging to the nose and jaw. Hideous, hollow laughter echoed on the wind—laughter from another time.

And then, as suddenly as it came, the vision was gone. The wind died and there was only the forest and the old, long-abandoned tank.

Jim ran a hand across his forehead and found it was covered with cold perspiration. "Bad case of jet lag. You've got to get some sleep tonight," he told himself as he began the slow, dangerous process of checking the Jagdpanther for booby traps.

Chapter Four

IT WAS ALMOST disappointing to find not a single booby trap, anywhere on the Jagdpanther. There were no Teller mines around the perimeter. Despite a noticeable absence of rust, all three roof hatches plus the escape hatch refused to budge. On the rear deck, however, the engine bay cover lifted easily after Jim spent several minutes convincing himself there was no grenade rigged beneath it. The problem was more or less academic, since forty-year-old booby traps almost never explode. On the other hand, he knew that anyone who had been smart enough to rig the main gun to fire when touched was somewhere well above the average intelligence of German tank commanders in World War II. Whoever he was, he might have left any number of surprises.

The twelve-cylinder Maybach engine was the first thing he saw that looked right. The screens over the air intakes had rusted away. Rotted pine needles jammed the cooling fans and, mixed with solidified oil and grease, were several inches deep around the crankcase. The valve cover was badly rusted, and the wiring seemed to be in a believable state of decay to have sat through over four decades of German winters. A quick look told him that it had not been stripped for parts and that there were no obvious signs of a breakdown.

He lowered the engine cover gently back into place and leaned against the escape hatch. Lighting his crooked meerschaum pipe, he gave the Jagdpanther another critical look. The gun tube caught his eye and he climbed back over the roof.

That tank commander—what was his name?— "Murrey" or "Murphy," Jim thought. The report said he felt the barrel move when he climbed over it. That was probably bull too, but perhaps some sort of trip had been rigged to the 88's hydraulic recoil system. It did not seem likely or even possible since the main gun fired electrically, and no battery, not even a German one, could have lasted forty years. There was, of course, a manual backup system, but it was a heavy lever that needed too much force. Just to convince himself, Jim climbed off the tank and put all his weight on the oval-shaped muzzle brake at the end of the 88's long gun tube. It did not budge.

He ran his fingers inside the muzzle brake and they came out black. "Gotta talk to this Murphy character sometime," he mumbled as he sniffed at his hand and walked back to the trail.

Michael was waiting for him there, leaning against the bumper of a five-ton wrecker that had just been driven up. "Are we ready to move her?" he asked nervously.

"It's risky. They were right about the hatches; gotta be locked from inside."

"Damn, that means we got a tank full of crispy Krauts."

"I don't know" Jim shrugged. "She didn't burn. I'm not even sure she was ever in combat. The engine looks pretty well trashed out, but there's no sign of battle damage, nothing but one dent on the fender."

He relit his pipe. "My guess is, she's already been stripped, at least on the outside. There's no spare track sections or road wheels on her hull. The rack with her pioneer tools is gone—everything." He paused and fiddled with the pipe for a moment. "Of course, if I'm wrong, and there is still ammo inside, those 88s might be getting pretty unstable after sitting around this long." At last he noticed the wrecker and added, "What does he think he's going to do?"

"We've got an eighteen-wheeler with a flatbed up on the main road. We'll use the wrecker here to drag her out of the woods and up the hill, then winch it onto the flatbed trailer."

Jim said, "No way."

"What?"

"Five-ton wrecker won't move it. Combat weight on that Jagdpanther is nearly forty-five tons. Besides that, her power train is probably locked up, and I can't free it up until I can get inside. We'll need either a tank or a tank recovery vehicle down here."

Michael gave his watch a worried glance. "Let's let the wrecker try. General Walker's going to be all over my ass if I don't get this relic out of here today."

The wrecker driver was an overweight Spec-5. He chewed on a cigar as he hooked up his cable to the Jagdpanther's towing hooks and climbed back into his cab. Black smoke boiled from the exhaust stack; the wrecker appeared to squat and then lurch forward. There was a squeaking of treads, and the Jagdpanther was towed slowly forward. The wrecker driver smiled behind his cigar as he passed by Jim and Michael: What the hell did a chicken colonel and some middle-aged civilian know about towing tanks?

Restoration Building #2, on the U.S. Army Tank Museum complex, was about the size of a football field. The Germans had built it in 1943, as a major overhaul shop for medium-class tanks, and the two-foot-thick, steel-reinforced concrete walls had withstood the months of Allied bombing that followed. During the late 1940s, the U.S. Army had used it as a repair facility before the museum had taken it over. Now, the walls were lined with an odd collection of dilapidated war machines—some in various stages of restoration, others cannibalized for parts and discarded.

It was well after dark before the tank transporter had finally been backed inside. There was then the

minor problem of getting the Jagdpanther unloaded. A steel cable, attached to the Jagdpanther's
bow, had been shackled to a couple of large steel
rings in the floor. When the eighteen-wheeler
moved forward, the Jagdpanther's treads, which
had rolled free all during the loading, locked tight.
The truck burned rubber on ten wheels and went
nowhere.

"Might have vibrated into gear somehow, I
suppose." Michael suggested.

Jim scratched his chin and grinned. "Maybe it
don't like the company," he said, pointing at a pair
of partially restored Russian T-34s.

Again the truck driver gunned his engine. His
vehicle lurched forward; the Jagdpanther rolled
easily off the trailer and onto the concrete floor.

Both men looked at each other and shrugged.
"You ready for a beer?" Michael said as the tank
transporter drove out the doors.

The Jagdpanther sat silently on the floor as the
doors were shut and the lights turned off. Outside, snow was falling in large, wet flakes which
collected in the corners of the building's old windows. Stirred by the night wind, more snow
drifted in little swirls, in under the doors, and
sparkled in the fringes of a cold, blue light that
began as tiny sparks along the edges of the Jagdpanther's frontal armor. It spread quickly across
the slanting bow and ran like electric snakes out
the gun barrel, until the whole tank was engulfed
in the glow.

From somewhere inside the Jagdpanther there
came a faint, ringing sound of metal against metal
as the breech dropped and a shell was loaded. The
gun moved, raising slightly as it swung a few degrees toward the two T-34s sitting amid a pile of

parts. It held there for a minute and then swung away, moving slowly over the other vehicles to its front. The light faded as the gun tube hesitated at the hulk of a German armored car, and pulsated brightly as it trained on an M-4 Sherman with no treads and with the gun tube cut off. One by one, it scanned the forlorn hulks with which it shared the building, and then the gun tube dropped back into its former position. The blue light faded. There was no enemy here, at least none that it had reason to fear, and so it rested.

Jim stood in the falling snow as Michael's staff car drove off into the night. For a minute, he looked up at the long, two-story bachelor-officers'-quarters building and then picked up his bags. His life, it seemed, was all here, in the few pieces of luggage he carried. He hated the nights. Only at night could he not totally lose himself in his work. Only in the darkness was he forced to look at himself, and each time he did, he saw little else but failures.

Marriage perhaps had been the biggest. It took a certain kind of woman to be the wife of an army officer. The social class system, determined completely by husband's rank, was something a woman either thrived on, withered away in, or ran from. Kristen had been smart enough to run. Perhaps, Jim thought, if he had risen to field grade, made major instead of becoming stuck in that often dead-end rank of captain, it might have been different.

Combat had really been the only part of military life Jim ever understood, and there he had always excelled. The bull all went out the window as soon as the first round went off, and then the choices were fewer, the decisions more final. Armor tactics, the fast-moving art and science of killing with tanks, came easily to him. It was, after all, nothing more than an accumulation of military knowledge, collected from centuries, perhaps millenniums of warfare. Arthur's mounted knights; the sweeping raids of Russia's cossack hordes or the American Apaches; Sherman's cavalry sweep from Atlanta to the sea. All the pieces had been forged long before Guderian, Rommel, Zhukov, and Patton began putting them together to form the doctrines of modern warfare. The evolution was continuous. Now, the Israelis were contributing their own improved and modernized version of Germany's *Blitzkrieg*, as they fought seemingly endless wars with their Arab neighbors.

He had come to believe there was an instinct for combat, one some men were born with. Some lost it quickly in the blood and misery of warfare, but others, like himself, remained somehow able to separate the horrors of war from the science of tactics. He had also observed that most men who accomplished this became excellent fighters and failures at most everything else, especially at love. Perhaps war was easier if there was not all that much else to live for.

Inside the sparse room that had been reserved for him on the second floor of the BOQ, Jim let his bags drop onto the floor, turned on the light switch, and pulled off his borrowed jacket.

Although his marriage had been short, the divorce dragged on, long and painful. By the time it finally ended, Jim had known that the regular army, then more or less at peace following the disgraces of Vietnam, was no longer the place for him.

He had resigned his commission and accepted a position as military adviser, first in Syria and then in Saudi Arabia.

The Middle East was good tank country—Rommel had proven that years before. The armor, during the time Jim had been there, was a museum mix of Shermans and M-48s, British Centurions, Russian T-34s, and Stalin IIIs with even a few old Panzer IVs still clanking around. It was the perfect place to become an expert on antique tanks.

Jim flopped onto the cot without taking off his clothes. Kristen. He wondered where she had ended up. "Think about now," he told himself, and forced his thoughts back to the Jagdpanther.

It was, of course, impossible for a five-ton, rubber-tired wrecker to drag a Jagdpanther with a combat weight of 92,000 pounds out of the woods, up a steep hill, and onto a trailer.

But he had seen it happen.

Digging a pocket calculator out from one of his shirt pockets, Jim began to calculate what the vehicle might actually weigh if it had been unloaded and stripped inside. Even after subtracting the weight of sixty rounds of 88mm, six hundred rounds of machine-gun ammo, all the fuel she could possibly have carried, plus her optics, gun breech, and everything movable including the driver's seat, he still had a vehicle that should weigh in excess of thirty-nine tons.

"Possibilities?" he mumbled, now half asleep. "Number one: The army's standard five-ton, rubber-tired wrecker has been vastly improved during the past six months and no one told me." He laughed quietly at his own poor joke. "Or number two: Our Jagdpanther is really an old prop left over

from some 1950s war movie." Again he started to
laugh, but it turned into a yawn. "None of us would
ever live that down."

"Gott im Himmel!" Rudy Bauer remarked when
he walked into Restoration Building #2 at 0800
the next morning. "Dat *Gott*-damn piece uh shit,
dey brung it here." He glared at the Jagdpanther.
"If Rudy was run things around here, dey drag
you ass out on da firing ranges and blow you to
bits."

He walked in a wide circle around the vehicle,
frowning behind his bushy gray eyebrows as he
scratched his chin and grunted thoughtfully. "In all
da war, I see maybe five or six of you. Always mit
der SS Panzers. So now dey bring in some big tank
expert, thinks he make you run again, *ja?*"

Rudy was poking around the road wheels when
Michael walked up. Jim was a few paces behind
him with a cup of coffee in one hand and a tape
measure in the other. "Morning, Rudy," Michael
said, and pointed a thumb in Jim's direction. "This
is James Fafner. He'll be working with us as a consultant on this one."

Rudy wiped his hand on his coveralls and extended it cautiously as Jim fumbled to get both
coffee and tape measure in the same hand and return the shake. "Vell, you make it run, *ja?*" Rudy
asked with a frown.

"We haven't even got the hatches open yet. Mike
says you used to work on these."

Rudy grunted. *"Ja,* forty years ago ven I vas
young boy. An dose were regular Panthers, not
Jagdpanthers. I saw very few of these vere I vas."

"The hatches are all either locked from inside or

jammed," Jim said. "They all look like standard types to me. Any tricks for getting them open?"

Rudy's weathered old face turned a little pale. "All locked, eh? Den der man who locked dem is still inside."

"Damn." Michael whistled between his teeth. "I'll have to contact the Bundesrepublik government. They'll want a representative here, probably a military funeral and all that. How soon will you be ready to open her?"

Jim walked to the Jagdpanther's rear. "We could drive the hinge pins out of any of the hatches, then lift them up and away from the locking mechanisms. Let's try it on the escape hatch first. That should be the hardest one to booby-trap, and it'll be the easiest to get in and out with body bags."

He looked to Rudy for support and the old German nodded grimly. "Might work."

"But I want to do a wash-down on her first," Jim added. "Maybe under all this dirt, we'll find some unit markings, something besides that one crest on the bow. With a little luck, the *Bundesarchiv* might come up with the names of her crew."

Michael looked at his watch. "I've got a meeting," he said. "Have fun. I'll see you for lunch."

Rudy left to round up some men to begin washing forty years of grime off the Jagdpanther. Jim set his coffee cup down on the left front fender and ran the tape measure across the width of the bow. "Three hundred and ten centimeters?" he said to himself. He scratched his head and frowned at the tape, then put on his reading glasses and read it again. "I'll be damned, seventeen centimeters short. The book's wrong, and I wrote it!"

Two hours later, Jim was leaning against a workbench, reading his own book, when Rudy told him they had finished the wash-down. "Anything but that one crest?" he asked.

Rudy shook his head, "No. Paint is in damn good shape; might be something underneath, but nothing I can see."

Thirty minutes earlier, they had finished cleaning the crest, and Jim had been sure he had never seen it before. This, in itself, was rather embarrassing, since his own book devoted almost thirty pages of color plates to cataloging German armor unit insignias. It was considered the most complete reference in the world—the Smithsonian used it. Yet, in the past two hours, he had found two mistakes.

"Nibilungen," Rudy said, pointing at the sneering face above the SS runes.

"Nibilungen," Jim echoed. Mythical forest creatures out of ancient Germanic folklore, he thought, but said only, "Elves."

"*Ja*, elves." Rudy nodded. "Und dat is a mean-looking one. Don't want to meet him in no dark forest."

"You ever see the crest before?" Jim asked, embarrassed.

Rudy took a long time to answer. Finally, he shook his head. "I'm not sure. I don't think so. Is not in the book?"

"No," Jim cursed quietly under his breath. "It's not in the book."

At noon, Michael returned, and Jim went to lunch with him. The snow had stopped and the sky had cleared to a crystal blue as they walked down between the line of tanks displayed at the museum entrance.

"The press is coming this afternoon," Michael said.

"I hate meeting the press."

Michael ignored the statement. "Of course we haven't told them anything to connect the brewed-up M-60 with our Jagdpanther, but rumors are flying. We've officially admitted that the M-60 hit some buried explosive device left over from WW II, near where the Jagdpanther was found, but that's all."

"And they're buying that?"

Michael shrugged. "Maybe. As I'm sure you know from the official report you read, none of this really makes any sense."

"I'm glad to hear you admit it. I was beginning to wonder if you actually believed any of that bull."

"Not hardly. But the brass has covered up this one good. I suspect we'll never know the real story."

"The gun did fire," Jim said thoughtfully.

"The 88? Are you sure?"

Jim nodded. "There's cordite residue inside the muzzle brake. It's fresh."

"I'll be damned."

They crossed the main road and walked another half-block to a small cafe where the odors of brat-wurst and beer mingled pleasantly with polka music. They took a booth tucked under a shelf of beer steins.

"Do you remember Gretchen?" Michael asked.

Jim nodded. "Yeah, vaguely."

"Ah, come on, the one with the boobs."

"Oh, her. Yeah, why?"

"She still works here. Still got the hots for you. I told her last week you were coming back."

"That's nice," Jim said, detached. "Mike, cover

the press for me this afternoon. I'm going to Koblenz."

"With Gretchen? Damn, you move faster than I remember."

Jim looked totally confused. "What? No—not with Gretchen. I haven't even seen her. I'm going to the *Bundesarchiv* to see if I can trace that crest on the Jagdpanther."

Michael looked disappointed. "You should take Gretchen."

"Not if I'm supposed to get any work done."

"Okay, but wait until tomorrow. You're the highly paid consultant on this project, and General Walker is going to be expecting you to explain things to the press."

"Yeah, I know. That's why I'm going to Koblenz now. I don't have any of the answers."

Chapter Five

AUGUST GNOKTE WALKED always with a limp and a cane. Yet every morning, he walked. It was six blocks from his flat on Stalingrad Street down to Primorsky Boulevard, which paralleled the rocky coast of the Black Sea. Then, with his back to the north wind, he could stroll high above the crashing breakers, all the way to the Potemkin Steps, which led down to the harbor. He usually rested there, at about the time the sun rose above the Caucasus Mountains. Odessa, "the Pearl of the

Black Sea." It was a good city, August believed,
for a retired agent of the KGB to live out his last
days.

On this morning, August arrived early at the
steps while dawn was still only a purple haze above
the sea. Last night, the dreams had come again,
and sometimes walking helped to drive their haunting traces from his mind. Today it was different.
This time there was more than just the dream. This
time, it was beginning again.

"A wise man does not believe everything which
Pravda puts into print," he told himself. "And even
a fool believes little of what the United States Army
tells its own press."

Had it been any other vehicle but a Jagdpanther,
he might have accepted it as coincidence, but he
could account for every one of the 384 Jagdpanthers ever built. Over the years, August had metic-
ulously traced each one of them. All through the
1940s and 1950s he'd had the help, and the bless-
ings, of the Soviet intelligence network. But in the
early 1960s, they had closed their files on the
project, convinced the trail had been followed to its
end. The Jagdpanther, any Jagdpanther, they believed, was obsolete. Most had been cut up for
scrap. A dozen had come into the Soviet Union and
all of them had ended up as tank and rocket range
targets. Norway had kept a few, but they were gone
now. The Swedes had studied them and developed
their S-Tank. Two remained in museums.

The five Jagdpanthers built for Project Mirtheil
were, of course, in addition to the known 384, and
August knew that they were the only ones that mattered. He had, with his own young eyes, seen four of
them burn, each in that unearthly blue fire that left
no trace.

August shivered as he sat on the steps. It was that blue flame that haunted his dreams more than any of the other horrors of war—the flames and the screams of the men inside as all trace of the Jagd-panther vanished from the earth. Once, when it had happened, he had searched the ground around them and found it not the least bit warm.

He rose stiffly with the help of his cane and walked back in the direction of the Odessa opera house. Only the fate of Von Norden's Jagdpanther remained uncertain. For the first few years, after the war, August had feared Von Norden might somehow have survived and that his Jagdpanther might turn up. But now, after forty years? It was impossible.

Or was it?

From the pocket of his coat, he removed a copy of last evening's *Pravda*. His hands were shaking more than usual as he reread the story on page seven about an accident on one of the American Army's tank ranges in West Germany.

The possibility of coincidence was remote, but now what could he do about it? Who was there still left? Who, in all the vast Kremlin jungle of political intrigues and red tape, would still believe an old worn-out spy who, long ago, had been put out to pasture? There was perhaps one man, almost as old as himself, but still deeply rooted in Kremlin politics. Moscow was 1500 kilometers away, but he would go there, and somehow, he would make him believe.

August turned his steps toward home. Odessa, he thought, was a beautiful city. The palaces and the opera house, the museums and the theaters, all sit in the near Mediterranean climate of the Black Sea coast. It was home, and home was worth whatever sacrifice might be necessary to protect it. For if he was right, it would not be too long before the Americans discovered what they had found. And then, all of this might soon be gone.

Reading microfilm always made Jim seasick. Since early morning he had been seated in front of one of the viewers at the German National Archives in Koblenz, scanning the microfilmed records of German tank production during the last two years of the war. They were, of course, incomplete. Despite the fact that the Germans were famous for the meticulous records they kept, the mountains of resulting paperwork had gone in many different directions at the end of World War II. The British took a lot of it. The Americans grabbed what turned up in their sector and kept most of it classified in their national archives until the late 1970s. The Russians burned much of what they took.

Whatever was left ended up here at Koblenz and was eventually transferred to microfilm. Jim was not sure if it helped or not. After six hours of staring at a screen and turning a crank that brought up page after page of unwanted information, he felt like he had been on a carnival ride all day.

Yesterday he had put a magnifying glass on every photograph and drawing that had anything to do with Jagdpanthers, as well as everything Koblenz had on unit insignias. He had found nothing. He had expected to find nothing, since he had researched here several years ago while writing *German Armor: 1939 to 1945*. But the crest on the Jagdpanther's bow was real, and the only explanation he could come up with was that somehow

he had missed something. Now, he was beginning
to believe he was missing it again.

At about three-thirty in the afternoon, he called
the museum and Michael informed him there had
been almost no progress made in removing the
hinge pin from the Jagdpanther's escape hatch.

"You better get your tail back here," Michael
insisted. "The Germans want their crispy Krauts
out of our tank. It's bad press, leaving them in there
this long."

Jim sighed. "Damn. They've been in there for
forty years, if they are there at all. I need another
day. There's something here and I'm missing it."

"What are you talking about?" Michael's voice
was sounding strained.

"I'll explain when I get back, maybe tomorrow
night." Jim finished the conversation and hung up.

Most of the following day was spent with the
files of the only two wartime companies known to
have produced Jagdpanthers: MIAG and MNH.
Jim was almost relieved to be told that most of
these files had never been microfilmed. By late
afternoon, however, he was ready to give up. The
files were a disorganized collection of old card-
board boxes, into which piles of mostly routine
paperwork had been shoveled and forgotten. Pay
records, monthly quotas of everything from running feet of tank tread to road-wheel bolts. None
of it appeared to be important. He fumbled
through figures on numbers of vehicles completed
during the early months of 1944. In one ancient
manila folder there was a collection of requisi-
tions dealing with the transfer of some various
pieces of heavy machinery and one comlete casting mold for a standard Panther lower hull sec-

tion. In faded pencil on the folder was scribbled one word: *Mirtheil.*

Jim frowned at the writing and tried to translate the word. He was pretty sure it was not German. Maybe Latin or French, he thought as he wrote it down in his own notebook.

He closed up the boxes and then asked the fat girl at the main desk to run a computer check on the word *Mirtheil.*

She looked at him blankly for a moment and then asked, "What language is that?"

"I'm hoping the computer will tell both of us." He smiled.

The computer was unimpressed and turned up nothing.

"I can try some other spellings," the girl suggested.

They tried several possibilities, none of which the computer recognized. Jim was suddenly out of ideas. He left the archives depressed and somewhat bewildered. He threw his briefcase into the back seat of his rented Volkswagen Rabbit and drove onto the east-bound Autobahn. He was halfway to Frankfurt when he conceded that the only lead he had was the insignia, and now he had no idea how to follow it any further. Perhaps it was all academic. Once the Jagdpanther's hatches had been forced open, maybe the questions would be answered.

The Moscow Express made the 1500-kilometer run from Odessa in just under twenty-three hours. It rolled into Kiev Station in midafternoon, but already Moscow was shrouded in a gray twilight. The sun was a pale yellow globe, surrounded by a halo of reddish purple. It struggled to filter a little light down through the clouds and factory smoke to the snowy city below.

August carried only his briefcase as he left the railway station, deposited five kopeks in the subway tollgate, and caught the metro for Gorky Park.

He had wrestled with the decision to call his former supervisor, Ivan Judenov, for nearly twenty-four hours. This meeting in the park, instead of in the Kremlin offices, told August that Judenov was meeting him out of friendship only and that nothing said here would be official. But, it remained his only hope.

There was a cold, mysterious beauty to Gorky Park. A mantle of bright, new snow, barely disturbed by passersby, lay on the pathways and covered the evergreens, making the scene almost glow in contrast to the gloomy afternoon.

Judenov was waiting at the designated park bench. He looked old, August thought, and then decided that the other man was probably thinking the same thing about him.

"Comrade." Judenov smiled behind a snow-white beard, and rose to embrace his old friend. "It has been much too long. But tell me, how is retirement?"

"It is good." August nodded.

"But you miss all this?" Ivan gestured at the park.

August shrugged. "I do not think so." The two men walked for a while and talked of many things: Old men and old wars. They had stopped at a small cafe and Ivan was stirring a spoonful of fruit jelly into his black tea before the real reason for August's visit was mentioned. He handed Ivan the copy of *Pravda*, open to page seven. Ivan looked at him for a moment, then sighed and read the article slowly.

"I had hoped you had put all of this out of your mind." Ivan said at length.

"How can I do that?" August snapped. "I was the agent planted inside the project. I saw the things which happened there. I saw the men go screaming insane." He was gripping Ivan's sleeve, twisting at the fabric of his heavy coat. "I saw what *it* can do. I know!"

"It was all so long ago," Ivan said soothingly. "You were under a great deal of strain in those days; we all were. There were a lot of insane projects going on then. Not only in Germany." He laughed quietly. "Look at the Americans. They are still trying to hide their 'Philadelphia Experiment.' We also have our big hole in Siberia which is not spoken of.

"August, my old friend, it was all so long ago. Surely whatever technology the Nazis may have stumbled on then has long since been made obsolete."

"Has it? Tell me, which of our tank guns today will pierce the frontal armor of an American main battle tank?"

Ivan looked sick. "That . . . that information is classified."

August agreed. "Of course it is. Because we do not have a gun with those capabilities, and you know it. That fact, in itself, is not good for our balance of power. If the Americans ever figure out what they have found, there will be no balance of power!"

Ivan looked nervous and released a long-held breath. "I make no promises, but I will see what I can do. Go home now and rest."

"Rest? How can I—"

Ivan raised his hand. "Rest, Comrade, while you can, because I may have to send you in, to the other side." He gave his words a moment to sink in. "Can you do it?"

"Back into the jaws of hell," August whispered, and then rose to leave. "I would expect nothing less."

Jim stood on the rear deck of the Jagdpanther as he connected the chain hoist to the bottom of the escape hatch. The hinge pin lay nearby and, by all his calculations, the hatch should now be free. At the top of the chain hoist was an electric winch capable of lifting the complete turret off a medium-class tank. But as the gears were engaged and the tension taken up, it soon became obvious that it was going to lift the Jagdpanther before the hatch pulled free.

"Amazing," Jim remarked as he signaled Rudy to shut down the hoist. "It doesn't budge."

"Amazing, shit!" General Walker bellowed up from the floor. He then turned his frustrations loose on Michael, who was standing next to him. "You and this overpaid college professor have had this piece of junk in here for almost a week and you can't even get a goddamned hatch open! What the hell are we paying you people for?"

Michael had been in the army long enough to sound totally unaffected whenever his ass was being chewed on. "We've moved very slowly on purpose. What with the vehicle being so extremely rare, and, with the likelihood of bodies still inside . . . I think we are making acceptable progress."

"That's another crock of your Irish shit, O'Leary, and you know it."

Michael managed somehow to keep smiling. "Perhaps just a wee bit of it here and there, sir."

"Disgusting. But the first time there's a slot open for public-information officer, I'm going to jerk your ass out of this overgrown toy room and put you where you'll do the army some good, throwing double-talk to the press and all those bleeding-heart liberals." With that he stalked out of the room.

Michael saluted his back as he left and waited as Jim climbed down off the Jagdpanther. "The general is impatient," he said. "What are we going to do?"

Jim shook his head as he ran his fingers along the edge of the Jagdpanther's hull, then wiped his hands on an oily rag. "This thing is different from any of the other known Jagdpanthers."

"Why's that?"

"Until now, there have been only two Jagdpanther variants, and the differences between them were nothing more than bolts on the gun mantlet and exhaust systems. This is a third variant, and I suspect its changes go far beyond bolts and mufflers."

Michael frowned at him.

"There are a few centimeters' difference in width and height," Jim continued. "And my guess is, it weighs a lot less than the forty-five tons it's supposed to."

Michael's expression brightened. "Then we've got an extremely rare vehicle here, the only known one of its kind."

"I think so," Jim said as he walked toward the Jagdpanther's bow. "And the only clue we've got to find out just how rare, is this damned crest."

Michael rubbed his chin. "Nasty-looking little

fellow, isn't he? Reminds me of a TAC officer we
had once back in officer candidate school." He almost laughed, and then tore his eyes away from the
leering face. "Dinnertime. Betty is expecting us at
six. She'll be mad as hell if we're late."

Rudy watched them leave and then stood staring
at the Jagdpanther for a long time. "Where is it I
know you from?" he whispered to the silent steel.
For years, he had pushed all memory of that last
year of World War II from his mind until it was
only a blur of dismembered horrors. Yet somewhere, along the dark fringes of his mind, some
memory of a Jagdpanther was lurking.

If he closed his eyes, he could see them: a column
of thundering steel, vibrating the ground in rhythm
with the boot-stomping cadence of some old march.
The road they traveled boiled in clouds of red-
brown dust, swirling from their spinning treads,
covering them, until they became vague shapes—
demons from the fires of hell.

The scene faded. It dissolved to cobblestone
streets in some forgotten village. On one side of
the street was a factory; he had no idea what it
produced. On the other was a small stand, built
from the rubble of bombed-out buildings. It was
serving beer. Factory workers, all old men or very
young boys, stood in line at the stand. Rudy had
been too busy to stop for a drink. Two SS officers
stood idly beside him as he struggled to change
an inside road wheel on some broken-down older
tank. As he worked, a column of Jagdpanthers
had rumbled down the road, and one ground to a
noisy halt in front of the beer stand. A tall man
with thin blond hair and dressed in a black tunic
with silver epaulets climbed down from the com-

mander's hatch. His cap was cocked at a jaunty angle, and the skull and crossbones of the SS Panzer divisions glistened in the sunlight. The young man, Rudy thought, had been a *Hauptmann* (captain), but he was not sure. He swaggered up to the stand, bypassing the line of workers, and demanded to be served.

"You must wait as the others do," he was told, and the workers laughed at him. Even from where Rudy had watched, it was obvious that the man was furious, but he said nothing as he returned to his Jagdpanther.

"This should be very interesting," one of the SS officers had remarked as the hatch dropped shut with an ominous, metal clang. The Jagdpanther turned on its treads. Its machine gun leveled on the line of workers and opened fire, dropping a dozen of them before they realized what was happening. And then the Jagdpanther rolled forward, spraying the stand with machine-gun fire and then crushing it beneath its treads.

The vision began to fade. There was more to it, Rudy was sure. There had been something said, some name . . . but it was gone now. Cold sweat ran down his face; his old hands trembled as he backed away from the Jagdpanther and hurried to lock up.

Michael's two-story house on Kalbach Strasse was surrounded by nicely shaped fir trees and had a high, pointed roof and lots of wood trim. It reminded Jim of a huge cuckoo clock. A fire was blazing in a big tile fireplace as they entered. Betty, Jim conceded, was still very pretty—a little heavier than he remembered, but quite attractive.

She smiled and kissed his cheek as he came in.

"Jim, it's so good to see you again. I hope you'll stay a while this time and not go running off so soon."

Before he could answer, Michael said, "I think he'll be here a while. We've given him something to keep him busy for a long time."

Betty was still a wonderful cook, and Jim over-ate. The kids were just larger and noisier.

Dinner was finished and Betty was doing dishes when Michael and Jim retired to in front of the fireplace.

"This is nice," Jim remarked.

"Can't really afford it, but well, we got a little tired of duplexes on Officers' Row. This gives us some privacy. Besides, I wanted the kids to do a little growing up somewhere besides on base . . . let 'em see there really is a world out here, outside the army. Two more years, you know, and I'll have twenty-five in. I'll be ready to retire then."

"Sounds good."

"You ever have regrets? About not staying in, I mean."

Jim shook his head and set his drink down beside a half-dozen comic books scattered on the coffee table. "I regret a lot of things, but that's not one of them. I make a better civilian then I ever did an officer."

Michael nodded and a sly smile spread over his face. "There any truth to that story about you fighting on the Golan Heights?" he asked quietly.

Jim almost laughed. "I was there." He nodded with a faraway look in his eyes. "Those old Israeli Super Shermans ate T-34s and JS-IIs for lunch. It was beautiful."

Michael sat silently. For a moment, that same

faraway look was in his eyes, also. "What could you have done with a platoon of Jagdpanthers?"

Jim laughed out loud. "Probably blitzed all the way to the Persian Gulf. That is, if I could get the damn hatches open."

They both laughed. Jim reached for his drink, and it toppled onto the comic books on the coffee table. The glass was almost empty and only a few drops sprinkled onto one cover. Jim brushed at it with a napkin and read the title: *Princess of Elfland*. He stopped in midsentence and stared dumbly at the comic's cover. A woman, beautiful, dressed as a warrior, and more or less human except for pointed ears, wielded a sword in a desperate duel against a male creature with pointed ears and a leering smile.

"What is it?" Michael asked.

"The face on the Jagdpanther! It's here, right here in front of me, on the cover of a goddamn comic book!"

Chapter Six

"THERE IS A resemblance," Michael agreed when Jim laid the comic book beside the crest on the Jagdpanther's bow first thing next morning.

"More than a resemblance," Jim echoed, and sighted through a magnifying glass. "There are too many similarities. The curves on the face lines, the curly hair in the ears—one of these is a copy of the other."

"What the fuck is going on?" Michael suddenly sounded mad. "Is this whole thing some kind of a goddamn joke?"

Jim continued to inspect the comic book. "If it is, I'm going to be looking for a new career and Walker is going to bust you back to lieutenant in charge of latrines."

Michael coughed nervously. "There are some things even I don't joke about."

Jim put down his magnifying glass and handed Michael the comic. "At least it's a lead, and one we ought to be able to follow pretty fast."

Michael perked up a little as he read, *"Princess of Elfland,* story and art by Sherri Vail, copyright Dungeon Graphics, New York, N.Y." He smiled for the first time that morning. "I'll call a friend of mine in counterintelligence. Their computers should be able to run down something on this Sherri Vail, or whoever she, he, or it really is."

"Of course, we could just call her publisher, tell them what we want, and see if she'll talk to us," Jim suggested.

"Now that's an interesting angle," Michael said. "But let's try both ways. You call the publisher and I'll call the spooks."

By noon, the CID's computer had determined only that Sherri Vail, Inc., was a U.S. corporation, solely owned by Sharron Dumbroskie. The registered agent was an accounting firm in San Francisco, California. During the past five years, they had paid the Internal Revenue Service considerable sums in income tax.

Because of the six-hour time difference between West Germany and New York, it was three

o'clock in the afternoon before the overseas operator connected Jim's call to the New York offices
of Dungeon Graphics. They refused to give him an
address or phone number on Sherri Vail, but
agreed to pass on his message to her. They expected to hear from her in about two weeks but
added that she sometimes took a year to answer
fan mail.

"I'm kind of on a deadline. Isn't there any way
she can be reached sooner than that?"

There followed a long silence, and the voice said,
"Well, she is doing a public appearance tomorrow,
if you happen to be anywhere close to something
called a Medieval Festival near Austin, Texas."

Jim hung up the phone and charged into Michael's office. "I found her," he announced. "All you
have to do is get me to Texas by tomorrow."

"Now, how the hell am I supposed to do that?"

Jim looked puzzled. "I don't know. It's less than
halfway around the world, and we're six . . . hell,
eight hours ahead of Texas time. Find me a military
jet headed that way."

"This is a museum, man. We don't have that
kind of priorities." There was that Irish twinkle in
Michael's eye as he spoke and Jim could see that
already his mind was working on the problem. It
was well after dark before they left the museum,
and by then the problem had been three-quarters
solved.

Rudy stayed after they had left, puttering with this
and that for another hour before he returned to
Restoration Building #2. Last night's unfinished
memories weighed heavy on his mind. What else
had happened? What was it that he could not quite
remember?

There had been laughter amid the screams of the dying workers. The two SS officers who had stood beside Rudy as he sweated to replace the road wheel—they had laughed at the horrible scene, and then one of them had said something to the other.

It came to him suddenly: "Von Norden is in a bad mood today." The weathered lines of age on Rudy's face hardened. The SS men had said it, but he had seen it also, stenciled on the Jagdpanther's hull as it rolled past. It was totally against regulations, but apparently Von Norden had been someone who had no fear of either regulations or the SS.

"Dere is no such marking on this Jagdpanther. Or is dere?"

Rudy hurried to one of the storage closets and returned with a small can of paint remover and a brush. "If it is dere, I vill find it," he whispered as he climbed onto the Jagdpanther. Beside the commander's hatch, he carefully applied a light coat of the paint remover and waited until it bubbled the first layer of ancient, yellowish paint.

He wiped at it with a rag, being careful to remove only the top layer. Years of working in the museum had taught him that most military vehicles were covered with dozens of coats of paint. "Painted every morning before breakfast," the saying went, but not this time. Below a single layer of mustard yellow was battle gray. As Rudy nervously wiped a bit more, the traces of white lettering began to appear: E. Von Nor. It was proof enough.

Rudy climbed off the tank and looked at his watch. Turning his back to the Jagdpanther, he walked nervously to the telephone on his workbench by the wall. He should call someone. "Herr

Fafner is gone, but is not too late to call Colonel O'Leary. Maybe Old Rudy find something dey can check out." He looked up a number on a list taped to the wall and dialed. Nervously, he waited as it rang once . . . twice. On the third ring it was picked up and a woman's voice said, "Colonel O'Leary's residence. Mrs. O'Leary speaking."

Rudy asked for the colonel.

"He's taken Mr. Fafner to catch a plane. I expect him back shortly. Can I take a message?"

"*Ja,*" Rudy said. "Dis is Rudy, at da museum. I think I find something."

The muffled metallic ring of steel against steel sounded behind him as he hung up the phone. Rudy turned quickly but saw no one and nothing out of place. There was a blue light coming from somewhere, he thought. "Who ist dere?" he called out, and his voice echoed off the building's walls. From the tool bench, he picked up a pipe wrench and cautiously began walking back toward the Jagdpanther. It was not until he was standing directly in front of the gun tube that he saw that the commander's hatch was open.

"*Verdammt!*"

With the pipe wrench gripped like a club, Rudy started to climb up over the treads. His hand touched the cold steel and found it damp and slick, like the skin of a hibernating reptile. He drew back, wiped his hands on his pants, and then climbed up, over the drive sprocket and across the machine-gun ball mount. For a moment, he stopped short of looking into the open hatch and steeled himself for what he might see. He expected skeletons, twisted in the unnatural poses of violent death—grisly, hollow-eyed remnants of all five of the crew. He expected to smell the sickening stench of moldering flesh, rotted and decaying in the disintegrating remains of once-proud German uniforms. Rudy took a deep breath and leaned over the open hatch.

Nothing could have prepared him for what awaited within the Jagdpanther.

A blue light bathed the interior. Everything was there, in the proper places. The gun breech was closed, and beside it was the gunner's scope and the range finder. The ammunition racks bristled with 88mm rounds for the main gun. Only the MG-42 machine gun was missing from the ball mount in front of the radio operator's seat. It was all clean and shining, but, he thought, it looked wet. The blue light danced on his face, mesmerizing him, riveting him to his perch. The interior seemed to move, swell slightly, and then contract, pulsating in an even rhythm. It was not the fighting compartment of a dead war machine, but the entrails of a living thing. Its breath was cold on his face, foul and sickening with the odors of diesel, cordite, and death. The steel tingled against him as if millions of tiny nerve endings sensed his slightest touch. The Jagdpanther was breathing! The Jagdpanther was alive!

Despite himself, Rudy screamed. Vaguely, he was aware that he had fallen onto the floor. Beside him, only inches away, were the Jagdpanther's treads, reaching for him like huge steel claws. They were moving—the Jagdpanther was moving, turning toward him. Still flat on his back, he tried to crawl away from it, but something was holding him. He raised himself on one elbow and saw in horror that his pants leg was pinned beneath the tread. Once more he pulled frantically as the tread inched against his ankle.

Rudy jerked at his belt, trying to free himself by crawling out of his pants. His belt buckle hung, he jerked it again, and it came loose, a second too late. His ankle was already halfway under the tread and he could only watch as his foot was crushed beneath the tons of sharp steel.

His screams echoed among the other discarded war machines as the Jagdpanther inched forward, crushing his lower leg to pulp. His own blood spattered on his face and squirted across the concrete. His weathered hands clawed at the concrete, tearing away his fingernails as he still tried to pull himself from the Jagdpanther's steel embrace. The tracks inched their way to his waist. He grabbed at the end-connectors with both hands as if he would reverse their direction and restore the damage they had already done.

Beneath him the concrete was slick with his own blood as the Jagdpanther inched its way onto his chest, crushing ribs and snapping his spine. Far away, he saw his own foot and the flattened, bloody stump of his leg emerge behind the tread. His tortured lips screamed silently now. In one final convulsion, he vomited a crimson torrent of blood and supper from both his mouth and nose before the grinding treads at last shattered his skull.

The Jagdpanther's treads dripped with gore as it rolled over the entire length of his crushed body. Yet, it remained unsatisfied, as if drugged by the power of killing. It reversed, backed over the scattered bits of flesh and bone again and again, until they were ground beyond recognition and scattered from one end of the building to the other.

*   *   *

It was almost midnight when Michael at last delivered Jim to the helicopter that would shuttle him to a Stratotanker bound for the States from Rhein-Main Airbase.

"You've got a long, cold trip ahead and I sure hope you come up with some answers. If Walker finds out about this, we're both in a heap of trouble, so good luck."

Jim had only nodded as he got out of the staff car. Michael watched as the Huey lifted off and disappeared into the night before he parked his car and walked inside the operations office to call home. There had been only one call, from Rudy at the museum.

"He said he'd wait for you." Betty's voice said on the other end of the line.

Michael took another look at his watch. "I doubt if he'll still be there, but I'll stop by the museum on my way home. I love you." He ended the conversation and hung up.

Twenty-two hours and eight time zones after he had flown out of Ansbach, Jim walked up to the gates of the Hill Country Medieval Festival, somewhere about thirty miles south of Bergstrom Air Force Base and the city of Austin, Texas. As he stopped at the castle gate in front of him, it was as if his flight here had been through time instead of distance.

The wooded hills were ablaze with the oranges and reds of fall. Beyond the castle walls was a street of rustic shops, seemingly carved out of the forest around them. A merchant, dressed in robes of heavy velvet and with a jeweled ring on every finger, dusted a large quartz crystal in front of a shop selling jewelry.

The odor of roasting meat and wood smoke drifted on the afternoon air from a stand in front of a barbecue pit where a dozen turkeys were being turned on a spit by two barbarian types dressed in leather. Next door was a stand selling Lone Star beer in paper cups. There was something about that combination that seemed a little out of place, but Jim stopped to buy a beer anyway before continuing.

At the ticket stand, he had been told only that the cartoonist Sherri Vail was still somewhere on the grounds, but she would not be signing autographs again today. He dodged out of the way as a knight, on horseback and dressed in full armor, brushed past him. Somewhere, someone was playing a mandolin. The musical strains, gypsy and haunting, settled over the scene and blended with it.

Farther down the row of shops, a crowd had gathered. On the dusty ground inside a roped-off area, two knights dueled with broadswords and shields. Jim approached with interest. Their blades, he could tell at a distance, were wood, wrapped with silver tape. The rest appeared quite authentic. As he watched, one knight with a black crow on his shield advanced savagely, forcing his opponent against the ropes. A final blow, deflected only partially by his shield, glanced off the opponent's helmet and toppled him. The winner backed away.

A richly dressed man with a black beard—the judge, Jim guessed—stepped from the sidelines. "Sir Basil," he announced in a deep and royal voice, "chooses to spare the life of his opponent. This is to be considered an act of chivalry and kindness on his part, and not required by the rules of combat."

To this, the crowd applauded. The victorious

knight bowed and then retired. His beaten opponent crawled, without ceremony, out under the
ropes.

"And now, O gracious lords and ladies," the royal
voice continued, "I present to you Catherine the
Terrible, Shield Maiden of Ator and champion of
all the southern kingdoms." There was moderate
applause as a tall woman with black hair braided
down her back stepped through the ropes. Jim
guessed that she must be at least six feet tall. She
wore a silver-colored chain-mail tunic, which
reached about halfway down her thighs, and
leather boots, coming to just above her knees. A
black shield was strapped to her left arm, and she
rested a broadsword on her shoulder as she swaggered to the center of the ring.

"Catherine has been challenged today by Sherri,
a princess from the western kingdoms," the judge
announced, and waved his arm dramatically.

Jim turned his attention to the challenger as she
stepped into the arena. The most outstanding thing
about her was her size—that is, her lack of it. She
stood, perhaps, five four and, Jim guessed, weighed
little more than a hundred pounds. Her gold tunic
was short and tight, hinting of small breasts and a
girlish figure. At her waist, a shortsword and a dagger hung from a wide belt. She wore sandals that
were laced like ballet slippers, and a second dagger
was strapped to her left leg. On her arm was a
small white shield with a brightly-painted dragon.
Flaxen hair with more than a touch of curl was tied
back with a beaded headband, and reached nearly
to her waist. Her small round face was dominated
by a pair of green eyes, so large that they almost
hid her turned-up nose and seemed out of scale to
the rest of her body.

"She's dead meat," Jim thought as the little blonde touched the hilt of her shortsword to her chin and the battle began. Catherine moved in fast, swinging her broadsword in wide slicing strokes. The blonde, Jim noticed, was smart enough to duck and dodge most of the blows, deflecting with her shield only when absolutely necessary. At one point, she ducked under a wide slash and jabbed for her opponent's abdomen. Catherine doubled up and the blonde hit her on top of the head, but the attack seemed only to anger Catherine. The big girl's next blow connected solidly with the blonde's shield and seemed to rattle her all the way down to her toes.

It was then that Jim began to notice something familiar about the blonde. "Sherri," he almost said aloud. That was who the judge had introduced. From a pocket of his flight jacket, he pulled out the copy of *Princess of Elfland,* and took a quick look at the cover picture. Her costume was the same, she fought with basically the same weapons, and her hair was similar. Her body? Jim took one more look at the now-retreating blonde. "Only in her wildest dreams," he thought. "But that's gotta be her. Now, I just hope she can still talk when this is over."

It was over before he could give the matter much more thought. Another solid strike rained off the blonde's shield. She staggered once, blinked her eyes, and then looked down at the ground as if she had lost something. She was still looking when Catherine the Terrible planted her boot in the seat of the blonde's tight tunic and pushed her over the ropes. The crowd loved it.

By the time Jim had circled the area, the blonde had been helped to her feet by a large, burly character dressed like Conan the Barbarian. "No autographs," he growled, and blocked Jim's approach.

"Oh, I'm not looking for an autograph—" Jim started, but the barbarian cut him off.

"No interviews."

"I'm not here for an interview, either." The growing anger in Jim's voice was becoming poorly disguised. "I've got something I'd like Ms. Vail to look at."

"Who is he?" the blonde's voice said from behind the barbarian.

"Just another starving cartoonist. Wants you to see his work."

The blonde pushed past him. "All right, I'll look at it. Melvin, where the hell are my glasses?"

The barbarian handed her a pair of thick glasses. "I lost my contact lenses out there, both of them this time," she said to Jim as her eyes blinked and focused behind the glasses. "Okay, let me see your work."

"I'm not an artist," Jim told her as he handed her a photograph of the Jagdpanther's crest.

Sherri Vail blinked behind her glasses and frowned. "You didn't draw this?"

"No."

"Then who did?"

"That's what I was hoping you'd tell me." Jim was not sure if the look on her face was fear or just concern as she studied the photo for a long moment.

"We can talk in my camper," she said, and then turned to the barbarian. "Alone, Melvin." She led Jim a hundred yards or so to a concealed parking lot behind the hill where several lines of campers and other vehicles were parked.

"All the conveniences of home," Jim remarked as he followed her into a motor home.

"Yeah, I do a lot of these festivals and stuff." She tossed her sword and scabbard onto the couch and sat down cross-legged beside them. "Okay, so who are you and where did you get that?" she asked, and began unbuckling the dagger on her leg.

"My name is James Fafner. I'm a consultant with the U.S. Army Tank Museum in West Germany. This crest was painted on the front of a World War II German tank."

"It's old."

"That, I know," Jim said. "The tank was built in 1944 or '45."

Sherri was on her feet again and heading for the kitchen. "No, I mean, like, old-old." She opened the refrigerator door and stuck her head partway inside, causing her voice to echo strangely as she continued. ". . . at least the drawing they copied that from is. You want a sandwich?"

"No, thank you."

Sherri returned and stuck half of a submarine sandwich in his face anyway. With a large bite of the other half in her mouth, she kept talking. "These are really great. They've got watercress and garbanzo sprouts, alfalfa, seaweed, and buffalo meat."

"I'm trying to cut back on buffalo meat," Jim said dryly, and tried to change the subject. "So, just how old is 'old-old'?"

"Antediluvian, at least."

Jim almost laughed. "Antediluvian? Meaning 'before the Flood'?"

Sherri nodded as she swallowed another bite of sandwich. "In this case, way, way before the Flood.

Twenty thousand years maybe, give or take a couple of dozen centuries."

Jim was beginning to feel that he had wasted his time coming here. "The face looks suspiciously like the pictures you draw," he stated flatly.

"Of course it does. The characters I create are quite accurate."

"So how did it end up on the front of my tank?"

Sherri shrugged. "How would I know? It's your tank."

Jim was totally disgusted. "Thank you for your time, Ms. Vail, but I really must be going." He was rising to leave when a telephone rang on the dashboard of the motor home.

"Excuse me," Sherri said, again with her mouth full. "Mobile phones—they can find me anywhere now . . . Hello, Sherri's Whorehouse." There was a long silence and she said, "One moment. I'll check." She covered the phone with her hand and turned toward Jim at the doorway. "For you. Some General Walker. You here?"

Jim gulped and turned a little pale, then took a deep breath and nodded.

"Fafner here, sir." His voice was a little weak.

"Fafner, can you get back here right away?" The general's voice sounded strangely sympathetic. "There's been an accident at the museum. Colonel O'Leary and Rudy Bauer have both been killed."

Chapter Seven

"FAFNER? YOU STILL there?" General Walker's voice sounded distant and hollow as the phone dropped from Jim's shaking hand and bounced on the motor home's floor. A numbness flooded over him, dulling his senses and making his stomach try to climb into his throat. Sherri took a couple of cautious steps toward him and picked up the phone.

"You all right?" she asked.

Jim could not answer. He knew only that he had to get out and get out fast. He reached for the doorknob, but his hand was shaking so badly that he missed it on the first try. In frustration, he forced his shoulder against it, snapping the lock and forcing his way out.

Michael, dead . . . and from an accident at the museum? It seemed an insane possibility. Four different times, on convoy escort in Vietnam, Michael's tank had taken hits, twice from mines and twice more from antitank rockets. He had lost treads and bogie wheels, jammed the turret ring. Once, one of the rockets had blown the engine bay wide open. But each time, Michael had gotten out without a scratch. To die now, after all of that and with only a couple of years left to retirement . . . it was wrong—damned wrong and damned unfair.

Jim forced his way along the crowded festival streets, barely aware of which way he was going and bent on nothing more than finding someplace away from everything. How could it possibly have happened? What kind of an accident at a museum could kill two men as experienced as Rudy and Michael? Of course, he tried to reason, tanks were dangerous by nature and never really cared who they hurt. There were a hundred ways to get killed just being around them, but both Michael and Rudy had worked with tanks and war machinery all their lives. Maybe they'd just gotten careless.

He passed beyond the festival boundaries where the forest closed in around him and muffled the distant, dull roar of the crowd. Only the muted notes of the mandolin drifted with the rustling of leaves. He slumped down with his back against a tree and sat there staring at the drifting leaves. It was his fault. He should have been there. The Jagdpanther was his responsibility and he was here, halfway around the world, talking to some dippy bimbo about elves.

Sherri found him an hour later. She approached him quietly and said nothing until he looked up. She stood with the sun filtering through the trees behind her, wrapping her in a soft golden glow and making her chain-mail tunic sparkle.

"You left these," she said, holding out his briefcase and the photo of the Jagdpanther's crest. He only nodded, so she sat the briefcase down beside him but continued studying the photo.

"About ten years ago," she said, "I was doing some stuff with Norse mythology, developing the characters I wanted to draw for *Princess of Elfland*. In the records of an Austrian monastery, I came across parts of an ancient manuscript. It was written in Latin, so I think one of the monks had copied it from some pre-Christian writing, or maybe from an oral saga. I don't know; so much of it was missing that I could never even figure out exactly what he was writing about. But in it, he described elves, and on some of the pages he had drawn sketches which seemed to match his descriptions."

She handed him the photo. "This particular drawing was not one that I saw, but it's so close that my guess is, whoever drew it had seen that same manuscript."

Jim looked up slowly and stared at her, trying to force his troubled mind back to the problem that had brought him here. Suddenly, she did not sound like such a bimbo. "If we pay you a consultant's fee and expenses, could you trace it any further?" he asked.

"Not without going back to Germany."

"We can arrange that."

Sherri shook her head. "Can't do it. I'm playing Dungeons and Dragons next week in London."

"All week?"

"Yeah, at least. It's a big game; can't miss it."

Jim rose slowly to his feet, feeling very, very tired. "Look," he said, "I need an expert on elves and it looks like you're the only one there is. What's it going to take to hire you?"

"You can't," she answered flatly. "Consulting is, like, really dull. I mean, before I sold *Princess of Elfland*, I once spent eighteen months in Scotland, doing a retranslation of the *Elder Edda* for the University of Edinburgh. You ever read the *Elder Edda?*"

"Read it? I never heard of it."

"Dull, like to drove me crazy," she said, then raised one arm dramatically and recited:

> *"Then sought the gods their assembly-seats,*
> *The holy ones, and council held,*
> *To find who should raise the race of dwarfs*

Out of Brimir's blood and the legs of Blain.

. . . Motsognir the mightiest made
Of all the dwarfs, and Durin next;
Many a likeness of men they made,
The dwarfs in the earth, as Durin said."

"It was terrible. By the time I finished, it took me six weeks to stop talking in verse."

Jim had heard enough. The girl, he decided, was not playing with a full deck. "Look," he said, "I just lost a pretty good friend. He grew up next door and then went though Vietnam with me. He was two damned years away from retirement with a wife and kids. Now, I got a mad-assed general to face back in Germany, so, thanks for your time."

He started past her and she asked, "Can I keep the picture?"

Jim handed it to her and kept walking.

Colonel Nikoli Malinkov shifted his weight uncomfortably in the cab of the big diesel truck and watched the East German Autobahn pass beneath him in the night. For the seventh time this hour, he checked his watch. 0230 hrs: There were still almost three hours to go until the border crossing at Hof. He looked over at the driver, who was proving to be an untalkative type. Perhaps, Malinkov reasoned, he was nervous about carrying agents over the border.

Relax, Nikoli, he told himself. You have done all of this before. This time is no different. Insertions into the American sector of West Germany were done all the time. He guessed that one truck driver out of every five on this run from Leipzig to the Hof crossing point was a Soviet officer gathering intelligence on American troop movements and defenses. It was a good system, cheaper than all the expensive spy planes, satellites, and listening devices that the West used to do exactly the same thing.

Malinkov's granite face was pockmarked from a childhood disease that should have left him dead at the age of ten. A wide scar, compliments of an Afghan grenade, meandered across his forehead and down his left cheek to end a half inch from his jugular vein. His frame was short and stocky, with a neck so thick that his face just seemed to melt directly into his chest.

He was just the right size to fit comfortably into a tank, and that was where he had spent most of his adult life. He marveled at the fact that only twenty-four hours ago he had been riding the turret of a T-62, watching another Iraqi offensive bog down and then stall a few miles inside the border of Iran. At least, this assignment would be a change from his dull, and usually unsuccessful, assignment as senior Soviet military adviser to an Iraqi armored division. What, after all, could be much worse than trying to make tankers out of a smelly bunch of ex–camel jockeys with sand for brains.

He lit a cigarette and inhaled deeply. Think, Nikoli, he told himself. Use your time; rehearse your cover.

This was, without a doubt, the strangest assignment he had ever had. Only this morning, he had been briefed by Marshal Judenov, handed his false papers, and sent on his way. "We want you to get a look at a certain tank, an old Jagdpanther from World War II. We are trying some low-profile plans to get it into the Soviet Union for evaluation. But if they fail, you may have to steal it."

"Why do we want it?" Malinkov had asked, totally astounded that the Kremlin would be interested in anything so old.

Marshal Judenov had looked a little embarrassed and said only, "We have some reason to believe that it could be more than it appears to be. We have to know for certain."

With little more information that that, he was told to contact the director of Civilian Personnel Services for the United States Army at Ansbach. He would receive more details there.

At 0530 the truck pulled up behind a line of other trucks waiting in line at the crossing point near Hof. Malinkov tried to visualize his position on a map of Western Europe. Nuremberg was southeast, about 140 kilometers. Hannover was almost due north, perhaps three hundred kilometers. To the northeast was the infamous, open stretch of rolling hills, known to both NATO and Warsaw Pact as the Fulda Gap. It is there, according to most of the military minds in Europe, that the first tank battles of World War III will most probably take place.

An American MP and a West German border guard approached the cab, and the driver rolled down his window. "Your bills of lading," the German demanded. "What are you carrying?"

"Potatoes."

"Driver's licenses," the guard demanded.

Nikoli reached into this coat pocket and handed his license out to the MP, who looked at it critically. "What's your name?" he snapped, looking straight into Nikoli's eyes.

"Hans Graff," Nikoli growled at the MP.

General Walker noted that Fafner looked like walking death as he sat down in Walker's office about thirty hours after flying out of Bergstrom. He had not shaved in several days, his hair was uncombed, and there was the distinct look of a hangover about him. He had come directly from the helicopter that had ferried him back from Rhein-Main.

"How did it happen?" Fafner demanded.

The general frowned. "The official report hasn't been written yet, and the way it looks, you may have to be the one who writes it. Unofficially, it looks like the Jagdpanther somehow rolled completely over Bauer and then crushed O'Leary against the wall."

"Wasn't anyone else there?"

Walker shook his head. "Everything was closed. For some reason, they were both working late at night. Did O'Leary say anything to you about why he would be there?"

"Nothing."

"Well, he called home right after he put you on that chopper for Rhein-Main. Rudy had been trying to get ahold of him earlier. So, he told Betty he was going by the museum on his way home."

"How's she taking it?"

Walker breathed nervously. "She's Army—she'll be all right." He paused, looked out the window for a moment, and then continued. "How the hell could that thing have rolled over them?"

"I don't think it could have."

"Well, it damn sure did. Hell, there were so many pieces of Rudy Bauer strung over that floor, they had to identify him by a wedding ring. Now, if that Kraut tank couldn't have rolled by itself, maybe we better consider the possibility that we got a couple of murders on our hands."

Jim stared blankly at the general. "For what possible motive?"

"I don't know, but you can bet your ass the provost marshal's office is going to keep digging until they find out."

He pointed a finger at Jim's nose. "If I wasn't absolutely sure O'Leary was alive when you got on that chopper, you'd be my number-one suspect."

Anger flashed in Jim's eyes as he glared across the general's desk. Then he was on his feet and headed for the door.

"Hold it a minute," Walker called after him. "I said 'if.' As it is, I'd like you to take over Michael's job as museum curator, at least until this investigation is all over and I can find someone else."

Jim stood by the door as if frozen in time for a few moments, and then turned around and nodded his head. "Yeah, I'll do it."

"Good," Walker stated with a note of finality in his voice. "Now, maybe we've got an easy way out on this Jagdpanther."

Jim said nothing but looked interested, so Walker continued.

"Odd thing happened today. The museum got a request from the East German government. They're building some kind of a memorial in honor of Russian and American cooperation in World War II. They asked that the Jagdpanther be donated so they can use it as part of the memorial."

Jim frowned, not believing what he had just heard. Alarm bells were going off in his head. "They want what?"

"You heard me," Walker growled. "It would look like a nice, friendly gesture on our part if we did."

"We'll give 'em another tank, any tank. Jagdpanther is too rare. We've got a Hetzer and a Mark IV that are both cosmetically restored. Either one would be perfect for what they want."

Walker looked doubtful. "There's a lot of pressure coming down on this one. But all right, I'll
stall 'em for a while. Something sticks in my craw
about giving a Russkie a tank, even an antique one
that don't work."

Jim rose to leave. "My sentiments exactly, sir."

Jim walked back to the museum, trying to let the
cold air clear his head. He had boarded the MATS
flight with a fifth of Wild Turkey and emptied it
long before touching down at Rhein-Main. He felt
terrible. He hadn't drunk like that since Kristen left
him years ago. About halfway there, he leaned
against a lamppost and threw up on the snow.

An hour later his footsteps echoed in the gloom of
Restoration Building #2 as he walked to the center
of the floor and stared at the Jagdpanther. Although
the concrete had been cleaned, a ragged line of dark
brown stains still traced the route the Jagdpanther
had taken as it crushed Rudy and then ground the
disjointed pieces of his body into the floor. There
were stains on the Jagdpanther's tracks also, like
canary feathers in a cat's mouth.

Jim turned away. They had found Michael's body
crushed against the tool bench and impaled on the
muzzle of the Jagdpanther's 88. Now, only the tool
bench remained, broken and bent against the wall.
The telephone caught his eye. It had been torn from
the wall beside the bench and now lay on the floor.
The receiver was cracked and there were bloodstains on it, also.

"Was one of them trying to call someone?" Jim
asked himself.

He looked over the fallen tools and other junk
that had accumulated on the bench. He tipped up
a coffee can and sniffed the odor of paint remover. Beside it was a brush that smelled the

same. With his curiosity now aroused, Jim probed through the debris with the end of a pencil: a flashlight, some metric bolts, a rag with dark yellow paint on it.

"Yellow paint, with bits of lusterless brown and green," he thought aloud, and picked up the rag with his pencil. The paint was military, late-war German. "Ambush scheme," it was called and the only vehicle in the building that was painted that way was the Jagdpanther . . .

Jim got up and walked back toward the glowering machine. He circled it completely one time, looking for any evidence of removed paint. "They had to be working on it somewhere," he muttered, and climbed up over the treads. He was standing on the left fender when he saw it—a smudged streak along the rim of the commander's hatch. Leaning closer, he wiped the spot with his hand and read "E. VON NORD . . . something. Looks like he stopped before he was finished." Jim took out his pocketknife and scraped away a little more paint. "E. Von Norden," he said, and climbed off the Jagdpanther, still talking to himself. "I wonder if there is anything else under there? Shouldn't take much to bring it out if there is."

"Hey, Fafner," a voice said from the doorway. "You look terrible."

Jim stopped and looked up. In the doorway stood Sherri Vail, dressed in a silver mink jacket with a large hood, faded blue jeans, and fuzzy pink boots. "I thought you were in London, playing out your fantasies," Jim said dryly.

"Short game." She smiled sheepishly and pushed back the mink hood. "I got ate by an orc."

"Is that bad?" Jim grunted, and started scratching around for the can of paint remover that should have been somewhere among the remains of the tool bench.

"Yeah, well, win some lose some. So, anyway, I thought since I was in the neighborhood, I'd pop in and take another look at your elf."

Jim found the paint remover and got up. "This way."

Sherri followed him toward the Jagdpanther and stopped a few yards in front of it. She pulled her mink tighter around her and buried her gloved hands deep in her pockets. For a long time she just stared at the tons of squatting steel, and then said, "It's evil."

Jim laughed and climbed back onto the fender. "There were probably a lot of Russian gunners who thought the same thing, just before they died." He put his hand on the gun barrel for support and felt it raise slightly. Instinctively, he jerked his hand away and almost lost his balance.

"It's evil," Sherri's voice cracked, "and it hates me!"

Jim was standing on the fender, scratching his chin and ignoring her. "The gun does move," he said, thinking aloud. "Well, I'll be damned, maybe it's got some sort of experimental stabilizing system for the 88. Counterweights or something like we tried on our early M-3s."

At last he looked down at Sherri. Her eyes were green saucers, wide with fear, and her golden-tanned face had turned pale. She was shaking all over as she backed with unsteady steps, away from the Jagdpanther.

"It wants to kill me!" Sherri cried, and stumbled. Her eyes rolled back and she collapsed.

Chapter Eight

§

"THE BIMBO IS obviously on drugs," Jim sighed, and climbed down off the Jagdpanther.

He lifted Sherri's unconscious body from the concrete and looked around for someplace to put her. Beside the front entrance was a doorway that led to a small storeroom, and in it, Jim remembered, were a couple of wooden seats taken from the back of a half-track. Seeing no place better, he turned his back on the Jagdpanther and started for the storeroom.

Sherri's head moved and she tried to say something he could not understand. Behind him, he thought he heard the clank of a tank's treads, and turned with her still in his arms.

For a moment, it looked as though the Jagdpanther had been following him. "No way. You're just getting jumpy," he said aloud, dismissing the idea and turning away. In the storeroom, he lowered Sherri onto the seats and covered her with her mink.

He found a dirty coffee cup and poured her some water from a drinking fountain outside. "Come on, wake up," he growled, and patted her cheeks none too lightly.

She was trying to say something again, whispering in a weak and distant voice. Jim leaned closer and managed to understand a little of it.

". . . beneath the misty mountain deep,
Where evil hides and dragons sleep . . ."

"Oh, this is great," he said, throwing up his hands. "She faints and recites poetry!"

*"There the Elfin forges blazed and, so the sages tell,
Shaped a mighty hero's sword of magical Mirtheil."*

"Mirtheil?" Jim repeated and then shook Sherri
by the lapels of her mink jacket. "Come on, lady,
wake up and tell me what the heck you know about
Mirtheil?"

"Stop shaking me," Sherri answered sleepily and
swung her small fist at the side of his head. "You've
got the manners of a troll." Her eyes popped open
fully, and some of the fear he had seen in them
earlier returned. "Where is it?" she asked, looking
around.

"The Jagdpanther? It's out there in the middle of
the floor where it has been. It weighs forty tons. Did
you think it was going to get up and follow . . . ?"
Jim's voice trailed off as he remembered that it had
to have moved in order to kill Rudy and Michael.
"You're all right," he added in a softer tone. "You
fainted."

She sat up slowly and shivered. "Wow." She took
a deep breath and released it. "I don't usually do
that."

Jim backed away and leaned against the wall.
"What have you been taking?"

Sherri looked up at him and frowned. "What? I
don't do drugs. I don't even take aspirin." She
paused and looked toward the door. "That thing is
evil."

"Yeah, you said that."

"It radiates evil." She looked back at Jim, who
was plainly unimpressed. "It was like . . . bad vibes.
You know, sometimes you feel 'bad vibes' around
people who don't like you or want to hurt you?

Well, it was sort of that same feeling, only bad, really bad." She rose unsteadily to her feet and took another deep breath. "Can we get out of here for a while? I need some air."

They walked out of the museum and down between the antique tanks lining the front drive. Sherri looked at each of them as they passed. "I don't feel anything from these," she announced.

Jim was not in the mood for another discussion on the forces of evil, so he changed the subject. "Back there, when you were out, you mumbled something about *Mirtheil*."

"I said that? Wow, I must have been really out of it."

"Does it mean something?"

"Of course, everything means something."

"You used it in a verse of poetry."

Sherri looked surprised. "Beneath the misty mountain deep, where evil hides and dragons sleep? Yeah, it's one of the lost verses from the *Elder Edda*, or at least I think it is. It keeps about the same meter and I'm pretty sure it was written about the same time."

"I saw the same word written on a file in the archives at Koblenz. I thought it might have something to do with the insignia on the Jagdpanther."

"No." Sherri laughed, and shook her head. "Not hardly. If the Nazis had had *Mirtheil*, we'd all be speaking German and wearing those funny little black mustaches."

Nikoli Malinkov climbed out of the potato truck two blocks from the office of Civilian Personnel Services in Ansbach. Wearing an old brown overcoat and carrying a leather briefcase, he walked the remaining distance briskly. He touched the two days of beard growth on his chin to be sure he was properly unshaven to pass for an unemployed tank mechanic who had been released from the *Bundeswehr* (West German armed forces) two years earlier. Inside the offices, he gave his name to the receptionist as Hans Graff and was told to take a seat.

He joined a line of waiting German civilians and, for over an hour, he sat in a hard, straight-backed chair waiting for his name to be called. When at last he was called, he had almost gone to sleep.

He was ushered into another office where a pudgy man with glasses, very little hair, and bad breath shook hands with him. "My name is Smythe. First, a few questions, Herr Graff." the pudgy man said, and shuffled through some papers on his desk.

"Of course," Nikoli answered.

"What unit were you with in the *Bundeswehr*?"

"First with the 44th Panzer Grenadier, but after maintenance school, I was transferred to fourth-echelon maintenance-shop facilities at Karlsruhe."

"And what were your duties there?"

"Third- and fourth-echelon maintenance of tracked vehicles. Primarily the medium tank M-48, M-113 armored personnel carrier, M-60A1, and Leopard. We performed engine overhauls, transmission rebuilds, track and suspension system repairs."

A look of relief spread across Smythe's face. "Very good, Herr Graff. You have the job you applied for with the American Army Museum."

"Thank you."

"And now, we will take a little walk."

Nikoli nodded and they exited through a back door and down a set of stairs which ended in an alley.

"This was all put together very quickly," Smythe said in a lowered voice. He handed Nikoli a set of keys. "Your apartment, 129 Volker Strasse, number 4. Everything you need should be there. A motorcycle is in the garage."

"What can you tell me about this mission?"

"Only that the Americans are using the museum to hide something. Maybe a new type of tank gun, maybe some new armor. Moscow would not say exactly what. But, it has something to do with a Jagdpanther they dragged in off one of their firing ranges. Two of the museum employees were killed in some kind of an accident three days ago."

Nikoli smiled. "An accident?"

Smythe looked almost embarrassed. "Actually it was just that. We had nothing to do with it, although it has worked out wonderfully."

They stopped where an alley opened onto the main street. Smythe kept in the shadows. "You will not come here again. I am to be your only contact. Do you know how and where to contact me?"

Nikoli nodded.

"Then, good luck and good hunting."

At the same *Gasthaus* where Jim and Michael had lunched only last week, Sherri sat with Jim as winter twilight settled outside. "The manuscript that I used is in Munich now," she said between mouthfuls of sauerbraten and red cabbage. "The monastery where I saw it went out of business a few years ago."

Jim looked up from the Bloody Mary he was nursing. "I didn't know monasteries could go out of business."

"Well, not exactly. I guess 'die out' would be a better word. This place in Munich has all the records from nine hundred of them that folded. Hey, let's face it, monks don't exactly reproduce like rabbits."

"You said they were incomplete. What could you gain by going through them again?"

"Probably nothing. Of course, I didn't do a lot of translation before. I was only interested in the descriptions and the artwork."

"I think I've got a better lead," Jim said. "A name: E. Von Norden. It was stenciled on the hatch, so he was probably the tank commander. With a little luck, I can get his service records sent down from Koblenz."

"What'll that tell you?"

"His unit assignments, among other things. The Jagdpanther couldn't have been in service before January of 1944 at the very earliest. So I'm only concerned with the last eighteen months of the war."

Sherri finished off the last of the sauerbraten and sipped on a glass of white wine. "You got access to a computer? Something with a 9600-baud modem and a bunch of disks. I want to access Cambridge University Library." She pointed at Jim's Bloody Mary. "You should eat something."

"No computer," Jim answered, and ignored the comment about food.

"Gee." Sherri smiled thoughtfully. "That means I get to go to either Paris or Munich. Let me see, since it's December, the fashion shows are all over. The Champs-Elysées just doesn't do anything for me once it starts snowing, and the Sorbonne will be closing up for Christmas in a couple of weeks. So, I pick Munich."

"Why?"

"Hard copy." She leaned forward and looked into

his eyes. "Do you ever sleep? Your eyes look just like a Swiss road map."

"Do you ever say anything that makes any sense?"

Sherri wrinkled her nose. "There's something I want to look at. There are copies of it at Cambridge, England; Goetha University in Munich; and the Sorbonne in Paris. If you had a decent computer, I could access it. Since you don't, I'm going to Munich to look at it."

"Have a look at what?"

"It's a surprise; but while I'm there, I'll breeze through those monastery records too," she said as she got up. "I'll tell you about it when I get back. Ciao."

Before Jim could protest further she turned and bounced merrily out of the *Gasthaus*.

The next morning, Jim went to see Betty O'Leary. As he drove up in front of the cuckoo-clock house on Kalbach Strasse, the first thing he saw was the moving vans in the driveway. Workmen were carrying out furniture and boxes, moving in a steady procession, back and forth from the house to the trucks. Inside, Jim wandered aimlessly through the bare living room and into the kitchen.

Betty was there, with her back to him, wrapping dishes in newspaper and putting them into boxes on the cabinets. She turned suddenly and saw him standing in the doorway. Her eyes were red and puffy, and she looked like she had not slept in days. For a long moment, they faced each other while they found no words to fit the occasion.

At last, Betty managed a weak smile. "I think you look worse than I do," she said, and almost choked on her tears.

"Where will you go?"

"Home," Betty answered dully. "Iowa. My parents' place for a while. And then . . . I don't know. We talked about retiring in Florida. I don't think so now."

Jim looked around at the bare kitchen. "I'm surprised they're moving you out this soon."

Betty put another dish into the box. "One of the few times the army moves fast. But it's best. Keeps me from thinking about it too much." She pointed at his dirty clothes and unshaven face. "Looks like you could stand to get to work yourself."

"I'm having everything from his office packed for you. I'll send it over when it's done."

Betty nodded and kept packing dishes. "General Walker said he had asked you to take over the museum until they can get someone else."

There seemed to be nothing else to be done here. "I think you're right," he said. "I need to work." He kissed Betty lightly on the cheek as he left, and said, "Take care."

He started driving back to the museum but changed his mind and turned instead toward the base hospital. He had been wanting to have a talk with the tank commander who found the Jagdpanther, and this seemed like as good a time as any.

In a fourth-floor room, he found Hank Murphy propped up in bed and watching television. There were bandages on his head and one arm. Murphy eyed him suspiciously as he walked in. "Well, you damn sure ain't Army," Murphy said.

Jim introduced himself and Murphy remained passively hostile. "I've told everybody from brigade ordnance to CID exactly the same thing. They all think I'm crazy."

"You're a tanker; you've got to have a few screws

loose," Jim said, and for a moment, he thought Murphy was going to come out of the bed after him.

Then the sergeant's expression changed and he almost smiled. "Look, it's just like I said; the tube moved, the gun fired, my M-60 went up like a star shell."

"Did you hear anything before it went off, some kind of a firing mechanism maybe?"

Murphy shook his head. "Just one thing: I heard the breech close inside." Jim was looking doubtful. "Yeah, yeah, I know, that's impossible."

"I didn't say that."

"There had to be somebody inside," Murphy insisted. "Why is that so hard to believe? They had plenty of time to get out. I got hit with something right away. I heard it was an hour before anybody got there. Hell, the army don't even believe that old gun fired."

"It fired, all right. I found fresh cordite burns in the muzzle brake. The part I'm having trouble with is the ballistics. That gun was an 88mm L-71. It's not supposed to be able to penetrate M-60 frontal armor, even at that range."

"So we've been told," Murphy growled. "But it happened, goddammit, whether any of you egg-heads want to believe it or not. It happened, and it looks to me like there's all kind of evidence to prove it!"

Jim left the hospital and drove back to the museum. He arrived in time to see the last of Michael's things being carried out of the curator's office. Inside a man about his own age was waiting for him.

"Hello," Jim said as he walked in.

"Herr Fafner? I am Hans Graff. The civilian employment services sent me."

"Ah, yes. A pleasure to meet you. They told me you were a tank mechanic."

"Yes," Malinkov lied. "Three years with the *Bundeswehr*."

"Good. We're maintaining several vehicles in running condition. A half-track, a Stuart, and a couple of Greyhounds for parades and shows. And, as you've probably heard, we've acquired a Jagdpanther, which I intend to put into running condition."

"Can that be done?"

"I think so. The engine looks like it's restorable and I saw a couple of spares in Israel a few years ago. If they're still available, we'll get them for parts. Of course, I've still got to get the damned hatches open. But, assuming we do, can you work on a Maybach 230?"

Malinkov only nodded.

"Good," Jim said, "I'll have one of the men show you around. Right now, I need a bath. We'll talk later."

Malinkov shook his hand and watched him go. He left the office before anyone could come to show him around. The Jagdpanther, he had already learned, was in Restoration Building #2, and he headed straight there. He entered the gloomy room where the Jagdpanther sat in the middle of the floor.

This is what the KGB is excited about? Nikoli thought. If there is any secret weapon here, it is certainly well hidden. He started walking toward the ancient tank killer. As he walked, it seemed to him that someone was turning on a blue light. He stopped in his tracks as little blue sparks danced over the Jagdpanther's hull and along the gun barrel.

He backed away and the light faded. Some sort of electronic security? he thought. Perhaps Moscow was right and there is more here than I thought. He scanned the ceiling for video cameras or motion detectors. Seeing nothing, he walked to one side and began to move behind the Jagdpanther. Again the blue sparks flew and the old tank glowed brightly. Nikoli backed away again, his excitement growing. So the Americans are hiding something, and never have I seen anything like it!

Chapter Nine

⚡⚡

IT WAS TUESDAY before the *Bundesarchiv* at Koblenz sent down what service records they had on German soldiers of World War II with the last name of Von Norden and a first initial of E. There were only seven: two Ernsts, an Evan, an Everett, an Eberhart, and two Eriks.

Ernst number one was a private in the 18th Motorized Engineer Battalion and stepped on a mine in France in February of 1941. Ernst number two was an *Oberleutnant* of the 334th Artillery Regiment, Afrika Korps. He was taken prisoner at Tunis and lived out the war in a Texas prison camp, emigrated to the United States after the war, and died of a heart attack in 1956.

Evan was the first name that looked interesting. He had been a tank commander with an SS Panzer division, but he burned in his Tiger I at Kursk, in the summer of 1943. Still, Jim considered it a long shot and laid the file aside.

Everett Von Norden was a sergeant with a paratroop regiment. A Sherman tank cut off both his legs during the Second Ardennes Offensive, December 1944. He died in a hospital, two months after the war ended.

Eberhart had been a cook with a Bavarian *Volksgrenadier* regiment, survived the war, and now owned the Edelweiss Restaurant at Garmisch.

One Erik was reported killed in action, April 1945. Jim perked up a little at this possibility and read on. He was a *Hauptmann*, 2nd SS Panzer Division, awarded the Iron Cross at Tobruk, the Knight's Cross at Kursk. He laid this file aside also.

The other Erik was also a tank officer, *Sturmgeschütz* Regiment, and was alive apparently until the final days of fighting in Berlin. By then, the record-keeping had pretty well fallen apart, and it was impossible to say exactly what might have happened to him. During that time, whole companies had surrendered to the French, volunteered for the French Foreign Legion, been given new identities and been shipped off to die in French Indochina. Jim left his desk and walked to the window, poured himself a cup of coffee, and looked out over the snow-covered tanks outside. He had not heard anything from Sherri since she had left the *Gasthaus* on Friday night. Not that this surprised him. Nothing about her surprised him, and if he never heard from her again, it would not have surprised him either. Still, he wished that she had told him a little more about *Mirtheil* before she left.

He turned back to the files on the desk. The two

Eriks were the most likely possibilities. A knock on the door interrupted his thoughts. "Come in," he said.

"Herr Fafner," Malinkov said as he stepped into the office, *"Guten Morgen."*

"Good morning, Hans. Coffee?"

The other man nodded and poured himself a cup. "Well, what shall I do today?"

Jim was standing behind his desk, studying the three files lying in front of him. "Take a look at these. One of these men may have been our Jagdpanther's commander."

Malinkov raised one eyebrow, walked over to the desk, and started reading through one of the files. Jim picked up the other and scanned it again. On page three, there was a report of a physical examination, dated July 1944. There was nothing unusual about this, except that there was also a mention of psychological tests, which he appeared to have passed with flying colors. The report was signed, but the paper was yellowed and badly water-stained. Jim took a magnifying glass out of the desk drawer and moved the report closer to the light. "Dr. Helmut Ehrler," he read half-aloud, "transfer approved, Project Mirtheil."

"Bingo," Jim said.

"You found something?" Malinkov asked, looking up from the file he was reading. He thought, what kind of a game is this fool playing? He has a tank wired with the most advanced security system I have ever seen, and he is telling me he is trying to find out who the commander was?

"This is our man, Hauptmann Erik Von Norden. Quite a man, Knight's Cross even. And our Jagdpanther may have come from something called 'Project Mirtheil.' "

"Project Mirtheil? And what was that?" Malinkov asked, playing his part while he worried that he was either being set up or was being fed false information.

"I haven't got the slightest idea," Jim said, and closed the file.

"I do," Sherri said from the office door as she walked in, unannounced. She wore a tight sweater and ski pants that could have been painted on. Her mink was slung over one shoulder. "Hi," she said to Graff, who immediately glued his eyes to her legs as she passed by. "You better believe I had to really force myself to come all the way back up here," she sighed, and dropped a big folder of papers on Jim's desk. "There is eight inches of new powder on the slopes at Garmisch."

Jim looked at the folder she had dropped in front of him. "If you ski anything like you handle a sword, this probably saved your life."

Sherri wrinkled her nose and cocked her head to one side, dumping a lock of blond hair down into her eyes. "Come on, she outweighed me fifty, maybe sixty pounds." She crossed her eyes and blew the wayward blond lock back into place.

To Nikoli, Jim said, "Hans, this is Sherri Vail, our consultant on weird things."

Nikoli only nodded and smiled.

"So what did you find?" Jim asked, and started to open the folder.

Sherri placed her hand over his and said, "Later. Tell me what you've dug up so far."

Jim turned to Malinkov. "We won't do anything on the Jagdpanther today. How about running some maintenance on our half-track? Walker wants to use it for Santa Claus to ride on in the Christmas parade in a couple of weeks."

Malinkov nodded, smiled at Sherri, and left the room.

"He's creepy," Sherri said as the door closed.

Jim shrugged. "Lots of things are creepy to you. Besides, he likes your legs."

Sherri sat down on top of the desk and listened while Jim told her about Erik Von Norden's personnel records. "Now if I can find out what this 'Project Mirtheil' was, I might be making some progress."

"Well, then you're in good shape, because *that* is what I've brought you!" Sherri announced and giggled as she opened the folder. "Right here . . . it starts with that verse, 'beneath the misty mountain deep, Where evil hides and dragons sleep, There the Elfin forges blazed and so the legends tell, shaped a mighty hero's sword of magical *Mirtheil*.' "

"I hate poetry."

"It figures," Sherri grumbled. "But this, even you should be able to appreciate. 'In high Moria, homeland of the dwarves, for centuries there, they bore . . .' "

Jim closed the folder. "Just tell me what it says."

"Oh, all right, if that's the way you want it. But it loses a lot going to straight prose."

"Yeah, but maybe I'll be able to understand it."

Sherri sighed and looked at the ceiling for a moment, then resigned herself to the boring job of explaining *Mirtheil*. "Translated from Elfish, it means 'gray star,' or, more idiomatically, 'Elfin steel.' This was the metal that was used to forge the weapons of the gods. It was probably the reason they became gods. Thor's hammer would be an example, King Arthur's Excalibur and, a little closer to good old Germany, Siegfried's sword. Remember in the *Nibelungenlied*, the sword that Siegfried kills the giant with, what was his name? Oh, yeah, Fafnir." She stopped suddenly and laughed. "That's your name. You're named after a giant!" Sherri kept laughing until she fell off the desk.

"Hilarious," Jim said dryly. "Is it possible we could continue?"

"Oh, yeah," Sherri giggled, and tried to catch her breath. "It's just that there's something about *you* being named after a *giant;* I mean, wow, with those reading glasses, and that pipe, and the way you always forget everything . . ."

"Oh, for Christ's sake," Jim growled. "When was all of this sword-and-sorcery stuff supposed to have taken place?"

"That is a very good question. And there is considerable disagreement about it. Some authorities believe it could have been going on as late as the time of Christ. I'm inclined to believe it falls into 'prehistory,' having happened at least before the Flood or before our own recorded history begins.

"But whenever it was, there were three dominant races on earth; elves, dwarves, and men, although elves were by far the most intelligent. Now, of course there's a lot of controversy over whether dwarves were, in reality, a true race, or a mutant race, like trolls and orcs."

Jim figured he had heard enough. "All right, so when you boil down all of these fairy stories, what you seem to be trying to say is that *Mirtheil* simply means metal, especially an advanced metal for its day. Right?"

Sherri started to protest that statement and then shrugged. "That's about like condensing the Constitution and the Bill of Rights down to the word *freedom,* but, if that's the way your mind works, I guess it might make sense to you."

"I would guess that *Mirtheil* doesn't mean anything, as far as the Jagdpanther is concerned, anyway. It was probably just a code name, used for whatever project developed this late-war Jagdpanther variant. Probably had something to do with better armor plate."

"Boring, boring, boring," Sherri sang, and walked across to the window. "I missed skiing Garmisch for this?"

"Win some, lose some," Jim grinned and picked up the personnel file of Erik Von Norden. "Dr. Helmut Ehrler?" he said, thinking aloud. "Let's see what we can dig up on him."

The street outside the Christl Hotel in Ansbach was crowded at noon, a condition that August Gnokte considered both good and bad. Although it was easy to blend into a crowd and remain unnoticed, it was also hard to tell if you were being watched.

He spotted Nikoli Malinkov instantly as he started across the street toward him. His pockmarked face alone was enough to trigger the image of the photo he had been shown only yesterday. The man beside him had to be Smythe, the KGB's operative working out of Civilian Personnel Services.

"This is highly dangerous," Smythe said as he and Nikoli stopped beside Gnokte.

Gnokte nodded but said, "We may have very little time. Tell me, what have you learned?"

Nikoli moved closer to speak. "There is something highly secret going on and I do not understand it. There is a Jagdpanther, or at least it looks like pictures I've seen of one. It is protected with some sort of electronic security device. Whenever I try to get near it, it glows. Some kind of force field perhaps. I have never seen anything like it."

Gnokte's hands began to shake and his face turned a little pale. "Go on," he whispered nervously.

"The museum curator is a new man, named James Fafner," Nikoli continued. "I don't understand this either, but he is spending all his time trying to figure out who commanded the thing in 1945."

To Nikoli's surprise, Gnokte nodded his head and asked, "How much has he found out so far?"

"He came up with a name, 'Erik Von Norden.' And also the name of some secret project, 'Mirtheil.' " Nikoli shrugged. "It means nothing to me."

"I wish only that I could say the same," Gnokte whispered. "What else?"

"Very little. There is a woman working with him. An American also, Sherri Vail, very young, very beautiful, but apparently insane. I suspect she is an agent, playing the part. She is not one of ours, I hope?"

"Working with him? What is she doing for him?"

"I am not exactly sure. When she came in, I was given work to do, so I listened from outside the door. She was talking about elves and dwarves and . . ."

Before his sentence was finished, Gnokte's shaking hand had dropped the folded newspaper he was holding. "Then there is almost no time left!" he whispered through clenched teeth. "We must stop them before they learn anything else. An accident, whatever it takes, but stop them!"

Smythe looked doubtful. "You know how the Kremlin feels about assassinations here in West Germany right now. They don't like anything to disturb the status quo, shake up the Americans, start them looking for things."

Gnokte grabbed at Smythe's collar. "If we don't stop them, it is not going to make any difference what the Kremlin thinks. There isn't going to be any Kremlin!"

"Nicht mehr haben Sie für Helmut Ehrler?" Jim asked with the phone cradled between his neck and his shoulder. As he listened, he jotted down a few more notes. *"Jawohl, danke."* He hung up the phone and looked over the scant information the Koblenz archives had supplied him on short notice over the telephone.

"Interesting," Jim said to himself.

Across the room Sherri giggled again. She was lying on her back on the office couch with her feet in the air, eating a brandy-filled chocolate bar and reading a comic book. "You know, the Smurfs are really hard to understand in German." She sat up and looked at him. "So, what's interesting?"

"Our Doctor Ehrler was not a medical doctor but a psychoanalyst. He was born in Bavaria, the village of Anshau, educated in Vienna, studied under Freud. Impressive credentials for the time."

"So what happened to him?" Sherri asked with her mouth full of chocolate.

"They don't know. They have no record of his death, so apparently he survived the war. He was still listing Anshau as home in 1944." Jim paused and stared out the window. "I wonder what we'd find at Anshau?"

Sherri tossed her comic book on the floor and stood up. *"The Road goes ever on and on,"* she quoted. *"Down from the door where it began. . . . And I must follow if I can."* In answer to Jim's questioning stare, she explained; "J.R.R. Tolkien, *Lord of the Rings*. In your case, I think he was right. So let's go to Anshau."

Jim looked at his watch. "It's too late today. We wouldn't get there until after dark."

"We might if I drove."

"No thanks. I may be old, dull, and boring, but I've still got a couple of years left. That is, if I don't get in a car with you."

"Oh, come on, what's a couple of years? Let's go."

"I can't leave right now. I have to pack a few things."

"So we'll stop and get your rubber duck on the way."

Jim took a long look around the office and then thought about spending another night either drinking or staring at the walls of his room at the BOQ. "Why the hell not," he said, and picked up his coat.

He left a few instructions with the secretary in the front office and, with Sherri on his arm, stepped outside. At the front steps, she jumped onto the railing and slid all the way down to the street. When Jim got to the bottom of the stairs, she was waiting for him.

"Haven't you ever grown up?" Jim growled, and walked past her.

Sherri's smile disappeared. She took a couple of quick steps after him and grabbed his sleeve, spinning him around. "Let's take mine," she insisted, pointing at the red Ferrari convertible parked at the curb behind his staff car.

"That's yours?" Jim said, surprised.

"I lease it when I'm in Europe because it's the closest thing available to the one that's in my garage in San Francisco. That one's parked right next to my Rolls Royce. I paid more income tax last year than a lot of major corporate heads. Not bad for a short Polack from Pittsburgh. Now, don't give me any crap about growing up. I tried it. It was no damn fun and I'm sure not going to screw up and do it again."

Jim could think of nothing appropriate to say, but made a mental note that underneath her shell of youthful insanity, Sherri was a woman capable of a great deal of anger.

"Now, come on, I'll get you to Anshau before dark." She walked up the back of the Ferrari and over the trunk, leaving small tracks in the light film of snow that had settled there. "Hurry up," she added, and dropped into the driver's seat.

"It's half full of snow," Jim said as he opened the door.

"No problem. We'll leave the top down and it'll all blow out long before we get to Nuremberg."

Nikoli watched them drive off, leaving a cloud of swirling snow behind them. He slipped unnoticed into the curator's office, quickly dialed a number, and waited nervously as it rang. "They are headed for Anshau. No, not in a staff car—a red Ferrari. Get moving."

Chapter Ten

§§

THE FERRARI'S SPEEDOMETER wavered around the 160-kilometer mark as Sherri drove south on the Autobahn. Most all of the snow had blown out in the first few miles and she had stopped long enough to close the convertible top. Now less than two hours later, the rolling hills of Franconia were growing into the foothills of the Bavarian Alps. Nuremberg and Ingolstadt were somewhere behind them. Munich was just to the west, and far in the distance, the snow-capped peaks of the Alps were a hazy outline against the southern sky.

"So what do you do when you're not restoring old tanks?" Sherri asked as she flashed her headlights at a Mercedes sedan almost a mile ahead.

"A little of this and a little of that. Wrote a couple of books about German armor development, some articles on tactics, military history, stuff like that," Jim answered as he tried to watch the road.

Sherri looked at him over her sunglasses. "I never knew anyone who did anything like that before."

"I never did, either. It just worked out that way." They passed the Mercedes as if it were standing still.

"So you were in the army, and then what? College?" Sherri started past a long convoy of U.S. Army trucks, followed by a couple of wreckers and a jeep with flashing yellow lights.

"Not exactly. My only degree comes from the school of hard knocks."

Sherri thought she detected a note of bitterness in Jim's voice. She glanced at him thoughtfully for a while. "Yeah, that's all right, Fafner," she said finally. "I got a doctorate in mythology and a master's in art. But the only thing I've been able to do to make money, I mean real money, is drawing pictures of elves. That I could do when I was twelve, and most of my art professors said I was wasting my talents. Dumb, really dumb."

Despite the Ferrari's speed, the sun set behind them a half hour before they left the Autobahn at

Frasdorf, some fourteen kilometers from Anshau. The road south wound through the Alps, twisting and turning as it climbed slowly. Just outside of Anshau, Sherri brought the car to a stop in front of a small hotel. "This look okay for you?"

Jim read the sign over the door. "Alpenstock Inn." He nodded and got out of the car. He untied their overnight bags from the luggage rack as Sherri pulled a large sketch pad out from behind the seat. "Got to work a little tonight," she said. They started inside without noticing the Mercedes sedan or the three men inside who watched them enter the hotel and then drove on.

After supper in the hotel restaurant, Sherri yawned and said she was going to sketch a story-board for her next comic book issue, and she went upstairs. Jim sat for a long time, sipping on a stein of dark beer, and then went upstairs also. He stopped for a moment at the head of the stairs where a well-worn mountain-climbing ax hung with a coil of rope and a Bavarian hat above a spray of artificial mountain flowers. He gave Sherri's door an uncertain look, started to knock, and then changed his mind. "Don't be ridiculous," he told himself, and went on to his own room.

Sherri pushed opened the window curtains. A full moon hung above the snow-capped mountain peaks, making the snow glisten magically in the cold, pale light. For a while she curled up in a chair with her sketch pad and tried to lay out a story-board for *Princess of Elfland*. After almost thirty minutes she was convinced it was not working, but the urge to draw was strong. She tore off what she had done and started on a blank page, letting her hand move the pencil without direction. It was a technique she used often when developing new characters, a kind of direct link between the sketch pad and the right side of her brain.

Her pencil flew over the paper and a face began to emerge, but long before it was finished, she knew it was the sneering elf on the Jagdpanther's hull. She abandoned it and moved to another place on the pad. The next face was human, square-jawed with short hair and eyes she did not like. The face was never finished. Instead, a sketch of the Jagdpanther emerged, superimposing itself over the face until, except for the eyes, it was hidden within the lines of the Jagdpanther.

Fascinated, as if the drawings were being done by someone else, Sherri watched the sketch emerge as little beads of perspiration formed on her forehead. The Jagdpanther was not exactly as she had remembered it. The gun seemed larger and longer. The treads had become steel claws, dripping with gore. She had the distinct feeling that it wanted to climb off the paper, rip her to pieces, and grind her bones beneath those treads.

There were other faces too: some with elfish eyes and ears; others with pixie faces and fairy wings. All of them were crying. They were her characters, she realized, all the imaginary creatures she had created for her comics. Her own portrait materialized, centered among them and dressed in her chain-mail tunic. She lay draped on a funeral pyre as the flames rose to consume her. She was dead, and there were only her characters to mourn her death.

She flung the pad across the room and jumped to her feet, tipping over the chair as she backed against the wall. With both hands over her mouth, she stood shaking for several minutes. Then, taking a deep breath, she ran for the door. Before she finished releasing the locks, she changed her mind. "No," she whispered to herself. "Whatever happens, you don't go running to him. He's not the one for you. You must wait. You know that."

Wiping a tear from her cheek, she backed away from the door and turned to the bathroom. She was still shaking a little as she walked around the crumpled sketch pad on the floor, pulled off her sweater, and tossed it on the bed. Inside the tiny bathroom, she turned on the shower and peeled off her boots and ski pants, then unbuttoned her French lace bra and stepped out of her panties.

"Relax," she said. "The elves are just playing tricks on you. They do that sometimes; you know that. They're just in a nasty mood tonight. Maybe you've been ignoring them and they're mad at you. So, you'll make it up to them. Now take yourself a nice, hot shower and go to sleep. Right? Right."

The black Mercedes sedan stopped only long enough for a man in a dark parka to get into the back seat before driving out of the parking lot of the Alpenstock Inn. "Perfect," the man said. "Rooms 14 and 16, second floor."

"Adjoining rooms," the man in the front seat asked. "Are they sleeping together?"

"No."

"Seems odd."

"It's good," the driver added. "She'll be nice and lively when I fuck her brains out before I slit her throat."

"Not tonight, *Schweinhund*," the man beside him said as he opened the glove box and removed a small case. As he talked, he opened it and removed two large syringes with long needles. "This is to look like an accident. So, since they are Americans, we arrange a drug overdose. Americans die of drugs all the time and no one ever looks very closely." He raised one of the syringes, inserted the needle into a small bottle, and smiled as it filled with a milky liquid.

"We'll take the girl first; she should be the easiest." The same man smiled. "Then we kill the man, put them both in the same room, and leave a little coke around for the police to find. It will look as if they were having a little friendly orgy and sniffed too much magic dust."

"All neat and routine," the man in the back seat echoed. He removed a 9mm Walther PPK from beneath his coat, chambered a round, and smiled at the satisfying clunk of metal against metal as the round chambered.

The driver cursed quietly and turned off the lights. He swung the Mercedes onto the narrow dirt road that ran behind the hotel and stopped. "Shit. I still want to fuck her brains out."

Sherri drifted in restless dreams. The faces from her sketch pad swirled in her mind shouting warnings she could neither hear nor understand. From out of the darkness came trolls—huge lumbering trolls with warts and ugly faces. They chased her through a dark forest and cornered her against a rocky cliff. She seemed unable to resist as they dragged her to a rough, stone altar and chained her. "The princess must die, must die," they chanted, and danced around her. "You are the one it fears, it fears."

The chanting stopped suddenly, the trolls backed away, dissolving into the darkness. Only the Jagdpanther was there, crawling toward her as she struggled. It was stalking her, like some wild lion stalks its helpless prey. It came closer, its clawlike treads ripping the ground. She could hear its heavy breathing. The steel tracks touched her.

Sherri awoke with cold sweat dripping in her eyes. The moonlight was still bright through her window. I'm all right, she thought. I'm here, in the hotel room. But it seemed as if remnants of the nightmare remained. There were figures in the room with her, dark silhouettes moving toward her bed.

She screamed and a gloved hand went over her mouth, forcing her head back against the pillow. The figures were faceless in the moonlight. They were grabbing her arms, holding her down on the bed.

One of them straddled her squirming body. In the moon's pale light, she saw him raise the needle. "In about two minutes, Blondie, this will make you feel real good," he laughed wickedly. "But then of course, you'll die."

Sherri bit at the gloved hand that covered her mouth until her teeth hurt. *"Verdammt!"* someone cursed in the dark, and then punched her in the stomach. Her nightgown was jerked from her shoulders. "Hold her tight," the same voice said. "I don't want any blood to mark the injection."

The needle moved toward her—a silver death lance in the moonlight. Her eyes were riveted to it, until she could see nothing else. Again and again she screamed into the gloved hand. The needle touched her body; she jerked with all her remaining strength against her captors, twisting her body a few inches. The needle missed its mark and scraped across her breast. She felt a trickling drop of her own blood, warm against her skin. The man on top of her cursed. As if in slow motion, the needle moved toward her again. This time she could not move. Tears filled her eyes and clouded the horrible scene as the needle pricked her skin . . .

Something hit the man with the needle, and he fell forward, covering her face. All around her were the sounds of fighting. Somewhere a lamp broke. The man on top of her was moving, trying to get up. His rough face brushed her own and left it wet. Sherri forced her hands against his chest and pushed, straining with all her might to free herself from his unwanted embrace. Her first attempt failed, but the second attempt rolled him off onto the floor.

"It's blown. Let's get out of here!" someone said in the confusion. The man on the floor was crawling and Sherri kicked him in the side. Sharp pains shot through her foot and up her leg as the man got to his feet anyway and followed the other two through the open windows.

The light, she thought, find the light. She staggered to where the lamp had been, but it was broken on the floor. There was another, she remembered, beside the bed. She found it, also overturned but still plugged in. With trembling fingers she turned it on and the light hurt her eyes. There was more movement against the wall. She spun around, with the lamp raised over her head.

"Fafner?" she said, and lowered the lamp. "You did pretty good."

Jim was getting to his feet. The climbing ax from outside the door was in his hand and one end of it was bloody. "I heard you scream," he said, and rubbed at his jaw. "What the hell did those characters want?"

"They wanted to kill me . . . I—I don't know why.

They tried to give me a shot of . . ." Sherri went pale as she looked at the scratch across her chest. "The needle," she gasped. "Find the needle! I don't know if they did it or not."

Sherri was on her knees, pulling off the bedcovers and looking under the bed, when Jim found both of the syringes against the far wall. One was still in the case. The needle was broken on the other, and he held it up to the light. "It's still full," he announced.

"Oh, wow, am I glad to hear that," Sherri gasped, and moved closer to the bed. "Now, will you excuse me, I'm going to faint." With that, she fell face down onto the bed and did not move.

Jim lifted her in his arms and carried her to the door, opened it a crack, and checked to be sure no one was in the hall. Then he carried her to his room, lowered her onto his own bed, and covered her with a quilt.

He fumbled around in his overnight bag for a moment and removed an Israeli-built, Desert Eagle automatic pistol. He had picked it up in the Middle East, just last year, and except for its large size and weight, he liked it. Somewhere else in his bag, he found its magazine and a box of .357 magnum shells. He had long ago decided that there was no perfect handgun. The Desert Eagle represented a unique trade-off. For the tremendous knockdown power of the .357 magnum combined with the rapid firepower of an automatic, you put up with a large, heavy-framed weapon. He believed it was worth the inconvenience of size, if you were not in the kind of work where you had to pack the gun very far into the bush. He rubbed his jaw again and wished that he had had it ready before he had heard Sherri scream. "Dangerous mistake," he said to himself as he stuck the Desert Eagle in his belt and went back to get Sherri's things from her room.

For the past several years of Jim's life, there had been people trying to kill him on a fairly regular basis. In Israel, the Middle East, or Africa, it was a way of life. But here in Bavaria, it bothered him. Especially since he was supposed to be involved in nothing more dangerous than the restoration of an antique armored vehicle. Two men had already died. Sherri had survived by only a matter of seconds, and he had not done all that much better himself.

He stuffed Sherri's clothes into her overnight bag and grabbed up her sketch pad. Deciding that it would be best to not draw any attention to themselves until he could figure out what was going on, he wiped the blood from the climbing ax and carefully replaced it on the wall outside the room. There was a small bloodstain on the floor and he moved a chair to cover it. He finished straightening up the room and decided it might pass unnoticed, for a while, at least.

Sherri was still unconscious when he returned. He lifted one limp arm, felt her pulse, and decided she was still alive and breathing normally. Her sketch pad caught his eye, and he sat down on the edge of the bed with it. The picture of the Jagdpanther sent a strange chill up his spine and made little hairs bristle on the back of his neck. It fascinated him and, as he studied it, he began to pick out the face within the drawing. "Goddamn!" he whispered when he traced his fingers over the SS collar tabs. It was the same, blond, Aryan face that had flashed in his own mind that day in the forest when he first saw the Jagdpanther.

Sherri stirred on the bed beside him. He should

move her, he thought, looking around the room. Put her on the floor between the bed and the wall, then stuff the pillows under the bedcovers, and make it look like she's still there. Then, if he took a position beside the windows and behind one of the chairs, it should give him the first shot at either possible entrance.

He reached for Sherri and she suddenly awoke. Her eyes popped open, and for a second, Jim thought she was going to scream. "It's all right," he said. "You just fainted. I want you to sleep on the floor—it's safer that way."

"Not now," she said. "I need a favor first. Would you hold me? Just for a little while?" Jim nodded and she snuggled into the crook of his arm. He pulled the quilt up close around her chin and sat back against the headboard. With his other hand, he laid the Desert Eagle on his lap and noticed that Sherri was already asleep. He brushed a few tangled curls from her face and smiled when he saw that she slept with her thumb in her mouth. He tried to guess how old she must be and gave up. Tonight she was a child.

Chapter Eleven

JIM AWOKE WITH the first, gray light of dawn. He hurt everywhere. Beside him on the bed, Sherri stirred and snuggled closer into the crook of his arm. With his free hand, he stiffly laid his pistol on the nightstand and carefully touched his face. He felt tenderly at a bruise on his left cheek and worked his jaw, again, just to reassure himself that it was not broken. Too old for this crap, he thought.

Sherri moved again, mumbled something about not wanting to go to school today, and then, with her face inches away from his, opened her eyes. For a second, she stared at him sleepily, and then jerked away, releasing a little scream as she bounced off the bed and dragged the quilt with her.

"Oh, wow," she said sleepily. "For a moment I thought I—I mean you . . . we had . . . that would have been terrible. We didn't, did we?"

Jim shook his head and got up. "Oh, no, nothing as horrible as all that," he answered sarcastically, and disappeared into the bathroom.

By the time he had shaved, Sherri had gotten dressed. "Come on," he told her, "let's get out of here." They left the room together and stopped at the office only long enough to pay the bill. Jim approached the Ferrari and set his bag down a few feet away. "Give me the keys," he said.

"What for?" Sherri demanded.

"So I can find out if it's going to blow up in our faces."

"Why would it—oh, yeah, good idea." As Sherri watched, he slid under the Ferrari, then crawled out and opened the hood. Cautiously, he checked over the engine, then eased the trunk open only an inch or so and took a long look inside before opening it the rest of the way.

"I guess whoever tried to O.D. us last night, is still committed to making our deaths look like an accident," she said as he started the engine.

"What is this 'we'?" He almost laughed. "I believe that was your room they were in."

"There were two needles, weren't there?"

Jim shrugged. "Probably a backup, in case you did something like break the first one. Besides, I'm just being paid to restore an old tank. I'm not involved in anything right now which would make me a target."

"Maybe you are."

Jim laughed again. "What? Magic metal?"

"Hey look, I'm not exactly in a high-risk profession either. Okay, so not everybody likes what I draw, but the mortality rate on comic-book artists is very low."

Jim grumbled and decided the conversation was going nowhere. Ahead of them, the village of Anshau was just waking up. They drove down the winding main street between neatly whitewashed houses standing gable to gable and decorated with brightly painted flowers, holy saints, and golden scrolls. As always in Bavaria, the church dominated the village skyline with its high-pointed spire rising like another mountain peak against a backdrop of the snow-capped Alps. They waited as a farmer and his wife guided a small herd of milk cows across the road and up into a steep pasture. They drove on, and Jim parked the Ferrari in front of the first cafe they found and slipped his pistol under his coat before they went in.

"I feel better," Sherri admitted as she turned her third cup of coffee into a syrupy mixture of sugar and cream. "I've never been so scared in my life."

"Almost being killed will do that to you."

Sherri nodded between bites of a sweet roll. "Oh, yeah, that too. But, when I woke up this morning, I thought, just for a moment, that I'd had sex with you. Now, that really scared me."

Jim glared at her across the table. "A fate worse than death?"

Sherri frowned at him as if she thought he should be more understanding. "Well, it's not that. I mean, I'm sure you're very good and all. Probably not very imaginative, or the least bit kinky, but you're, you're . . ."

"Next time I hear you scream, I'm going back to sleep."

Sherri released a heavy sigh. "You're impossible to communicate with. Look, let me explain it this way: do you believe in reincarnation?"

"No."

"You should."

"When you're dead, you're dead."

"No, definitely not. I can remember most of my past lives. And through all those lives, I have loved the same man, or 'being,' I should say. Because in one life, he was a unicorn. But that's all right; I was one too. And in a couple of other lives we were both elves."

"And so what does all that mean?"

"Very simple: I've known him since time immemorial, so I should have no problem recognizing him when I meet him in this life. And, well, believe me, you are not him."

Jim dropped a few marks' tip on the table and got up.

"That's refreshing to know. Now, come on. We've got a man to find before somebody finds us again."

They spent the morning checking the likely sources for a Dr. Helmut Ehrler. He was not in the phone book and had no post office box. Courthouse records showed several Ehrlers had owned property in the area, but in every case, they had sold their holdings many years before. At the police station, they were told that no one by that name lived in Anshau, but if they did, they were not permitted to give out any information about them.

At the church, they did a little better. "There is no one by that name among my congregation," the young priest told them. "But perhaps we can find his name among our funeral records." He led them up a winding stairway to a room in the church tower that was crammed with old record books. The priest squinted behind his big glasses as he searched and finally removed a large, leather-bound volume from a dusty shelf. He sat down with it at a heavy oak table and searched through it for a long time.

"This is interesting," the priest said after a while. "I have here the death of a Frau Helen Ehrler in February of 1956. My records go back only to 1950. Perhaps your Dr. Ehrler died before that time and this was his widow?"

"Perhaps," Jim echoed. "Where was the body buried?"

"Outside, in the churchyard. That is the only cemetery we have."

"And is it still there?"

"I am not certain, but we can look and see." The priest got to his feet, and they followed him back down the stairs.

"What do you mean, still there?" Sherri whispered, grabbing at Jim's arm. "Why wouldn't it still be there?"

They left the chapel and were passing a wall lined with weathered gray shelves. "Because cemetery space is very limited," Jim answered. "If no one pays the rent, they dig you up and put you in there." With a hand on Sherri's arm, he turned her toward the shelves, where a neat line of human skulls, each surrounded by a small collection of bones, sat stored and forgotten, except for a small brass name tag in front of each.

Sherri drew back. "Yuk," she whispered. Jim grinned at her and walked on.

"Yes, Frau Ehrler's grave is here," the priest called. In front of him was a small gray tombstone surrounded by a well-tended grave.

"Tell me, Father," Jim asked. "Do you have records of who pays the cemetery rent?"

The priest nodded. "Somewhat, I will check."

Jim thanked him and he disappeared back into the church.

"So what are you going to do if the priest comes up blank?" Sherri asked.

"Somebody's taking care of the grave. Whoever it is, knows the Ehrler family—simple."

"I doubt it," Sherri said as the priest returned, looking disappointed.

"The fee was paid ahead for five years. It was in cash, so there is no record of who paid it. That was three years ago, just before I came here."

They thanked the young priest and left the church. "Well, Fafner, you got any more ideas?" Sherri asked as she gunned the Ferrari out onto the road.

"If we stay around here too much longer, we're apt to get hit again. I don't think the guys who visited you last night can afford to give up just yet, and red Ferraris are pretty easy to spot on the Autobahn." Jim removed a map from the glove box. "Maybe we should stay visible until dark and then slip out of here on some back road." He studied the map for a while. "And then on the other hand, maybe we're overlooking the obvious."

"I'm listening."

"On this map, the village we are in is actually called Hohenanshau, which translates to Higher Anshau. Five klicks down the road is Niederanshau, Lower Anshau. Maybe we're in the wrong Anshau."

"Once in a while, Fafner, your mind works pretty good," Sherri admitted, and floored the Ferrari.

The road to Niederanshau was two-lane and as crooked as a snake. Halfway there, Jim pointed at a turnoff and said, "It looks like there's a back way in; take it just in case we've got a tail."

Sherri nodded and downshifted as the Ferrari drifted onto a dirt road, which led in through a half mile of forest and then meandered out across a rolling snow-covered field and approached a house perched on a knoll at the forest's edge. The house was still fifty yards away when she hit the brakes and pointed.

"Elves," Sherri said, looking at the house.

"Elves?"

"Yeah, all over that house. Look at the carvings under the roof and the paintings on the wall."

The house was typical for the Bavarian Alps. Built low with a lean-to roof protected with heavy rocks, it looked out over the fields, with mountain peaks rising behind it. The walls were timbered, and under the wide eaves were carvings of various small characters with large ears and pointed shoes.

Sherri drove closer, stopping in the driveway and shutting off the engine. "I got a feeling—this could be our man," she said and got out. Jim followed her, and together they walked up the stone pathway. The front door was heavy wood and carved also. "More elves and they're like the sketches in the monastery." Sherri pointed out.

Jim shrugged, but had to agree with her logic. He knocked on the door and waited. There was no answer, so he knocked again. They heard movement inside, and at last the door was opened by an elderly man with snow-white hair and thick glasses.

"Excuse us," Jim said in German. "We are looking for Dr. Helmut Ehrler."

There was a long silence while the old man looked them over. "*Ja?*" he said finally in a rasping voice. "I am he."

"We wanted to talk with you about Project Mirtheil."

There was the strangest look in the old man's eyes. Jim had never seen anything quite like it. It was somewhere between the look of man at the instant he knows he is going to be killed and the distant, aimless eyes of shell shock known as the thousand-yard stare. If Jim had any doubts that this man was Helmut Ehrler, they vanished instantly.

"Get out of here," the old man rasped, and tried to push the door closed.

"Please, it's very important or we would not bother you," Jim said, putting his foot in the door.

"Who are you?" Ehrler demanded.

Jim told him he was with the U.S. Army Tank Museum. "I have a tank, a Jagdpanther which I believe has something to do with Project Mirtheil."

"Then you are wrong," Ehrler snorted. "They are all gone, destroyed."

Sherri ran a finger over one of the carvings on the front door. "This one has an elf painted on it which was copied from sketches in the same monastery as these carvings were."

From a coat pocket Jim removed a handful of photos he had taken of the Jagdpanther. The first was a close-up of the insignia. He handed them to Ehrler and waited.

"This is an old photograph; you copied it."

Jim shook his head. "This vehicle is in Ansbach right now. We don't have a vehicle number, but we are pretty sure the commander's name was Erik Von Norden. You approved his physiological profile for Project Mirtheil."

The old man wilted. He backed away from the door and, with a shaking hand, motioned for them to come inside. He closed the door behind them and locked it. Everywhere inside the house was wood, oiled and varnished—light pines, dark cherry, and mahogany. The stuffed heads of deer and wild boar and elk hung above the huge, stone fireplace and along the walls. There were mountaineering trophies also, climbing axes and rope coils, pitons and framed photos.

Everywhere were books. High shelves of them lined every room. Sherri noted the titles of several. "You are a scholar in the grandest tradition," she said.

Ehrler ignored the compliment. "So Von Norden is still alive," he said sadly. It was not a question but a statement, as if there was no possible doubt. "I never believed even he could survive all this time."

Jim said, "We have no reason to believe he is still alive."

"Then you know nothing. You have Von Norden's Jagdpanther; Von Norden is not far away."

Jim did not understand. "We haven't been able to open the hatches. It's possible he is dead and still inside."

"*Nein, nein!*" The old German exploded. "If the

Jagdpanther exists, then Von Norden lives, and God in Heaven help us all."

A smile crossed Jim's face. "Oh, I think we can handle one obsolete tank destroyer, especially since it's been parked in the woods for forty years."

"You know nothing," Ehrler sneered. He turned to Sherri. "You have seen the manuscript from Tauenkopt Monastery?"

"There were a lot of pages missing."

Ehrler nodded. "They were removed in 1936 by Fredric Linth. His doctorate was metallurgy. His obsession was folklore." Ehrler began to pace nervously back and forth in front of the fireplace. "The manuscript was, of course, a translation, made, we think, somewhere around the eleventh or twelfth century. It was translated from elfish runes. Apparently the Church had ordered all elfish records destroyed centuries earlier, so it is anyone's guess where an eleventh-century monk learned elfish. But he did, and he also learned two of their greatest secrets."

"*Mirtheil?*" Sherri whispered with trembling lips.

Ehrler nodded. "Where to mine it and how to shape it," he said. Sherri half-whispered:

"Beneath the misty mountain deep,
Where evil hides and dragons sleep,
There the Elfin forges blazed and, so the legends tell,
Shaped a mighty hero's sword of magical Mirtheil."

Ehrler looked very pale. "Correct, except for one thing. Swords, even those made of *Mirtheil*, were useless in World War II. So Fredric did not shape swords. He shaped Panzers!"

Chapter Twelve

"YOU'RE TRYING TO tell me that the Jagdpanther sitting in my museum is made out of *Mirtheil?*"

"That's what he's saying." Sherri was bubbling over with excitement. "Wow, do you know what this means? This is going to rewrite all the history books. It proves all the theories about other races. Fairy stories aren't going to be fairy stories anymore; they are going to be history."

"So, just how tough is this *Mirtheil* supposed to be?" Jim asked, turning to Ehrler.

Ehrler shrugged. "Once it had accepted a master, we never found anything that would penetrate it."

"If it is that good, how come you didn't win the war?"

"The project was a failure. We could not control *Mirtheil* and we could not control Hauptmann Erik Von Norden. But wait, I think you know so little that you must be told the whole story."

Jim nodded and sat down. "Sounds like a good idea."

Ehrler continued to pace as he began his story. "Fredric Linth and I were old school chums. I shared his interest in folklore; he shared mine in psychoanalysis. As I told you, it was in 1936 that he found the manuscript at Tauenkopt. He knew enough about the legends to see that it was a . . . a monumental find—one that could change history. He smuggled out the pages which told where the mine and forges were located and described the process for refining *Mirtheil*.

"The mines were not so easy to find. Elves hide their secrets very well, and humans, by elfin standards, are nearly blind. It was 1942 before Linth and myself finally found them. By then, we had the resources of Hitler's Reich behind us, but still it took another year to understand the refining process and actually produce the steel."

Ehrler sat down in one of his big padded chairs and sighed. "The real problems did not at first become apparent. The metal, once it was properly refined, was lightweight and quite easy to shape. There was considerable argument, beginning with its correct application. Since it was forty percent lighter than steel, we thought first of aircraft. Perhaps that would have been a better application.

"But the Führer loved his panzers. We asked for a vehicle to use for testing the strength of refined *Mirtheil*. We were sent an American Sherman tank which had been captured somewhere in Italy. To it, we mated glacis armor plates made of *Mirtheil*. We made them exactly one half the thickness of the original Sherman's armor. *Mirtheil* was so easy to work with that we also built a thin sheath to protect the turret. Then we cast new road wheels and treads of *Mirtheil*, added some small shields to protect the drive sprocket and the rest of the Sherman's inferior suspension."

"And it worked?" Jim asked doubtfully.

Ehrler nodded and got back up. "All too well." From the mantel, he picked up a long, ceramic pipe and began filling it with tobacco from a silver container. "A demonstration was arranged and Hitler himself attended. We drove the modified Sherman onto a tank range and surrounded it with an entire platoon of King Tigers, all with the latest L-71, 88mm main guns. At a range of less than one hundred yards, they fired until all of their ammunition was gone. Then we started up the Sherman's engine and drove it away."

Jim frowned doubtfully at him but said nothing.
"The Führer was insane with happiness." Ehrler's excitement built with each word he spoke and,
although his English was excellent, his accent increased with his excitement. "He proclaimed dat
Siegfried hiself, der greatest of all Aryan heroes,
hat returned and handed to Germany his own
sword, mit which ve vould crush the invaders und
conquer *die ganze welt*!" He slammed his fist down
onto the mantel.

It took a minute for Ehrler to regain his compo-
sure. "The project was given the highest priority,"
he continued after a deep breath. "The caves in
which Linth had found the elfin forges were en-
larged to create a huge, underground factory complex. Everything we needed was brought there to
produce panzers."

"It was a sacred place," Sherri said, with a touch
of anger creeping into her voice. "You shouldn't
have desecrated it."

Ehrler shrugged. "Perhaps that is what cursed
the project. The Jagdpanther was chosen as the
best panzer design to produce. With it, there were
no problems with casting a turret, and it was all
relatively easy, flat armor plates. It was fast enough
as it was, so when we produced it in lighter *Mirtheil*, it could disengage from any enemy tank whenever it wished and outrun them. Of course, it would
never have reason to run from any fight. We also
built the ammunition for it of *Mirtheil*, which, of
course, produced an armor-piercing round which
was unequaled."

Sherri was squirming with excitement. "Did it
do all the neat things that the legends say about it,
like glowing?"

Ehrler nodded his head. "If only that was all it

had done. But there was more, so much more we were never able to understand."

"Glowed?" Jim smiled a little as he asked.

"Yeah," Sherri interrupted. "According to Norse legends, *Mirtheil* glowed in the presence of an enemy."

"True, *Fräulein*. And it was the glowing which caused the first problems with the project."

"How?"

"It was, how does one say this, a problem of mating technology with magic. They do not mix well." Ehrler looked at Jim, who obviously thought he was nuts. Sherri, at the same time, stared at Ehrler with the hypnotized eyes of a child seeing Santa Claus.

"A sword does not have a lot of choices to make when determining who an enemy is. For a tank, we found the choices were harder. For example, one time, early on in the project, a mechanic went to remove an injector pump from one of our Jagdpanthers. The panzer identified him as an enemy. The same thing happened again, when we were inspected by some accountants who wanted to cut the project's budget. We found out very quickly that a panzer has many more enemies than a sword.

"Tell me, *Fräulein*, do you know the other magical properties of *Mirtheil*?"

"Well, let me see. It seems like there was something about it accepting a master before it could work right."

"We never completely understood that whole process. It was not apparent during the first tests with the Sherman, but after we built the second Jagdpanther, there was an accident. We were running some ballistics tests, considering arming the Jagdpanthers with a smaller-caliber round, but using a projectile made of the *Mirtheil*. We fired a small, 20mm, conventional projectile and it passed completely through the Jagdpanther, killing one man inside.

"So we went back to the legends, determined that *Mirtheil* would serve only one master, and that it must first accept the master."

"How in hell did you get it to do that?" Jim asked as he got up and walked to the window.

"That is where I became most heavily involved in the project. It was my job to evaluate potential Jagdpanther crews and decide if they were capable of accepting and believing in the power of the steel. Everything, you must remember, depended on the tank commander—the master. The tank had to accept him, and he had to accept it, knowing that he could never be promoted or replaced. And if he was killed, then that was the end of the tank and the rest of the crew."

Jim was standing at the window, looking out across the snowy fields that stretched away to the treeline, when he saw the car. "Are you expecting company?" he asked.

"No."

"Then I think we better get out of here," Jim said just as the car's lights went out.

"Is it Von Norden?" Ehrler asked in a shaky voice.

"We don't know who it is, but they tried to kill us last night," Sherri answered as she got up.

Ehrler looked confused and nearly scared to death. "All right," he agreed. "Take me to see the Jagdpanther. Perhaps I can find some way to stop Von Norden, if it is not already too late."

Jim grabbed his coat. "I don't know what you're talking about, but it sounds like as good a place as any to head for." Ehrler picked up his own coat and they hurried out to the Ferrari. "You drive," he told Sherri, "and put Ehrler behind the seats. I think there's enough room."

As the Ferrari's engine roared to life, Jim strapped into the seat beside Sherri and chambered a round in his Desert Eagle. "Now, just drive like you always do, and they haven't got a chance."

"Go to the left," Ehrler said. "The road winds up into the forest and then hits the main road into Hohenanshau." As he spoke, the dark outline of the Mercedes pulled into view in front of them, driving cautiously toward the house with its lights out. Sherri floored the Ferrari just as a single pistol shot flashed from the Mercedes's window. They passed inches apart and Jim fired into the Mercedes's windshield. The .357 magnum autoloader belched a foot-long tongue of flame and, for an instant, turned night into day.

The Ferrari drifted into a tight turn between two fences and slipped far enough to remove a section of rails before getting back onto the road. Behind them, the Mercedes had as much trouble on the same corner and scattered another section. Another pistol shot thudded into the Ferrari's rear fender just as they topped a hill where the road dropped off into the trees.

"Can you see where the hell you're going?" Jim yelled at Sherri as she sped down the winding forest road without lights.

"Sure, I see like a cat," she assured him just as a tree scraped the entire length of the Ferrari's right side, leaving a pile of bark and broken twigs in Jim's lap.

The road dropped again, down to a small stream crossed by a narrow bridge. Sherri managed to

straighten out the Ferrari seconds before it would
have hit the stone posts guarding the bridge railing. With rooster tails of snow and gravel spewing
behind them, they crossed the bridge. The road
made another tight turn. Sherri swung the wheel
over hard and for a second it looked as though the
Ferrari would claw its way around. Then, the tires
broke loose. Sliding sideways over a bump and into
the shallow ditch beyond, Sherri jammed the gears
and hit reverse, but the tires only spun.

"Get away from it," Jim yelled as he fought his
way out of the Ferrari's tiny cockpit. Sherri's door
was jammed against a tree, so she released the
convertible top and started to climb out with
Ehrler right behind her. Jim looked quickly around
him, hoping he would come up with a better idea
than the only one he had at the moment. He did
not, so grimly he placed himself just at the turn in
the road where he had a clear field of fire directly
across the bridge.

"Fafner, what are you doing?" Sherri yelled at
him as she struggled to free herself from the Ferrari.

Jim ignored her. He could hear the Mercedes
coming down the hill, just on the other side of the
bridge. He dropped to one knee, leveled his pistol
with a two-handed grip, and waited. It occurred to
him that he had done something like this only once
before. Only then, he had been in an Israeli-mod-
ified Sherman tank, waiting just over the military
crest of a hill as an Egyptian T-54 climbed up the
other side. This time did not feel any better. T-54s
have weak spots in the bottom of the hull which are
exposed when they top a hill. He wondered where
the "soft spots" were on a Mercedes sedan.

Before he could give the matter further thought,

the Mercedes was in front of him, speeding across the bridge with its lights still off. Jim began firing, letting the Desert Eagle rock comfortably in his hands, and fighting back the urge to rush his shots and run like hell. With round number four, the Mercedes swerved slightly and clipped one of the bridge railings. Still, it was round number seven before he got results. As the Mercedes cleared the bridge, it seemed to lose control and began to slide. Jim held his fire, keeping the remaining rounds in reserve in case he had to finish off anyone still alive inside. The sedan kept sliding. He dodged out of its way and then ran after it as it joined the Ferrari in the ditch. The driver's door opened as he approached and a man staggered out. Jim aimed at the center of his chest and dropped him with a single round. A bullet, fired from inside the Mercedes, whined passed his ear as he moved closer. Without hesitation, he stuck the automatic inside the Mercedes and fired twice.

"You killed them?" Sherri said suddenly from behind him as he reached into the Mercedes and came out with another pistol.

"Yeah, I killed them. Did you think I was going to spank their little bottoms and send them home to mommy?" Without giving her time to answer, he held out the gun he had just retrieved. "Can you shoot?"

"Well, sort of, I—"

"I can," Ehrler interrupted, and took the pistol.

"Good, now let's see if we can get the Ferrari out of the ditch and get out of here."

"What the hell's the hurry, Fafner?" Sherri said, still angry. "You already killed everybody."

"Maybe, maybe not. As bad as these guys fucked up last night, I'm afraid their boss didn't send them out alone tonight. Now get in and drive, we'll push."

Sherri glared at him for a moment. "Sometimes, I don't think I like you." she said.

"Drive, damn it!"

She stalked away from him, dropped into the driver's seat, and started the engine. In less than fifteen minutes they had pushed and shoved the Ferrari back onto the road. Ehrler tapped Jim's shoulder. "Look, up the hill." Through the trees, they could see the lights of another vehicle. Apparently it had a spotlight because a beam of yellow light was sweeping the trees on both sides of the road.

"Maybe it's the police," Sherri suggested.

"Maybe it's not. Let's get out of here."

Sherri started to protest but then changed her mind and drove silently. They hit a paved road only a few kilometers away and turned south. "This will keep us off the Autobahn as far as St. Heinrich, on the Starnberger See. That should be far enough."

As they drove on through the night, they continued to talk about Project Mirtheil. Jim asked, "You said that everything depended on the tank commander, and that if he died, then that was the end of the crew. Why?"

"Simple," Sherri interrupted. "For exactly the same reason they never found Excalibur."

"What are you talking about?"

"King Arthur's sword, Excalibur. Don't you read anything? It had to have been made out of *Mirtheil*. When he died, the sword died with him."

"She is right," Ehrler admitted. "I do not know anything about King Arthur's sword, but *Mirtheil* does die with its master."

"Oh, come on, you two," Jim insisted. "This story

is getting a little out of hand. Now maybe, just maybe, I can believe that your friend Linth discovered a better steel than existed in 1944, but metal is metal; it just lays there. It doesn't live or die or anything else. It just lays there and keeps on laying there."

Ehrler answered very quietly. "I wish, more than anything else in this world, that I agreed with you. But I have seen too much.

"Not long after the project began, there was another accident. One of the tank commanders was walking between two of the Jagdpanthers. The engine was running and the driver was at the controls inside. His leg hit one of the steering clutches; the Jagdpanther jerked over and crushed the commander between itself and the tank beside it."

"That's about the most common accident there is around tanks," Jim said.

"Yes. When we reached the commander, he was still alive, but he was crushed so badly that we knew he was dying." Ehrler's voice began to tremble. "As the life drained out of him, his Jagdpanther began to turn blue. And then, at the moment he died, it burst into flame. But not a flame like I have ever seen before. It burned cold and blue, and in a matter of seconds, the Jagdpanther and everyone in it had vanished."

"There wasn't any wreckage left?"

"Nothing. I felt the ground where it had been and it was not even warm."

"It must have been very hard to continue the project after that," Sherri said.

"*Ja*, it was that, all right. Several men went completely, screaming insane. There were three suicides in the first month after the accident. I believe that if Von Norden had not come into the program at about that time, the project would have been abandoned."

"What was so special about Von Norden?"

"He was different. He was everything that a panzer officer was supposed to be. First, he was a Nazi of pure Aryan blood—blond hair, blue eyes, and above all, a racist. Second, he was a young but highly experienced panzer officer from the SS Totenkopf Division."

"Yeah, I saw his service record," Jim said thoughtfully. "I can see why you'd pick him."

"Third, he was smart. He operated very well without any orders from higher command. He got his Knight's Cross at Kursk for taking command of an attack after all of his superiors were killed. And, like most men with those same qualifications, he was ambitious and power-hungry.

"I detected those qualities during his psychological testing. It seemed at the time that they would be assets. But, there was so much about *Mirtheil* we had no way of knowing."

"It grew stronger with age, didn't it?" Sherri asked.

"Yes, just as in the legends of old. An ancient sword which had seen many battles was better than one newly forged. But did you also know that *Mirtheil* learns from its master?"

"No. I never heard that part."

"Because it was never written. I do not know if even the elves who forged it knew of its ability to learn. They only forged swords, spears, suits of armor, and perhaps some arrowheads. Those are simple weapons. After all, how much can a sword learn? But when *Mirtheil* is used to build a complex weapons system, such as a tank, things are different. We gave it a gun, a six-hundred-horsepower engine, and the ability to move quickly over almost any terrain. Suddenly, it had a great deal to learn. And we, fools that we were, gave it a master who not only taught it how to kill, but how to hate.

"Von Norden's Jagdpanther broke all the records for rate of fire. It became faster than the others of its kind—we never knew why. But even Von Norden admitted once that he felt the Jagdpanther was anticipating his commands."

Jim shifted nervously in his seat as Sherri rounded a tight curve only inches away from the guardrail. "Did any of these Jagdpanthers ever actually get into combat?"

"Only one, Von Norden's, and then only very late in the war. Fredric had become very frightened of the project. He had realized by then that there was too much about *Mirtheil* which we did not understand. Von Norden was furious, accused him of treason for stalling the project and keeping the Jagdpanthers out of combat. In March of 1945, Fredric was killed. Officially it was an accident: similar to the first one, he was crushed between Von Norden's Jagdpanther and a wall. There was no sense in trying to prove anything different."

"And then Von Norden took his Jagdpanther into combat?"

"Of course, there was no stopping him. For a while he led a platoon of regular Jagdpanthers, but soon he drifted off, began to hunt on his own, and even those of us on the project crew which was supposed to be supporting and evaluating him could not keep up with where he was.

"I am sure of one thing, though: the Jagdpanther also became stronger with each enemy it destroyed."

Sherri said, "That makes sense, I guess. It's an-

other ancient belief. That's usually the real reason
cannibals eat their enemies—to take their power."

"We lost track of Von Norden for a couple of
weeks," Ehrler continued. "In February of '45, we
thought perhaps somehow he had been killed. Then
he turned up again. There was a large battle near
Ansbach. Some of the last remains of the 7th Panzer
Division disintegrated there. As near as I was able
to determine, Von Norden's Jagdpanther was the
only operational panzer left after the first two days.
Yet he delayed the advance of an entire U.S. tank
regiment for another four days."

"And then what?"

"And then . . . he disappeared."

"You mean, his Jagdpanther was destroyed?"

"No," Ehrler said. "One of Von Norden's crew,
his loader, was brought into a field hospital, and I
spoke with him there. He was terribly wounded
with an arm and most of one leg shot away, but he
told me there had been a break in the fighting and
Von Norden allowed his crew to get out of the Jagdpanther for long enough to cook a meal. They were
all outside when an artillery shell exploded almost
in the middle of them. The gunner and the radio
operator were in so many pieces they could not tell
one from the other.

"Von Norden, so the loader said, had a terrible
wound in his stomach and another which had
nearly severed his arm. But somehow, he managed
to pull himself back up onto the Jadgpanther. The
loader saw him drop into one of the hatches. Then
the engine fired up and the Jagdpanther drove off
into the forest.

"The loader died a few hours after I talked with
him. The Jagdpanther was never seen again. I as-
sumed Von Norden had died and, with him, his

Jagdpanther had vanished into the blue flame, just like the others."

"I think your theory is falling apart," Jim argued. "Von Norden would be in his sixties now, if he is still alive. But one thing I'm sure of is that nobody has touched that Jagdpanther for many years. So if Von Norden lives, he is somewhere far away."

Ehrler looked doubtful but conceded, "Possible, I suppose."

"It seems to me that he probably just abandoned the Jagdpanther when it ran out of fuel or ammunition. You said he was a smart man. Only a complete idiot couldn't see the war was lost by March of 1945. Maybe he got out, or surrendered, hid his SS tattoo somehow, did his couple of years in the internment camps and went his merry way."

"For that, we should pray," Ehrler said. "Because the other possibilities are too horrible to consider."

Chapter Thirteen

JIM HAD TAKEN over the driving by the time they reached the museum. Sherri had moved behind the seats and was now fast asleep. Ehrler sat beside Jim, silently staring ahead into the night—like a man on his way to the executioner. They passed the main entrance to the museum and parked the Ferrari beside Restoration Building #2.

"Wake up," Jim said, shaking Sherri.

She groaned and then sat up sleepily, looking at her watch. "God, it's three o'clock in the morning."

"The underground factory and the forge?" Jim asked Ehrler as he unlocked the door. "What happened to it?"

"Just before the Allies arrived, I burned the manuscript, drove the Sherman test tank inside, and sealed the tunnels myself."

"Will you tell us where it is?" Sherri asked.

Ehrler looked at her for a long moment and then shook his head. "Not yet, and not unless it becomes the only way. I think *Mirtheil* is a secret best kept by the elves."

Sherri nodded and smiled at him. She followed as they entered the building and turned on the lights. Jim watched Ehrler as his eyes adjusted to the light and he stared at the Jagdpanther. Slowly, he approached and brushed his hand over the crest. Backing away then, he still said nothing—as if he refused to believe what he saw.

Sherri noticed it first. "It's turning blue," she whispered.

"Oh, bull . . ." Jim snapped, and then he saw it also. Blue sparks danced along the barrel. Electric blue squiggles of lightning materialized on the edges of the Jagdpanther's hull, and suddenly, it was surrounded by a haze of iridescent blue.

"Wow, neat," Sherri gasped. "Just like the legends say."

Ehrler was backing away from it with unsteady steps, but the blue light remained intense and pulsating. "Von Norden!" Ehrler said. "He's here; I feel his presence. He's in the panzer!"

"There's nobody in there. The hatches have been locked for years," Jim assured him.

"No matter, he *is* here!" As Ehrler spoke, the gun

barrel rose slightly and leveled at his head. From the Jagdpanther's rear came the grinding sound of its engine turning over.

"It can't do that. This has got to be some kind of a joke," Jim babbled, not believing his eyes. The Maybach V-12 engine fired, and clouds of black smoke spewed from the twin exhausts.

"It just did," Sherri disagreed, and moved closer beside him.

"Von Norden!" Ehrler screamed over the engine's roar. "I know it's you in there!" He ran at the Jagdpanther and beat his fists on the steel bow.

The Jagdpanther began to move, its tracks clanking heavily on the concrete floor. Ehrler tried to move away, but one tread locked and pivoted slightly to the right, throwing him off balance.

"Get out of there, Ehrler!" Jim yelled, and started toward him, but he was too late.

The sleeve of Ehrler's coat caught on an end-connector of the slowly turning tread. It pulled him down, under the tank. His screams vibrated against the walls as his arm was ground to bloody pulp. When Jim reached him, his legs were still visible between the tracks. He grabbed his pants legs and pulled Ehrler away from the treads, leaving a bloody trail where his arm had been.

Again the tracks pivoted. The Jagdpanther pointed its bow at Sherri and began to pick up speed. Jim released Ehrler's body: there was really nothing he could do for him anyway. "Run, Sherri! Get your ass out of here!" he yelled, but still she did not move. Instead she seemed entranced, hypnotized by the horror that was unfolding before her. Jim ran to her with the Jagdpanther closing the distance behind him. Grabbing her around the waist, he pulled her toward the storeroom door just as the Jagdpanther's gun tube took down a piece of the wall beside them. They dived into the storeroom and were at once half-buried by the falling ceiling.

The Jadgpanther loomed above them for a moment, then swung away and started for the overhead doors at the far end of the building. It hesitated for a moment as it passed the place where Ehrler lay bleeding on the concrete and then rumbled on, steadily building up speed as it aimed at the steel doors. They lifted off their hinges and then disintegrated as the Jagdpanther struck them head-on and drove out into the darkness.

Jim staggered to his feet and pulled Sherri up after him. "Ehrler," he whispered, and went to him. The old man's arm was gone—pieces of it lay smeared across the concrete. Most of his shoulder was crushed to a bloody pulp with bits of his coat mixed in it. Jim was sure he was dead, but as he knelt beside him, his lips moved and he spoke. "The worst . . . it has happened." He coughed, and blood flowed from his mouth and nose. "Von Norden and the Jagdpanther . . . have become one. The evil now cannot be conquered."

"Tell us where the forges are," Sherri demanded from over Jim's shoulder.

Ehrler's lips moved again, faintly this time. "Where dragons sleep . . ." he whispered, and fell silent. His tortured body jerked once and went limp.

"He's dead," Jim said and stood up.

Sherri turned away and took a few steps. "I think I'm going to be sick."

"Do it later. Right now we've got to catch a Jagdpanther." With Sherri right behind him, they ran out into the night. Tank tracks in the snow showed the Jagdpanther had kept going. "We'll take the Ferrari," Jim said, and guided Sherri toward it.

"I don't think I want to catch up with that. It wanted to kill me."

Jim ignored her as he took the wheel and they drove off. The tracks crossed the main street in front of the museum, angled across a park area beyond, and then turned onto the pavement again. "I think it's headed for the training areas," Jim said as he drove.

"Is that bad?"

Jim said, "I don't know. There are thousands of acres out there, but you can't hide anything that big for very long."

The tracks led down an alley between two warehouses and ended at a railroad spur. "Where'd he go?" Sherri asked, looking all around.

"He's smart, whoever he is. He's running with his treads up on the rails, so we can't track him." Jim put the Ferrari into reverse and backed out of the alley, then ran parallel to the tracks. "Watch over there," he said. "We might get a glimpse of him."

"What happens if he gets a glimpse of us?"

They slid around a corner and were again headed in the direction of the tracks. Suddenly the Jagdpanther was there, sitting still and bathed in the headlights. Its gun barrel was pointed directly at the Ferrari. As he hit the brakes, Jim said, "I think he's going to shoot."

Without encouragement, Sherri went out the right-hand door. Jim dived out the other and into the snow. A blast of hot air and gases hit him, and the Ferrari dissolved into a ball of bright orange. The explosion left a ringing in his ears as pieces of car settled around him. As soon as it was quiet, he raised his head and saw the Jagdpanther turning away. He watched as it crossed the road that bordered the training area and disappeared among a black line of trees.

"All right, Fafner, let me hear this one more time," General Walker sighed. "You are trying to tell me that hunk of Nazi junk you dragged off my tank range is not really junk but is made out of some experimental type of armor which, you figure, the Russians stole."

"I don't know who stole it and I especially don't know how they stole it," Jim answered for the thirtieth time in the past four hours. "But since the Russians tried to get it donated to some cockamamie memorial in East Germany, I figure that puts them on the top of the suspect list."

"There are those who would put you and the blond bimbo on the top of that list. CID questioned her for six hours and came out mumbling some crap about elves and dragons."

"Come on, General, you saw the tracks in the snow and you saw what was left of her Ferrari. Now, if I was going to steal the Jagdpanther, don't you think I could have been a little neater than that?"

"I don't know what the hell to think. But it's open season on Jagdpanthers. The 45th has three battalions scheduled to run live-fire exercises starting tomorrow. With them will be three more *Bundeswehr* battalions. Whoever has it can't hide out there on the tank ranges very long. And I don't believe the Nazis invented any goddamned newfangled armor that our M-60s can't chew up and spit out."

"I hope you're right, sir," Jim got tiredly to his feet. "Will there be anything else?"

"Yeah," Walker snapped. "Don't leave town. Pro-

vost Marshal wants you and Ms. Vail in the stock-
ade and I'm just a millimeter or two from letting
them have you both."

Jim looked indignant. "On what charge?"

Walker began to count on his fingers. "Murder,
espionage, treason, destruction of government
property . . . shall I continue?"

"No, sir."

"Then get out of here. And, Fafner—don't fuck up
again!"

Jim walked out of General Walker's headquarters with a frown on his face and an idea germinat-
ing in his brain. He found Sherri sitting on the hood
of the museum's staff car.

"So where are we off to now?" she asked as he
ignored her and got into the car.

"I'm going panzer-hunting. You're going somewhere else, anywhere else."

"Come on, Fafner, you really think I'm going to
walk away from this? This is the greatest piece of
elfin lore to turn up in centuries."

Jim did not feel like arguing with her. "Have it
your way, but you can't go where I'm going this
afternoon. I'll drop you at the museum or your
hotel."

"Where are you going?"

"I said I was going panzer-hunting. But first I've
got to get something to kill it with."

"What do you think is going to kill it?"

Jim shrugged, "A guided missile, if I can find
one."

"You still don't understand, do you?" Sherri
sounded frustrated. "You can't kill it with anything
you can get from the army."

"How then?"

"I don't know yet. For some reason, it wanted to

kill me! I'm the one it really came after last night, Ehrler just got in the way."

"It looked to me like it was after all of us."

"I don't know, but I think the answer to destroying it is somewhere in the place that it was made."

"We don't know how to find the cave where the factory complex was."

"Ehrler was trying to tell us. He was reciting that verse from the *Edda*. I've just got to figure out what he was trying to say."

"Do that," Jim said as he stopped in front of the museum to let Sherri out. "I'll see you a little later."

Jim drove back to the base hospital and asked if Sergeant Murphy had been released yet. He was informed that he had been, three days ago and had now rejoined his unit; C Company, 1st Battalion, 4th Armored Brigade. It took a while, but Jim finally found him at the battalion motor pool, inside the turret of an M-60.

As Jim lowered himself down through the cupola, Murphy looked up from the machine-gun mount beside the main gun breech. "You. Fafner, isn't it?" he said. "What brings you down here?"

"Couple of things," Jim answered. "First, you were right. Everything you said was true about the Jagdpanther. Sorry I had a little trouble believing you."

Murphy nodded. "Yeah, so did the army. Right now, I'm feeling real lucky I still got sergeant's stripes and I'm still running a tank."

Jim leaned closer and lowered his voice. "I gotta find that Jagdpanther, and I got to kill it. Will you help me?" Jim asked and watched as a look of pure horror spread over Murphy's face. "I need a missile."

Murphy released a long breath. "Shit, man. No way."

"Yeah, there is. They can be had, I just need to know who, and where."

Murphy began to fidget. "Up to now I been just sweatin' maybe a Section Eight. What you're talkin' about is good for twenty years in Leavenworth, minimum."

"I know," Jim said evenly.

"Shit!" Murphy cursed, and banged his fist down on the gun breech. He took a deep breath and then said, "Okay, maybe, just maybe. I'll call you, but it's going to be expensive."

Jim slapped his shoulder. "Thanks," he said simply, and climbed out of the turret.

Sherri was gone when Jim got back to the museum. He stayed in his office until closing time, then switched his phone to forward calls to Restoration Building #1.

He walked to the back of the museum where the operational vehicles were parked. He patted the fender of a Whites half-track and checked its fuel levels. The heavy armored door banged as he opened it and climbed in behind the wheel.

Yes, he thought, this is the best choice.

He turned on the ignition switch and watched as the gauges came up, then pulled the hand choke and stepped on the starter. The engine turned, slowly at first, and then picked up speed. It fired, almost died, and then settled down to a pleasant, even rumble. Jim listened to it for a while with a knowing ear and decided it was strong. He drove the half-track out and then backed it into Restoration Building #1. He let the engine idle for a while, charging the batteries as he closed the overhead doors. The next two hours were spent adjusting the track tension, tightening bolts on the machine-gun ring mount, and balancing the tire pressure. He was under the half-track, checking oils levels in the transfer cases, when he looked out and saw Sherri's pink boots.

"Fafner, you under there?" she called.

He answered her and crawled out with a grease rag in one hand and a crescent wrench in the other. "Where you been?" he asked.

"I went to get another car," Sherri said glumly. "Would you believe the leasing company wouldn't give me another Ferrari? I mean, I told them that it had been shot by a tank, and they got really upset. They said that in all the years they had been in business, they had never had a tank do anything to one of their cars."

The phone on the wall interrupted her. Jim hurried over and picked it up. "Yeah?" he said into the receiver.

Murphy was on the other end. "See a man named Buchalder, Master Sergeant Eddie Buchalder. They call him Fast Eddie. Tonight in Nuremberg. There is a bar called Lillie Marlene. Bring cash, one thousand dollars, U.S."

"A grand?" Jim laughed. "It must be too hot to touch."

"I don't know nothing about it. But watch your ass; Fast Eddie is a psycho."

"Thanks," Jim answered, and hung up. "I gotta run," he said to Sherri, and started out before he realized that he should not drive to Nuremberg to buy a hot missile in a government car with U.S. Army printed on the side. "What kind of a car did you get?"

Sherri sighed. "A Volkswagen Rabbit."

"Could be worse. Come on, I'll buy your gas."

It was just after midnight when Sherri drove up in front of the Lillie Marlene. It was in the worst section of Nuremberg, and the lights were so dim that they could barely read the name on the sign over the door.

"Circle the block or something. I don't have any idea how long I'll be," Jim said as he started to get out.

"I'll come in and you can buy me a drink."

"No way," Jim insisted. "The only women in a place like this are hookers. With that mink of yours, you'll look overpriced." Before she had time to protest further, he got out of the car.

An official-looking sign on the door read *Off limits to all U.S. Service personnel.*

That figures, Jim thought as he entered. Inside, it was dark and he had to stand at the door for a minute to let his eyes adjust. There was a lot of smoke, which smelled like pot and hung in a gray fog over some dimly lit tables and a bar. In the center of it all was a round stage, bathed in red light where a slightly overweight stripper was down to her G-string and armpit hair as she gyrated to bad rock music.

Jim approached the bar and asked for Fast Eddie. The bartender looked at him for a long time and then jerked his thumb toward a table in the corner. "Buchalder?" Jim asked as he approached the table.

Fast Eddie was a thin man with a Flatbush accent who talked fast. "Yeah. You got the money?"

"I got the money. What am I buying?" Jim sat down.

"Sagger AT, one each, complete."

"That's a Soviet missile. Where the hell did you get that?"

"C'mon, trade secrets." Fast Eddie smiled and showed a couple of gold teeth. "My friend said you wanted the best. This baby will punch sixteen inches of armor at 3300 yards. Soviet, U.S., or Third World—it does not discriminate. And like you so aptly noted, it is Russkie. Very hard to trace."

"But not exactly famous for being accurate. I'll need the manuals, too."

Fast Eddie nodded. "You got 'em, I guess. There's books with it, but I don't read no Russian."

Jim reached in his pocket and withdrew five one-hundred-dollar bills. "Half now; the rest when I see the missile."

Fast Eddie did not look happy, but he nodded and took the money. "Ten minutes; the alley in back."

"Ten minutes," Jim echoed, and left. He came out of the bar just as Sherri was pulling up at the curb. "Circle the block again and then pull into the alley."

"You mean you got it? You just walked in there and bought a guided missile?"

"Only a little one. Now listen, this Fast Eddie character is probably going to try to rip us off, so stay behind the wheel and be ready to get out fast."

Sherri sighed. "Ever since I've known you, I've met such nice people."

She drove the Volkswagen into the alley, where a van was parked at the back door of the Lillie Marlene. As she turned off the lights, Fast Eddie stepped out carrying a large suitcase. Jim got out and walked toward him as he set the case on the Volkswagen's hood. Jim reached into his jacket again, but this time he came out with his Desert Eagle instead of the other five hundred dollars. "Back up against the van," Jim said, "so your buddy inside will have to shoot through you to hit me."

Fast Eddie did not back up. He pointed a finger at Jim and said, "Hey, you, nobody rips off Fast Eddie."

"Damn it, Fafner," Sherri interrupted from the car. "Are you going to shoot him, too?"

Eddie suddenly lost his confidence and backed against the van.

"I'm not ripping you off," Jim told him as he opened the suitcase with one hand. "I'm just making sure I'm getting what I paid for." From his jacket pocket, he pulled out a small flashlight and used it to examine the Sagger. The motor section was all there, with its four fins folded. He lifted the warhead and felt that it weighed properly. The control stick and sight was in its proper place. Yes, it was all there. He closed the box and, while still keeping his pistol leveled at Fast Eddie's head, removed another five hundred dollars from his pocket and handed it over.

"Pleasure doing business with you," Eddie said without any trace of a smile.

All the way back to Ansbach, Sherri kept insisting that Jim's plan would not work. By the time she left him at the museum, she had still failed to convince him. "Oh, all right, don't listen to me. Go get yourself blown away. I'm going back to my hotel and I'm going to sleep. It you're still in one piece, you can call me tomorrow—late." With that, she drove off into the night, and Jim carried his missile inside.

Two nights of no sleep was having its effect on Sherri by the time she arrived at the small hotel where she was staying. She yawned as she fumbled for her keys and dropped them once before she managed to open the door to her room. Her hand reached out in the dark for the light switch and missed.

"It's got to be here somewhere," she cursed sleepily, and then her hand touched warm flesh. Strong fingers gripped her as she tried to pull away. Something hit her hard across the back of her head and she was on the floor, struggling to get up. Other hands were holding her, hurting her, and touching her in places she hated to be touched. Odors of tobacco smoke, liquor, and sweat assaulted her. She wanted to scream but there was something around her neck, choking her in the darkness. Something else was being forced into her mouth and she could no longer breathe. The darkness was spinning around her. She was falling, somewhere in an endless black nothing.

Chapter Fourteen

CONVOY CHARLIE VICTOR 3 rolled south in the darkness along the snowy Autobahn between Erlangen and Nuremberg, midway on the supply route from Rhein-Main to Munich. In the second truck behind the convoy commander's jeep, PFC John Weston shivered as he drove, and watched snowflakes swirl in the yellow cone of his headlights. Just ahead, a pair of red dots marked the taillights of a two-and-a-half-ton fuel tanker.

Weston had been driving "deuce-and-a-halfs" (as

the army called two-and-a-half-ton trucks) in West
Germany for almost a year. In fact, that was just
about the only thing he had done since he completed basic training and driving school at Fort
Leonard Wood, Missouri. He had figured army life
would be a little more exciting than this. The ten-
wheeled truck he drove had really been designed to
carry supplies and men off the road in combat
zones. On the Autobahn, it was a real dog; and
besides that, the heaters never worked.

Weston reached into the pocket of his field jacket
for a pack of cigarettes as he steered around a wide
bend. He removed a crumpled, empty pack. "Hey,
Raymond, you got a smoke?"

The man in the shotgun seat was half asleep. He
yawned and handed Weston a pack. "Where are
we?"

"Comin' up on the turnoff for Ralston Barracks.
Maybe we can grab some coffee there."

"Shit, man. That chicken-shit lieutenant up there
gonna keep our butts humpin' all night, right
straight through to Munich."

Weston didn't answer, but figured he was right.
He down-shifted and followed the fuel tanker off
the Autobahn and down to a road junction at an
underpass. There the convoy turned to the right
and the road narrowed. On the right-hand side of
the road was a high, chain-link fence that bordered
one of the training areas. Across the road from it
were only a few scattered houses.

There was an unlighted cigarette in Weston's
mouth and he was fumbling with his lighter when
he saw the brake lights brighten on the fuel truck in
front of him. The driver had hit them hard and the
tanker began to slide sideways in the road. And
then, very suddenly, it exploded.

"Sonofabitch!" Weston breathed as the still-unlighted cigarette fell from his lips. Instinctively he hit his own brakes and his truck slid to a stop as flaming, high-octane fuel poured out across the road and ran like a fiery waterfall into both ditches. Silhouetted within the inferno were jagged, torn steel edges, like the petals of some hellish flower belching flame into the night sky. Weston thought he could see the driver—his name was Billy Joe Needam. He was still sitting in the remains of the cab although the roof was gone and the windshield was only a twisted frame.

A shadow moved beside the burning truck. The Jagdpanther came at them, bursting through the flames with its treads splashing liquid fire in all directions. "It's a tank," Weston said.

"Don't look like no tank I ever seen. It ain't no-thin' but a big fucking gun on tracks."

"Yeah, and the mother's coming right at us!" Raymond yelled out his last words in this life just as the muzzle of the Jagdpanther's gun shattered the windshield and drove into the cab, breaking his skull and then tearing off the cab roof.

Weston could neither think nor move as the strange monster pushed his truck toward the ditch. Steel treads began to claw their way up the hood. They no longer looked like tank treads; instead, there were rows of black steel claws, ripping the truck to pieces as a lion or panther would rip apart its prey and devour it. The deuce-and-a-half's front suspension snapped with a jolt. The steering column broke loose from the firewall mounts and hit his chest, crushing his ribs and jamming him hard against the seat. His truck was being flattened, Weston realized dully. The Jagdpanther was going to crawl completely over it. He could see the tracks closely now, through the shattered glass of the windshield. The hull was inches away from him. Its engine sounded strange and uneven, more like breathing than something mechanical. Yes, it was breathing. Weston knew suddenly that this was not some bizarre training accident. He was being killed by a living, breathing monster. The windshield frame snapped like a twig and hit him on the forehead. Blood ran in a steady stream down into his eyes. He screamed out his last breaths of life just as the truck burst into flame.

Sherri realized that her head hurt. It throbbed with a constant drumlike beating as consciousness slowly returned. It hurt more when she tried to open her eyes, so for a while she lay with them closed, trying to remember what had happened. It also hurt to think. She could remember coming back to the hotel, and then there seemed to be only a blank.

She at last forced one eye open and was confronted by the fuzzy vision of a woman bound spread-eagle to a bed. White tape was across the woman's mouth and a tousle of blond hair spilled in all directions around her face. As the last threads of unconsciousness left her, she tried to move and help the woman. A lightning bolt of stark terror shot through her. It turned her stomach and she wanted to vomit. The woman she saw was herself, reflected in a mirror suspended above her.

Her heart beat faster as the reality of the situation slowly and painfully soaked in. The gag made it hard to breathe, but as her panic increased, her lungs cried for more and more air. She tried to force her tongue against the inside of the tape, but something else had been stuffed into her mouth behind it. Her nostrils flared with each ragged breath.

Stop this, she thought. If they just wanted to kill you, they would have already done it. Several thoughts of what else they might want to do to her raced through her mind. Maybe they just want information from me. Something about the Jagdpanther.

Her breathing subsided a little. She twisted her head to one side, trying to see more of where she was. The lights were dim—oil lamps, she thought. The walls of the room were stone. She looked back up at the mirrors suspended from the ceiling. She could see the foot of the bed; her mink jacket and her boots were lying there on a red carpet.

Escape? She tugged at her bindings and then turned her head enough to see what was securing her hands. It looked like some sort of nylon strap, wrapped several times around her wrist and knotted out of reach of her fingers. The other end was pulled tight and tied to the bedpost.

Sherri jumped and released a little scream into her gag as the door opened suddenly. A man entered, wearing an overcoat and walking with a cane. She watched as he approached the bed and stood looking down at her for a moment. Then, he sat on the edge of the bed. She cringed as his hand touched her face.

"Hold still," he said in a quiet voice. "This will probably hurt." Before she realized what he was doing, he had pulled the tape away from her lips. Then he pulled a piece of towel from inside her mouth.

Sherri breathed deeply, gulping in air until her lungs were again satisfied. "Thank you," she said weakly.

"Where is the Jagdpanther?" August Gnokte asked.

"Jagdpanther? I don't know."

He sighed. "I am a very old man. I do not like being here, and I would not be here if the fate of my homeland did not rest on my either obtaining or destroying the Jagdpanther which you and Mr. Fafner stole."

"We didn't steal that thing. I don't like it and it don't like me. As far as I'm . . ."

Gnokte touched her neck with the silver head of his cane and shook his head. "No games, please. But I will give you a history lesson, little girl, because I want you to know how little your life means.

"As I said, I am an old man. I lived through the Second World War. Do you know what the Germans did to our women when they invaded Russia?"

Sherri shook her head and gulped. "No, and I don't think I want to."

"They raped them, of course, all of them—old women, girls, and everything in between. Then they drove nails through their hands and feet and crucified them on the front doors of their homes. Most all of them died there in the cold—very, very slowly."

"That was inhuman," Sherri said, her voice a little stronger.

"No," Gnokte answered thoughtfully. "Actually, it was extremely human. There is no creature on earth, except man, who kills for pleasure alone. And you may be assured that we returned the favor to German women when we marched into Germany."

Gnokte moved his cane away from her throat and pointed it at the door. "Right now, there is a man in the next room who is already looking forward to all the things he will do to you, before he lets you die. You must understand that your youth, your sex, your beauty, they mean nothing . . . Now, where is the Jagdpanther?"

"We didn't steal it. We didn't even know it would run," Sherri pleaded. "Someone else did . . . or maybe it just drove away by itself. It killed Ehrler and it just drove off. We lost it after it shot my car."

Gnokte released a breath and nodded. "Very well. I suspect you will see things differently in a little while." He rose tiredly with the help of his cane and walked to the door. He nodded to Malinkov, who stood waiting in the doorway. "I believe you two have already met, briefly. There is time now for you to become much better acquainted."

Gnokte looked back once more at Sherri just as Malinkov slapped her across the face. He shook his head and left the bedroom. She would talk, of course. Sooner or later, everyone did.

In the next room, a fire was blazing in a large stone fireplace. Gnokte walked to a table where Smythe was sitting with a telephone beside him.

"All right," Gnokte said. "It is almost dawn. Make the call." From the bedroom, Sherri's first screams sent a chill up his spine and brought back horrible memories of the past. He moved closer to the fireplace and tried without success to warm himself.

Jim laid out the Sagger missile on the floor beside the half-track and carefully examined each part. He checked the batteries and was satisfied they were fully charged. The Sagger was a neat, little missile, he decided. It weighed only about twenty-five pounds and was about two feet long. The carrying case opened up to form the launching ramp, which was supposed to be secured to the ground with stakes and straps which were also provided. The warhead attached to the motor section of the missile with built-in clips. Then there were four plugs, which connected the rear of the missile to the control box. On the control box were two switches and a joystick that looked like it belonged to a video game. The Sagger was wire-guided, which meant that it was controlled in flight by a couple of tiny wires that played out freely from the missile while it was in flight. The operator had simply to "fly" it with the control stick. Just like a model airplane, Jim thought.

After taking a few measurements on the launching ramp, Jim wheeled out a portable welding torch and looked around for a couple of pieces of scrap steel. These, he welded to the machine-gun mount on the half-track and drilled two holes in each. To them, he bolted the Sagger's launch pad and backed away to admire his work.

The Sagger could now be turned 360 degrees on the half-track. Jim set the controller beside him in the cab and decided he would have to fire it from a standing position on the driver's seat. It would have been better if it could be fired while the half-track was moving, but there did not appear to be any practical way for one man to do it all. If the situation permitted, he could aim the half-track at his target, stop, and stand up to fire. If opportunity gave him a few more seconds, he could stop the half-track in any direction, turn the Sagger on the machine-gun mount, and then fire it.

"Should work," he told himself and looked at his watch. It was 0530, almost dawn. He would have to wait until darkness came again to go hunting. But maybe by then, he could get some idea of where the Jagdpanther was, if it was still out on the training area.

He covered the missile with a tarp, locked the doors to the building, and walked back to his office, deciding to catch a few hours' sleep on the office couch.

His head had barely hit the pillow when the phone rang. Seven rings vibrated the office walls before he finally dragged himself to the desk and answered it.

"Mr. Fafner? Mr. James Fafner?" The voice had a slight German accent and the slightest hint of a lisp.

"Yes."

"I have something I want you to hear," the voice said, and there was silence for a moment. A woman's screams echoed in the background and grew louder, as if the phone was being carried closer to her. Then there was sobbing and someone else said in the background, "Talk to him."

"Jim?" It was Sherri's voice. "They're hurting me. I tried to tell them about the Jagdpanther, but they won't . . ." Her voice faded as the phone was moved away.

"I believe you now understand the situation?" the man's voice said.

Jim was wide awake. "The only thing I understand is that if she gets hurt, I hunt your goddamned ass down and blow it to hell!"

"She will be alive until tonight. That is when you will deliver the Jagdpanther to us. Is that clear?"

"Hell no, it's not clear! Somebody else stole the damned thing. She doesn't know where it is and I don't either!"

The voice sighed. "Then that is most unfortunate

for your late lady friend here. Perhaps you will be more eager to do business with us if we send a little of her back to you. We could start with a finger or two, or maybe one of her nipples."

Jim was thinking as fast as he could. "All right, you've made your point. I'll get you the Jagdpanther, but I need some time. As you know it's not right here, and you can't hide a tank just anywhere."

"Tonight, no longer. We will be in touch." The phone went dead.

A terrible feeling of helplessness swept over him. Sherri, laughing, nutty Sherri, was going to die a slow, horrible death because of that damned tank. Just like Michael and Rudy Bauer and Ehrler, all dead because of a bunch of insane myths and legends. There seemed to be no way of stopping it.

"Approach the problem logically," Jim said aloud, trying to calm himself. "There must be a way."

The phone rang again, interrupting his thoughts. "Fafner?" It was General Walker's voice. "I'm sending a helicopter to pick you up. There was a terrorist attack on one of our supply convoys last night. They found some very suspicious tank tracks I want you to look at." He paused and added an afterthought. "Oh yeah, I hope to hell you've got an airtight alibi for last night."

As Jim hung up the phone, he felt even worse then he had before. "No problem, General Walker, sir," he mumbled to himself. "I was out buying a hot antitank missile last night and then I came home and mounted it on a half-track."

The thought flashed through his head that he should run: take the half-track, drive it out onto the training area, find a place to hide until dark, and then . . . "And then what?" he asked himself. "No, you need to see those tank tracks. They're the best lead you've got right now."

He took time to shave and change clothes before the chopper arrived, figuring that he should not look like he had been up all night. Then, he loaded his Desert Eagle and slipped it beneath his coat. Ingrid was at her desk in the outside office by the time he heard the *thump-thump-thump* of the chopper's rotor blades in the distance.

"Has Hans Graff come in yet? I want him to clean up some of the mess in building two," Jim said.

"He's not here yet. He didn't come in yesterday, either."

A small alarm bell went off somewhere in Jim's subconscious mind. "Call him at home and see if you can find out where he's been," he said, and hurried out.

The helicopter was a UH-1D Huey with the door guns manned and the rocket pods bristling. Its pilot lifted off fast and flew low, barely skimming the treetops. It was obvious that security had been suddenly tightened and trigger fingers were itchy.

One of the training areas passed beneath them. It was an even mix of open land and groves of thick pines. All of it was crisscrossed with tank trails. A single tank might hide out there for a long time if it moved at night and hid in the trees during the day.

The Huey turned north, following a road and a chain-link fence that ran beside the training area. No one had to be told when they arrived over their destination. The blackened skeletons of a half-dozen trucks lay scattered along the road and in the ditches on both sides. Each one was surrounded by a blackened circle where the snow had melted and the grass burned away. It was much the same scene as Jim had seen on the day he had flown over the burned-out M-60. Here, it was repeated six times.

Military police, ambulances, and troops in full combat gear were everywhere on the ground. The road had been blocked off in both directions, and the area was apparently sealed. A captain motioned for Jim to follow him just as the chopper touched down.

General Walker was waiting beside the blackened wreckage of what looked to Jim like it had been a fuel tanker. He pointed at the asphalt. "There, Fafner. Looks like he rolled past this truck after it was burning hot enough to soften the pavement." He moved closer beside Jim and lowered his voice. "Those tracks belong to your Jagdpanther?"

Jim knelt and examined them carefully. From his pocket, he removed a tape measure and checked their dimensions. The tread pattern was right and the dimensions were close, although in places, they appeared a little wider than in others. There were other marks in the pavement Jim could not explain either: small clawlike scratches a few inches on either side of the tracks as if there were some kind of hooks extended out from the end connectors.

"Not much doubt." Jim nodded and stood up. "Which way did it go?"

"We're still checking. It headed that way, back up the road, but we lost it on the pavement. Apparently, it came out of the training area, because it tore down a few yards of fence about a half-a-mile up the road."

"Anybody see it?" Jim asked.

"Yeah, about six men, including the convoy commander, saw it really close, but they're all dead. We got a couple of survivors who got glimpses of it, but no real good ID in the dark." Walker paused and then looked straight at Jim. "Okay, Fafner, let's hear it. Where were you last night?"

Jim coughed nervously into his hand. "Well sir, I'd rather not say."

"You better say and you better say good," Walker growled. "Everybody from the provost marshal to Interpol is involved now."

"All right, sir. I was with a woman."

"Which one?"

Jim took a deep breath. "Sherri Vail."

Walker grunted. "She'll verify it?"

"Sure, no problem."

"Good, because I'm sending someone to talk to her right away."

Jim tried to look calm and confident. "I need to get back to the museum and check some figures on the range of this thing. I should be able to give you some idea how far it could go."

Walker looked at him suspiciously and then nodded. "Miss Vail better tell me that you were the best fuck she's ever had or you're out of excuses."

Jim tried to smile as he backed away and headed for the chopper. He knew that there was virtually no one left who was going to believe him much longer. And when the lies began to surface, all of Europe was going to be after him.

"Think fast," Jim told himself as he boarded the Huey.

Chapter Fifteen

≶

BY THE TIME the Huey dropped Jim in front of the museum, he had decided that there was no possible way he could find the Jagdpanther in time to have any chance of saving Sherri. In his mind, this left only one possible alternative: find her—and find her tonight.

Ingrid stopped him at her desk. "I tried to call Hans Graff's apartment, but there was no answer. Would you like me to try anywhere else?"

"Yeah," Jim said. "Give me his address and then find out who recommended him." It was a long shot, he knew, but he had to start somewhere, and once Walker failed to find Sherri, he would be on the run anyway.

The address Ingrid gave him for Hans Graff was an apartment building across town. Jim climbed the stairs to the second floor and knocked on the door. He waited, knocked again, and then began studying the lock. Deciding that it did not look too difficult, he took a credit card out of his wallet and slipped it between the door and the facing, wiggled it a little, and then pushed on the door. He opened it slowly and stepped inside.

Perhaps he had hoped to see a cleaned-out apartment or one that obviously was lived in by someone besides Hans Graff, but he did not. There was food in the refrigerator and a few dishes were neatly stacked in the cabinets. There were magazines on the coffee table, all German publications and all December issues. In the bedroom, a single bed was also neatly made up. Jim pushed open a closet and thumbed through a few clothes: one gray suit, two pair of wool pants, three shirts. There was even one tie. "Neat," he commented, "maybe too neat."

He was not completely certain until he examined the bathroom. Everything was there as he expected. Shaving cream, toothpaste, comb, brush, soap, towels. He picked up the toothbrush and ran the bristles across his thumb. "Bingo," he whispered. "This stuff is all brand-new; none of it has been used more than once or twice."

From the phone beside the bed, he dialed the museum. "Ingrid, this is Fafner. Anything on who hired Graff?"

"Of course; he was sent by the Civilian Personnel Office. The director himself recommended him, a Mr. Smythe."

"Thanks."

"The military police were here," Ingrid said.

Jim gulped. "Did they say what they wanted?"

"You."

"Great. Good-bye." Jim hung up and left the apartment. Mr. Smythe was the next logical stop; but now, since the MPs were already on his trail, he would have to make one more stop.

A block away from Sherri's hotel, Jim parked his government sedan at the curb and walked away from it. He found Sherri's rented Volkswagen in the hotel parking lot and stole it.

Bernhart Smythe disliked anything that could upset the status quo. It had been risky enough to establish an identity for Colonel Malinkov at such short notice and get him hired onto the museum staff. Now, with the kidnapping of Sherri Vail, the situation seemed to have escalated to the point where it could explode in his face at any moment.

The visit to his office around noon by the American military police ruined his lunch and kept his stomach upset all afternoon. They had been looking for Jim Fafner, and although Smythe believed he had acted natural enough, the very thought that Fafner might be somehow alerted to his involvement turned his stomach into knots.

He knew very well that if Malinkov's cover was blown, his own could be next. He had advised the Russian colonel to stay at the museum, even after the tank had disappeared; but Malinkov had refused, saying that he needed to be on the other end of the operation when the tank was delivered. And, perhaps he did. There were massive problems in obtaining a truck that could have any chance of transporting the Jagdpanther out of West Germany without suspicion. Malinkov was even considering a plan to drive it out by overrunning a border crossing. Smythe had to admit it would probably work—after all, the Americans were not used to anyone or anything trying to escape into East Germany.

Smythe felt a little relieved when closing time finally arrived. He put a few things in his briefcase, left by the back entrance, and walked into the winter twilight. He had unlocked his car and started the engine before he felt the press of cold steel against the base of his neck.

"Drive," Jim said as he eased himself up off the floor and into the back seat.

"Faf ... Fafner?" Smythe stuttered. "The military police are looking for you. What do you want with me?"

"Drive," Jim said again, his voice colder this time as he forced the Desert Eagle's barrel harder against Smythe's neck. "Sherri Vail. Where is she?"

"What are you talking about? I already told the MPs I don't know her."

"Yeah, I thought you'd probably say that," Jim said. "Fact is, you'll probably say that for several hours before you break. If you're even a half-ass agent, you'll probably hold out until after your friends kill her. Of course, then I'm going to send you back to them in pieces. Want to make any guesses on what parts go first?"

"You're crazy, Fafner," Smythe cried. "Look, I could drive you to the Swiss border, help you get out of the country before the police catch up to you."

"Yeah, I bet you would. Just drive to the museum. I'll tell you where to park."

Smythe said little more during the drive back to the museum, but Jim could see the beads of perspiration form on the back of his neck and soak his shirt collar. Jim directed him to drive back to the building where he had parked the half-track and hoped that the MPs had not searched the museum yet.

"I figure this is about the last place they'll look for me tonight," Jim commented as he jerked Smythe out of his car and shoved him toward the building. Smythe stumbled in the snow and Jim kicked him before he could get up.

Smythe looked around him as Jim turned on the lights. The room was empty except for the half-track and a tool bench against the wall. He watched as Jim locked the door behind him and then walked toward him. The pistol he carried looked huge, out of scale with the rest of his hand. Smythe did not think he had ever seen a handgun that big before.

"All right, asshole," Jim started. "How would you like to do this? You can either tell me where she is now, while you still look more or less like a human being, or later, after I've turned you into a vegetable."

"I don't know anything about any woman. I work at the personnel office; I hire civilians to work for the American Army. Why do you thing I'm a—?" Jim hit him in the stomach and he doubled over with pain. Before he could stand up, Jim kicked him in the face, knocking him backward and onto the floor.

"Your voice," Jim snarled in his face. "It was you on the phone this morning." His own hand was shaking badly. He slipped the pistol into his belt. He was forcing himself to act slowly, let each bit of new pain soak in. Give him time to think about dying, Jim thought.

As Smythe got to his feet, wiping blood from his mouth, Jim landed a left hook which closed one of his eyes and knocked him back against the cold steel fender of the half-track.

"Tell me what they did to her!" Jim sneered at him as he grabbed his collar and pulled him close. "Did they cut off her fingers? That's what you said they were going to do on the phone." He jerked Smythe toward the tool bench. "I think that's where I'll start with you—just a couple of joints off the little finger first."

Smythe screamed as his hand was forced into the big vise attached to the tool bench. He felt the steel jaws cut off his circulation and watched as his hand began to turn blue. When he looked up, Fafner was holding a pair of bolt cutters.

Smythe felt his stomach revolt. He vomited, spilling his half-digested lunch of bratwurst and dark beer over his own hand in the vise. He gasped for breath and tried to talk. "He did not hurt her!"

Tremendous relief flooded over Jim. Until now, he had not been sure if he had the right man or not. "Now we're getting somewhere."

Smythe spit up a few last traces of sausage and wiped his free arm across his mouth. "They only made her scream to impress you. Gnokte, the old man, would not let him do anything else—unless you failed to tell them where the Jagdpanther is by tonight."

"Where?"

Smythe hesitated. "I don't know, they—"

Jim tightened the vice. Bones cracked in Smythe's hand and his screams echoed off the building's walls. "A hunting lodge, outside of Ansbach."

From his jacket pocket, Jim pulled out a road map and dropped it on the bench in front of Smythe. "Show me exactly where," he said, and stuck a pencil into his free hand. After Smythe had marked the map, Jim released his broken hand from the vise and Smythe dropped to his knees, almost fainting from the pain. Jim thought for a moment about exactly what to do next, and then brought the butt of his pistol down on Smythe's head and he collapsed onto the concrete.

"Just in case you lied," Jim muttered as he threw Smythe in between the personnel seats in the back of the half-track, "you're going with me." He bound the unconscious man with tie-down straps from the half-track's equipment racks and left him gagged with an oily rag.

Jim returned to his office. From a shelf in the closet, he pulled down a couple of army blankets and then filled a thermos from the coffee maker. He compared his road map with a large area map on his wall. If he was careful, he could take the half-

track across the training areas and then have only
a few miles to where Smythe claimed the hunting
lodge was. For part of that distance, he could move
on a railroad track which should hide his tracks for
a while. There were two small villages he would
have to pass through, but armored vehicles were
pretty common, and at night, with a little luck, the
half-track might slip through without raising too
much attention—he hoped.

With a ruler and a pencil, he laid out a compass
course to take him across the training area and
decided he was as ready as he could be. He took the
map off the wall, folded it, and stuffed it into his
jacket as he went out the door.

Smythe did not move when Jim fired up the
half-track's engine and drove out into the night. He
guided the vehicle cautiously around the museum
with his lights out and then followed the same route
the Jagdpanther had taken only forty-eight hours
earlier.

Thirty yards from the road that bordered on the
training area, he halted just beyond the reach of
passing headlights and waited in the shadows as a
pair of MP jeeps passed by. As soon as the road was
clear, he gunned the half-track across the road and
onto the training area. The night sky had cleared
and a pale moon hung just above the trees. He felt
almost relieved as he drove. The waiting was over.
The half-track rattled along beneath him with its
engine purring. He was doing the things he did
best: driving an armored vehicle and going into
combat.

Nikoli Malinkov looked first at his watch, and then
across the room at August Gnokte, who was staring
out the window. "Something has gone wrong," he

said. "We should kill the girl and get out of here. We can't reach Fafner, and Smythe should have reported hours ago. I think they are onto us."

Gnokte turned slowly from the window and met Malinkov's eyes. "No," he said simply. "There is too much to lose."

"Then, we must make her talk." Malinkov's hand moved to his pocket and withdrew a long switch-blade. He held it up and released the blade, which sprung open. "Give me an hour with her."

Gnokte looked thoughtfully at the blade for a moment and then said, "No." He walked across the room to where Malinkov was standing. "I do not think that will work on her, at least not quickly. She has a spirit, that one does. I have watched her secretly today. Even now, after almost eighteen hours, she is still struggling with the ropes. Her wrists and her ankles are bleeding, yet still, she is trying, trying everything she can think of to break free."

"Then there is another way. Give her a clear choice—life or death," Malinkov said. Gnokte stared at him as though he did not understand, so Malinkov sat down at the table and said, "Go and bring her out here."

Gnokte nodded reluctantly and disappeared into the bedroom. Shortly he returned, leading Sherri by her arm. She stumbled, and caught herself on the table. "Tell us where the Jagdpanther is," Malinkov demanded.

Sherri rubbed her wrists and answered, "I've been trying to tell you idiots all day, I don't know!"

"Very well," he said. "Now take your clothes off."

Sherri took a couple of unsteady steps away from the table and backed into Gnokte. "What?" she asked, and her voice almost cracked.

"You heard me. If you like, I would be delighted to help you."

She looked to Gnokte, but he only nodded. Malinkov was smiling at her and running his thumb over the edge of his switchblade. She turned her back to them, pulled her sweater off over her head, and threw it on the table. The two men stared at her. "Pants, too?" she asked. Gnokte nodded, and she took them off also. "There, you filthy pig!" she cursed, standing in front of the table wearing only her bra and panties. "Does that make you happy?"

"Outside," Malinkov said.

Jim navigated by the moon and checked the green glow of the half-track's compass occasionally to be sure he was still on course. The snow was a brilliant white in the moonlight, and the half-track left only shallow tracks on the frozen ground as Jim approached the high chain-link fence that marked the military reservation's boundary. The road just beyond it was deserted, so he eased the half-track up against a fence post, pushed it down, and drove over the wire.

Across the road were two railroad tracks. Jim gunned his vehicle up onto them and headed south. Two miles down, he found a grade crossing and turned onto a paved road. He turned on the half-track's lights then and drove into the village of Königsbad. The streets were narrow here, built centuries ago when the widest things apt to meet each other were two mounted knights.

Jim kept the half-track's speed up, hoping to look like a vehicle in a hurry to be somewhere important. Only one sleepy German policeman noticed him and just stared as he rumbled by. Jim had learned a long time ago that to ninety percent of

the world's inhabitants, one armored vehicle
looked just about like another. Just because the
U.S. Army had not had a half-track in service for
nearly thirty years did not mean it would draw
undue suspicion.

Jim kept on the road as the village lights faded
behind him. He pushed the half-track up to its top
speed, which seemed to be close to 45 miles an
hour. The night air whistled in his ears and
whipped at his face as the half-track rumbled beneath him. Just outside the village of Dorfen, he
slowed down to orient himself once again. In the
moonlight he could see rolling hills with neatly
cleared fields bordered by forest. The hunting lodge
should be to the south, beyond the second line of
hills. He turned off his headlights. It was time to
get back off the road.

He plowed the half-track through the ditch and
flattened a rail fence as he headed out across the
fields, climbing steadily up the first line of hills.

On the crest of the first hill he stopped and focused his field glasses across the top of the half-
track's windshield. It took several minutes, but he
finally picked out a dark streak in the distant snow
which marked the dirt road leading to the lodge.
"There it is," he whispered to himself. "Now, let's
figure out the best way to get there without being
seen or dropping into some hole we can't crawl out
of." He moved his glasses over the ground slowly,
looking for anything that might stop a half-track.
Another shadow on the snow caught his eye. It
looked at first like another trail, and he drove toward it. Just before he got there, he realized it was
tank tracks.

Jim climbed out of the half-track and shined his
flashlight on the ugly marks in the moonlit snow.

"Jagdpanther," he whispered, "and real fresh." He stood up suddenly, realizing that he and his vehicle were badly exposed here in the open. He hurried to the cab, tore the tarp off the Sagger, and moved the firing controls closer to him. The tracks led off up the hill in the same direction he was headed.

What the hell is that thing doing out here? he thought, and then Sherri's words came suddenly back to him.

"It hates me," she had said the night Ehrler had been killed. "It was me it wanted to kill, Ehrler just got in the way."

"What are you doing to me!" Sherri cried as Malinkov pushed her out the door. He kicked her legs from under her, and she fell on her face in the snow.

"I am doing what we should have done this morning—making you either talk or die," he hissed as he tied her hands behind her and then jerked her to her feet.

Sherri was already shivering when he backed her against one of the wooden posts that supported the porch roof and pulled a rope tightly across her chest. "I told you I don't know. Why don't you believe me?"

Malinkov knotted another rope around her ankles. "For your sake, you had better be lying, because if you don't come up with a story we believe, there will be no reason to untie you before you freeze to death, which should be—he stood up and checked his watch—in about two hours."

He was smiling at her. He was enjoying this, she knew, loving her pain, her helplessness, her nakedness. His face was suddenly only inches away from her own. He smelled like tobacco and stale beer. Her skin crawled as his hand touched her throat

and moved to her jaw. He kissed her hard, hurting
her lips as she struggled unsuccessfully to turn her
head away.

"Pig!" She spit at him and he slapped her face.
She tried to scream, but he taped her mouth again
and backed away as she continued to struggle.

"I'm going inside where it is nice and warm. We
will check on you in an hour or so to see if you are
ready to talk. If not, then in a little while longer,
you should be dead, frozen stiff as a board." He
pinched her breast and went inside.

Sherri could not stop herself from shaking. A
light wind was blowing, chilling her quickly.
Through much of her ordeal she had clung to some
hope of rescue, her knight in shining armor from
some other life, perhaps. She pulled with all her
might against her ropes. She must get loose or die.
There were no other options.

The ropes held and the cold grew worse. Her
whole body shook in uncontrollable spasms of cold,
and she could no longer feel her toes. She forced
herself to move her fingers although the pain was
unbelievable. Her body was becoming numb all
over, and there seemed to be nothing she could do
to stop it.

Visions began to invade the fringes of her mind:
laughing trolls, chanting and dancing around her,
chanting that she must die. Why, she tried desperately to remember, did all this horrible scene seem
familiar? Why did she have to die?

"It fears you," the voices in her mind sang.

The dream, she realized. That night in the hotel
when they tried to kill me, I was dreaming about
all this.

She shook her head several times, trying to separate the visions from reality. The presence was

real. She felt it with a sudden crystal clearing of her mind. Straining her eyes, she tried to see into the forest shadows beyond the small clearing in front of the lodge. The Jagdpanther was out there, hiding from the moonlight, moving in the shadows. It was coming for her as if she were some human sacrifice, offered up to a pagan god.

A tiny vibration rippled through the post to which she was bound. The ground was trembling slightly beneath her. A shadow moved on the edge of the trees. It was coming closer. She could hear its engine, rough and more like breathing than anything mechanical. It echoed through the forest and grew steadily louder.

A dark shape materialized at the edge of the clearing. Moonlight washed the Jagdpanther in a cold, eerie light as it moved cautiously into the open and stopped. Its engine breathed nervously now, revving and dropping back to idle again and again. The muzzle of its 88 rose and leveled itself at Sherri.

Inside the lodge, Gnokte heard the Jagdpanther first. "Panzer," he said suddenly, and broke into a smile.

Malinkov frowned. "Does not sound like any tank I ever heard."

Gnokte was already getting up. "You are not old enough to have heard a Panzer. There is no sound like them." He opened the door with Malinkov right behind him.

"By Lenin's ghost," Malinkov gasped, "it's here. He's brought it here to make the trade."

"Yes," Gnokte agreed hopefully. "It certainly looks that way." He pointed to Sherri. "Quickly, get her clothes; I'll cut her loose."

Malinkov disappeared inside as Gnokte removed

her gag and cut the ropes that held her to the post. Sherri tried to stand, but her numbed legs failed her and she dropped to her knees. Gnokte was behind her, about to cut the last ropes that bound her hands, when he heard the Jagdpanther's engine rev up and shift gears. To his horror, the old tank-killer was bathed in a blue halo of light and it was coming at him, its treads churning up the frozen snow. They had lost—he knew it then without any doubt. There was still time to kill the girl. His knife moved toward the back of her neck. One quick stroke would cut the jugular vein and it would be over. He hesitated and looked up at the charging Jagdpanther. Why? he thought. Why should I die with any more blood on my hands? He threw down the knife and backed away.

Sherri tried to get up as the forty tons of steel rolled toward her. She saw the clawlike treads ripping the ground in front of her, saw the knifelike bow glowing blue and cutting toward her through the night. The elfin face on the Jagdpanther's fender leered at her, laughing with wicked delight. Somewhere, beyond the distant fringes of her memory, she knew she had seen that face before.

Someone was yelling at her, telling her to lay down. Without understanding why, she let herself fall forward. Her face buried in the snow, cold and numbing. She did not hurt anymore. She could sleep now.

Chapter Sixteen

JIM DROVE THE half-track cautiously forward, keeping it in the Jagdpanther's tracks. He followed the tracks through a stream and downshifted into his lowest gear to let the half-track claw its way up the steep hill beyond. They entered a narrow forest trail where the trees grew like black walls on both sides and only a pale archway of moonlight was visible ahead, where the trees thinned out. Ambush alley, he decided. Setting the hand throttle to a comfortable speed, Jim sat up high on the back of the driver's seat, steered with his feet on the steering wheel, and kept the Sagger's firing control in his hands. If the Jagdpanther was waiting for him in here, he would have to shoot very fast.

He was almost surprised to reach the opening in the trees without getting hit, and it occurred to him that perhaps the Jagdpanther was after something else. He halted again with only the half-track's hood exposed beyond the trees. He was beside the dirt road that should lead to the hunting lodge. With his field glasses, he scanned the moonlit land in front of him. The lodge was there: a low, single-story building with rocks on the roof. The windows were shuttered, but cracks of light showed around one that faced onto a porch. There, he picked up some slight movement and refocused.

"Sherri!" he whispered, and cursed under his breath as he focused his glasses on her. "She won't last long out there." With effort, he restrained himself from charging in with the half-track. He was still deciding how best to approach the lodge when a familiar blue glow caught his eye and he saw the Jagdpanther. It moved slowly through the trees and then halted in front of the lodge. Jim knew he was out of time. He dropped into the driver's seat and gunned the half-track forward.

The front door of the lodge opened, spilling yellow light out onto the porch and the snow. Two men came outside. One of them looked like he was untying Sherri. Out of the corner of his eye, he saw the Jagdpanther move forward. By the time he had turned the half-track and picked up the Sagger's firing control, he knew the distance was too close. Any hit on the Jagdpanther from this range would surely kill Sherri. He saw her fall forward, struggling on her knees in the snow. The Jagdpanther was close beside him now. He swung the half-track hard, ramming its bumper into the Jagdpanther's drive sprocket. The half-track recoiled, skidding away from the encounter with the bumper gone and most of one fender twisted over the hood. The Jagdpanther continued forward, unaffected.

"Get down!" he yelled at Sherri as the Jagdpanther charged toward her. "Get down, between the treads!"

The Jagdpanther blocked his view as it passed over her, and it was impossible to tell if she had made it or not. There was no doubt about the man with the cane who stood up behind her. The sharp bow caught him in the chest and threw him over the fender. For a moment, he scrambled backward in the snow, and then the Jagdpanther turned slightly and swallowed him beneath the tracks. His screams echoed above the roar of engines, and Jim saw his head and shoulders protruding from beneath the treads in a dark pool of gore as the Jagdpanther climbed onto the porch and crushed it with a vengeance.

Jim swung the half-track across the Jagdpanther's rear and hit the brakes. He clambered over the windshield and jumped to the ground. In front of him, the man's body was in two distinct pieces, but directly between the tread marks was Sherri. He cut the rope that bound her hands and rolled her gently onto her back. She felt terribly cold as he carried her to the half-track and placed her in the front seat.

The roof collapsed as the Jagdpanther rolled completely through the lodge. Flames, fed by falling lumber, were beginning to leap from where the fireplace had been as Jim started to get back into the cab. He noticed Sherri's mink, lying in the snow with tank tracks across it. As he picked it up, he found the rest of her clothes with it and threw them into the half-track.

He drove straight for the forest while the Jagdpanther seemed content to vent its fury on the lodge and whomever else might still be there. He did not stop until he was several hundred meters away and the fire was only a dim, orange glow in the distance. There, he backed the half-track into a thick grove of trees, so that only the Sagger missile was exposed with a clear field of fire. Finally, he shut off the engine.

Sherri continued to shake uncontrollably as he wrapped her in one of the blankets and brushed some of the snow from her matted hair. After managing to force a little coffee down her, he dressed her, laid her on the front seat, and wrapped her in her mink. It was only then that he remembered he still had Smythe in the back. With his pistol in hand, he walked around to the back of the half-track and found Smythe just as he had left him. He pulled the gag from his mouth and then untied him.

Smythe was shivering so badly he could hardly talk. "What, what are you ... going to do?" he asked.

"Take off your coat and your sweater and empty your pockets," Jim said. Smythe nodded, and did as he was told. "Now start walking, and don't look back." Smythe did not believe his ears. "Yeah, start walking. I was going to shoot you, but I'd rather let you try to explain all this to your superiors. I suspect they'll do a lot worse than just shoot you."

Smythe was too cold to think or reason, he just turned silently and staggered off into the night. Jim watched him go, and then returned to the cab and wrapped Smythe's coat around Sherri's legs.

"Jim?" Sherri said weakly. "You did it. You rescued me. I never thought you had it in you."

"Your confidence is so very reassuring," he said, and raised her head enough to give her some more coffee.

The moonlight reflected in her eyes for a moment—liquid pools of pale blue, framed with the matted strands of her golden hair. She laid her head on his shoulder and drifted off to sleep.

Sometime later, distant screams woke them both. Jim opened his eyes but did not move. Sherri stirred beside him and he told her to listen. A distant wail, shrill and bloodcurdling on the night air, drifted through the forest once again, and then there was total silence.

"Smythe," Jim whispered. "I think the Jagdpanther found him." Jim sat up and turned on the ignition. "That means it's hunting us, so we've got to move."

"Where are we going?" Sherri said sleepily from beside him.

Jim was already easing the half-track out of its hiding place. "I'm going to double back, stay about fifty yards off my own tracks, and try to get behind him."

"Then what?"

"Then I'm going to put that missile right up his exhaust pipe."

"I don't think it will work."

"The thickest armor he's got back there is less than forty millimeters. The Sagger will punch sixteen inches."

"Not of *Mirtheil*, it won't," Sherri insisted.

"Oh yeah? We'll see. Up to now, that relic hasn't taken on anything tougher than a truck. Tank-killing has changed a whole bunch since it rolled off the assembly line, so let's just see how it runs with a missile up its ass."

"Okay." Sherri sighed. "But I think we are going to get in a lot of trouble."

Jim ignored her and concentrated on driving and watching the forest around him. He eased the half-track along at barely more than an idle, avoiding most of the trees and pushing over only the smaller ones. He was working his way along the side of a hill, keeping to the high ground above the trail he had followed when they left the lodge.

"There," Sherri said suddenly, and pointed over the windshield. Jim stopped the half-track and killed the motor. Below them, through the trees, there was a familiar, blue glow.

"It's following our old tracks," Jim whispered. "Now we'll just sit tight and let it get past."

"Then what?"

"Then we slip onto the trail behind it and let the Sagger brew up a nice, hot panther stew."

They waited, barely daring to breathe as the

Jagdpanther prowled past them. They could hear the distant sighing of its engine and the squeaking of treads as it moved cautiously along the half-track's trail. Jim waited until the blue light was but a tiny flicker through the trees before he moved. With his engine at an idle, he guided the half-track down the slope and turned into the Jagdpanther's tracks. Far ahead, they could still glimpse the blue glow; the Jagdpanther was getting very close to their former place. Jim picked up his speed a little. Climbing a little rise, the trail turned slightly to the left. Suddenly, they saw the Jagdpanther, its rear still turned toward them.

Jim eased the half-track to a stop—the range looked good. "Now," he whispered and took the missile's firing control out of Sherri's hand. "Get down real low. When this takes off, there's going to be a lot of smoke and fire. Believe me, you do not want to be anywhere behind it."

Sherri did not answer but moved closer to him and got down onto the floor. Jim rested the firing control on top of the windshield and rechecked the connections and flipped the arming switch. The Jagdpanther was still there, still with its rear to him. "Here goes," he whispered as he took a good grip on the joystick and pressed the fire button.

The noise was tremendous—a high-pitched, ear-splitting scream which ripped at the stillness of the night and shattered it. Jim saw the missile's bright, flarelike exhaust as it streaked down the trail, flying true and straight. The Jagdpanther glowed a brilliant, electric blue a split second before the missile hit directly between the twin exhaust pipes, centered on its rear hull.

The explosion was blinding. White light with an orange center turned night into day. A shock wave rocked the half-track, and branches fell all along the trail. Rolling thunder echoed across the hills. "Bull's-eye!" Jim yelled.

Sherri was standing beside him, staring up the trail. Smoke and snow had mixed into a dense, drifting fog where the Jagdpanther had last been seen. The fog turned blue. "The blue flame?" Jim said.

"Maybe," Sherri answered, but even as she spoke, the Jagdpanther materialized out of the fog, glowing brightly and charging straight at them. "And maybe not!"

"Oh shit," Jim said as he dropped into the driver's seat. He hit reverse and floored the half-track, backing over a half-dozen trees as he hurried to get off the trail and down the hill. The treads began to slide sideways in the snow and he used the opportunity to shift into forward. The result looked much like a fancy "bootleg turn," only done with a half-track instead of a car.

"Can we outrun it?" Sherri asked yelling over the roar of the engine as they snapped off a six-inch pine tree, which fell across the hood and then rolled off.

"Theoretically, yes," Jim yelled back as he put the half-track into a tight S-turn. "Assuming that he doesn't get a clear shot at us with that 88."

"Oh," Sherri said. "Then why is he gaining on us?"

Jim shot a quick glance over his shoulder and, just as she had said, the Jagdpanther was only a few yards behind, the end of its gun barrel looking as if it was almost touching the half-track's rear armor. "Goddamn it, why didn't you tell me he was that close?"

"I just did, you idiot!"

Jim turned the wheel hard over. "Never mind, just jump—now!" He pulled the hand throttle wide open and stayed aboard only long enough to see Sherri leap, and then followed her. He was still in midair when the 88 fired and the half-track exploded. Jim glanced off a tree, took some branches off another, and hit hard in the snow. It seemed to him like he rolled a very long way and hit a lot of hard things before he finally stopped moving. For a while he lay perfectly still, listening to the Maybach diesel fade slowly into the night. When he at last raised his head, the first thing he saw was Sherri lying close beside him with her head propped up on one elbow.

"I told you it wouldn't work," she said.

Sergeant Hank Murphy had only been this scared once before in his whole life. That was the day the Jagdpanther had brewed up his tank and his crew. Now he was running platoon point, hunting what the operations order had called a "hostile armored vehicle being operated by terrorists."

The memory of Fafner's visit and Murphy's own call to set up the sale of a stolen AT missile both weighed heavily on his mind. It had to be the Jagdpanther they had been sent out to hunt, and Murphy, better than anyone else, knew exactly the damage it could do.

At 0700 that morning, his platoon had been lined up on Tank Table Six, with the ammo racks full of 105mm SABO rounds and the fuel tanks topped off. It should have been an average day on the live-fire ranges. Instead, they had received an operation order, all nice and standard, just like any other training exercise, except this time they were headed south, off the training areas away from Ansbach, down through the village of Dorfen and into the forest beyond.

Murphy's platoon rolled past the smoldering remains of the hunting lodge and saw the crisscross of wide tank tracks. The German police were there, stuffing things into a shiny black body bag and, from the M-60's cupola, Murphy had a good view of bloodstains on the snow.

"Hold it, driver," Murphy said into the intercom as they crested a small rise. There was something in the snow ahead of him. A burned-out vehicle, maybe.

He touched the radio button. "One-six, this is one-four, I got something up here. Give me some cover while I take a look."

Murphy glanced back, over the top of the open hatch as three tanks left the trail behind him, plowing through the trees and moving up to covering positions. "Move out, driver. Gunner, look sharp."

They eased forward as Murphy scanned the forest nervously. Visibility was poor. A fog hung over the snow. The forest faded quickly into a gray void and even the tops of the pine trees were invisible.

"One-four, one-four, what have you got up there?" the platoon leader's voice crackled over the radio. Murphy's M-60 idled up alongside the wreck.

Murphy leaned out of the cupola and looked at the ground. "Armored vehicle, burned out but still hot. It's U.S.—looks like an old half-track."

"Roger, one-four. Anything else?"

"Tank tracks, too wide to be one of ours. Headed south."

"Roger, one-four, follow 'em."

Murphy acknowledged, and told his driver to

move out. Yeah, we'll follow 'em, you chicken-shit lieutenant. While you're nice and safe back there somewhere, he thought.

The tracks led in a straight line south. Whoever was driving was making no effort to avoid anything. Streams were crossed in places where the banks were steep and slick, even if only a few yards away the banks were nearly flat. Murphy rolled over trees two feet thick that had been pushed down when only a slight course change would have avoided it.

"One-four, one-four," the radio crackled again. "Be advised, we've got a West German platoon on our right flank, about one klick west. They are Leopard IIs. They should be moving parallel our axis, over."

Murphy acknowledged and eased his tank up to a treeline that bordered a rolling meadow. The fog was thinner here. Far to his right, he saw the Leopards break from the trees. They were running fast, boiling up clouds of frozen snow in their wakes as they maneuvered into a ragged line formation. Halfway across the meadow, the center tank shuddered and turned, out of control. Black smoke began to pour from the engine bay. Only then did he fully realize that the Leopard had been hit.

"Come on, bail out, bail out," Murphy was whispering, but the hatches never came open, and the whole tank burst into flames. "One-six, one-six," Murphy almost shouted into the radio. "Krauts have a contact, one Leopard hit and burning." As he spoke, tree branches shuddered and snow stirred across the meadow as a hidden gun fired again and its muzzle blast gave away its position. Road wheels and sections of tread flew from a second Leopard, bringing it also to a halt, just as the remaining three opened fire on the treeline.

The platoon leader's tank rocked to a halt beside Murphy's. The lieutenant had his binoculars resting on the front of his cupola. "He's moving," Murphy said into the radio, "across our front. Range about one thousand meters."

"Identified." The lieutenant's voice sounded like an excited kid. "He's ours; let's go get him!" In only a slightly more formal voice, he barked out his orders: "Charlie one-six to all one-six elements. Warning order. Tank red, moving east, range one thousand; mission, destroy." There was a moment's hesitation and he continued. "Move out and close it up, echelon right."

The platoon commander's M-60 gunned its engine and broke out into the meadow with Murphy running just behind and to his left. Seconds later the platoon's other three tanks followed and began maneuvering for position. "SABO in the tube," Murphy's loader reported.

The fox had been flushed and the chase was on. Murphy dropped into the cupola and closed the hatch behind him. Despite his fear, he felt the adrenaline pumping in his veins as his excitement grew. There was something about tanks that did that to him. The roar of the engines, the speed of the attack, the tremendous weight and firepower at his fingertips. This time it was real, and there was revenge too; sweet revenge for the fiery deaths of his old crew.

Through his vision blocks, he glanced at the Leopards on his right. Only the two burning hulks were still visible. The others had made it to the treeline. He turned his own attention there: if the enemy chose, he could have the first shot once again. The treeline remained peaceful. Beneath him the M-60's 750-horsepower diesel roared at its top RPM, pushing the tank up to a speed of near forty miles per hour.

They broke into the trees, snapping off tall pines as though they were matchsticks. Only within the relative safety of the forest did the platoon slow down. Gray mist clung to the forest. All around them were the black silhouettes of tall straight trees.

"Platoon, right turn; form line," the lieutenant ordered, and six tanks executed a cartwheel turn. Murphy eased open his hatch and raised his head so that just his eyes were visible above the cupola. Any engagement in here, he figured, would be close, real close. He needed to see better than he could when buttoned up.

Even with the muffled roar of the engines and the cracking and snapping of trees and brush beneath the treads, the forest seemed ominously quiet. The enemy tank should be to their front, trapped now between the platoon and the three West German Leopards. "Driver, halt!" Murphy ordered as a brush-choked ravine suddenly appeared ahead.

"One-three and one-four cover; I'll cross first," the radio barked, and the lieutenant's tank swung its long gun tube to the side and plowed off into the ravine. Its engine screamed at a fever pitch as it fought, half-submerged in dead limbs and brush, across the ravine's floor, then began climbing steadily up the far side.

Murphy saw the end of the Jagdpanther's gun tube move slightly through a tangle of branches. The lieutenant's tank was already halfway up the ravine; in another two or three seconds it would be crawling out, belly up and totally exposed. There was only time to fire. He grabbed the override switch, swung his turret a few degrees left, and dropped the gun tube an inch. "Main gun," he yelled, and squeezed his firing control. The M-60 rocked back on its suspension. The muzzle blast was hot and sharp against Murphy's eyes as he sighted over the cupola. The 105mm SABO round exploded exactly where Murphy had seen the muzzle.

"Got the goddamn mother! You owe me one, sir," he cheered into the radio just as the lieutenant's tank topped the ravine. A gun fired in front of him, shaking down tree limbs and stirring the snow. The lieutenant's tank shuddered. The cupola and the loader's hatch both blew straight up into the air. The tank turned sideways, as the left tread slipped, and then slid backward down the ravine and turned over at the bottom, with black smoke pouring from the engine bay.

"Jesus Christ! SABO, left front!" Murphy ordered another round.

"Up!" the loader confirmed, and then something hit Murphy's tank. He could hear only a tremendous ringing sound, like some giant hammer had banged against the hull. Murphy realized that he was no longer standing in the cupola but sitting on the turret floor, staring at the gun breech.

The loader was lying beside him, all, that is, except his head, which was nowhere to be seen. Orange tongues of flame were licking around the turret floor. Murphy tried to stand up. He grabbed for the gun breech and pulled himself up a little. The gunner was still in his seat, slumped forward and unmoving. Blood was dripping onto the turret floor from a gaping hole in his back. Through a gray haze of smoke, Murphy reached for the fire-extinguisher-system handle and pulled. Nothing happened. He dragged himself toward the hatch far above him. His pants leg was on fire. He swatted at the flames with one hand, and then his sleeve was on fire also. Flames danced around the ammo racks in the turret's rear.

He could not breathe. The smoke was choking him as flames consumed all the oxygen within the limited confines of the turret. With one hand, he reached the commander's seat just as the padding on it began to smolder. Flames were everywhere around him, blending into a white-hot curtain; yet he was still moving, climbing and climbing, inch by inch, up over the seat and behind the machine gun in the cupola.

His head emerged above the open hatch, but he could move no farther. He could no longer feel the winter air on his face or fill his lungs with the crisp air. Across the ravine, he saw the Jagdpanther one last time with unreal, crystallike clarity. It was backing away. Flames leaped around him; he felt himself slipping, slipping back into the boiling inferno below.

Chapter Seventeen

THE FIRST, GRAY hint of dawn showed through cracks in the barn wall. Jim shivered in the morning cold as he stuck his head out of the hay that he and Sherri had slept in for the last few hours. He had no idea how far they had walked after the half-track had been hit, but this had been the first refuge they had found.

The hay stirred beside him. A tangle of hair, almost the same color as the hay, but somewhat dirtier, rose up and shook. "God, I feel terrible," Sherri croaked as she tried to brush her hair out of her eyes. "I hurt in places I didn't even know I had." She yawned and looked sleepily around the barn. "And next time, *I'll* choose the hotel."

"Yeah? Well, I've had better times with a woman in the hay myself."

"Don't be tacky. Where are we, anyway?"

"South of Ansbach, a little way."

Sherri nodded thoughtfully. "That's good. We have to keep going south."

"Whatever for?"

"What for?" Sherri looked disgusted at not being understood. "Because that's where Ehrler said the forges were."

Jim pulled the map out of his jacket and tossed it to her. "Okay, so which mountain?"

Sherri shrugged and picked up the map. "That's the only part I haven't figured out yet, but I think there is some—"

Jim touched his finger to his lips. "Listen," he whispered. Somewhere outside was the distant rumble of tanks.

"The Jagdpanther?"

"I don't think so—sounds too modern. M-60s or Leopards."

Sherri perked up a little. "Oh, good. Maybe they'll have something to eat; and we can get a ride out of here and then go get cleaned up and—"

"There is one little problem with that," Jim said cautiously.

"What problem? They're probably out looking

for us right now. You did tell them you were coming to rescue me, didn't you?"

"Oh, they're looking for us all right. But it's because they think we stole the Jagdpanther and used it to attack a supply convoy."

"Us? Why us?"

"By now," Jim said as he looked out through a crack in the wall, "General Walker's tried to check my story and can't find you to confirm it. So he's convinced we are in it together."

"What story?" Sherri was frowning.

"The one I told him about where I was the night I bought the Sagger," Jim tried to say casually.

"Yeah, right. That one."

"I told him I was in bed with you."

Sherri took a deep breath and held it for a moment, like a bomb about to explode. "Good grief, Fafner! You have got one vivid imagination," she said, trying to sound angry, but the hint of a smile turned her lips.

"Walker bought it, for a little while, anyway."

"And they let him be a general?" She giggled.

Jim ignored her and watched one of the Leopards roll slowly up to the barn.

"Why's he stopping?" Sherri wanted to know.

"Maybe he's just checking his map. Maybe they'll search the barn. Either way, you better get under the hay . . . and save me a place."

Sherri started burrowing. "Do you realize what they'll think if they find us under the hay together?"

"They're soldiers. They'll think that wherever they find us."

A hatch on the Leopard banged open and one of the crewmen emerged, carrying a submachine gun. Jim ducked and followed Sherri into the haystack. She giggled when his hand touched her leg, and he told her to shut up. Outside, there were footsteps in the snow; the barn door opened and the soldier stepped into the barn. From inside the haystack, they could hear him walking, pushing over barrels and boxes and rummaging through everything.

"Niemand ist zu Hause," he said finally, and moments later, they heard the Leopard move off through the forest.

Jim and Sherri watched them go and then waited a half-hour before leaving the barn. "There's a village this way," he said, and started down the hill.

"What do we do when we get there?" Sherri asked as her short legs hurried to keep pace with him in the snow.

"I don't know yet."

For the next hour, they trudged through the forested hills, keeping to the cover of the heaviest timber and skirting any field or clearing that might give them away. They had just crossed a small frozen stream when they heard the shooting; a single round followed by a second. There was a few seconds of silence, and then four rounds in rapid succession, but each a little louder and sharper.

"Sounds like the Leopards found the Jagdpanther," Jim said as he listened. "Jagdpanther got off two quick rounds before they spotted him and returned fire."

"You can tell all that by hearing a few explosions? What happened?"

"Either they got him, or the Jagdpanther pulled out."

Minutes later there was a rapid succession of rounds, fired so closely together that it was impossible to tell one from another. "I don't think they got him," Jim said, and kept walking.

It was afternoon before they walked down the

main street of the village of Dorfen. There was a
church with a high steeple, a few shops, and a *Gasthaus* which had a few rooms to rent on the second
floor. Jim and Sherri drew a few suspicious stares
as Jim rented a room and they went upstairs.

When Sherri finished taking a shower, she found
Jim had left the room. She curled up on the bed and
began studying the map again. Jim was right—
there were a lot of mountains, but many of them
had names which were printed on the map. Perhaps the clue was there.

Jim returned before she had gotten very far.
"How do you say 'dragon' in German?" she asked.

"*Drache*, I think."

"How about 'evil'?"

"*Böse*, with an umlaut. What are you doing?"

"Looking for a mountain that's big enough to
hide a whole factory in. The clue is written in that
verse from the *Edda*, it's been there for centuries.
It's just a matter of finding it."

"But there are just a bunch of mountains south of
here. They start in southern France and run all the
way to Asia. We don't have any idea where to start
looking."

"You're right." Sherri sighed, and laid down the
map. "Where did you go just now?"

"Looking for the whorehouse," Jim said dryly.

"Good grief, Fafner, you didn't look that horny."

Jim ignored the comment and offered no explanation. "Get your coat; there's a restaurant just
across the street from it. I'll buy you dinner."

Sherri came off the bed with a bounce and picked
up her coat. "Now, that's about the first good idea
I've heard all day."

They walked three blocks in a lightly falling snow
to a tiny cafe, where the odors of smoked sausage

and sauerkraut mingled with those of beer and fresh-baked bread. Jim and Sherri slipped into a booth by one of the windows which gave an excellent view of a small, and somewhat seedy-looking hotel across the street.

Sherri said little until she had ordered and the food arrived. "There," she said as she began devouring a bratwurst. "I always think better when I eat."

The meal was finished before she said anything else except, "Pass the bread."

With a clean plate in front of her, she was thinking clearly again. "Ehrler said that Von Norden and the Jagdpanther have become one. I think I know what he meant now. Like Ehrler said, one of the legends of *Mirtheil* is that it can learn from its master and become a better and better weapon. Obviously, this was happening with Von Norden's Jagdpanther. That's why he could shoot and move faster than anyone else."

Jim only nodded his head as he watched an army truck pull into an alley across the street and stop.

"Okay," Sherri continued, "let's project the theory to a logical conclusion. Ehrler also talked of the problems of mating magic and technology when they tried to use *Mirtheil* to build a complex weapon like a tank. This had never been done before, right? Von Norden and the Jagdpanther fought together long enough for the Jagdpanther to learn everything he could teach. When he died, it no longer needed him. It *was* him. And it still is!"

Jim at last took his eyes off the street and looked at her. "If I hadn't seen that missile bounce off its engine bay, I'd say you were crazy," he admitted. "And I hope to hell that the only reason I'm starting to believe any of this is because I haven't gotten a decent night's sleep in so long that I'm starting to hallucinate."

"There weren't any hallucinations last night."

Jim smiled thoughtfully and looked back out the window. "The Panzer Spirit."

"What's that?"

"The panzer divisions; they were the spearhead of the greatest army that every rolled across Europe. To the men who fought in them, the panzer was undefeatable, almost immortal. So, like you said, if you project that theory to its logical conclusion, then all their esprit de corps—all the fighting spirit of the panzers—was mated with the cruelty, the racism, and the hatred of the Nazis. Then, it was all condensed and concentrated into one bloodthirsty, killing machine with a mind of its own. If that exists, it might well be an unconquerable evil."

"It does exist!" Sherri insisted. "And to fight it, we have to find the forges where it was built. Ehrler was trying to tell us when he died. He started reciting that verse from the *Edda*. 'Beneath the misty mountain deep, where evil hides and dragons sleep, there the Elfin forges blazed . . .' It's perfectly clear to me."

"And if you do find it, what then?" Jim asked, and shifted his eyes to the three GIs who had gotten out of the truck and were now coming into the cafe.

Sherri ignored their stares as they passed the booth. *"Guten abend, Fräulein,"* one of them said in bad German.

She lowered her voice and leaned closer to Jim. "I don't know exactly, but that would be the only place a weapon could be made capable of destroying the Jagdpanther."

The three GIs clambered into the booth just behind Sherri. "Man, we gotta be real careful stoppin' here."

"You wanta get laid or not?" another answered with his voice lowered.

"Hell, yes, I wanta get laid. It's just with all the terrorist attacks going on, we gotta be careful."

"No sweat."

"No sweat, shit. That convoy the other night was bad enough, but man, when they start wastin' tanks like they did today . . . I'm surprised battalion even let us make this run without some kind of an escort. Now, those MPs we talked to back at Ingolstadt were talking about some truck just exploding on the Autobahn this afternoon."

Sherri gave Jim a questioning look, and he touched his finger to his lip and kept listening.

"Come on, we're carryin' C-rats and field gear—who'd want to blow that up? Now drink your beer and let's go get laid." The three GIs downed their drinks and got up to leave.

"Wieviel uhr ist es?" one of them with sergeant's stripes asked Sherri in German, and leaned across the table.

Jim answered him quickly. *"Halb acht."*

The sergeant turned to Jim, who stared coolly at him. *"Danke,"* he said and left.

"I could have told him what time it was, thank you," Sherri said when he was gone.

"Oh, I'm sure you could. But would you have handled it in German or English?"

"Actually, I was considering Gaelic."

"That would be almost as bad. Let's try not to stand out any more than we already do."

"Give me the map," Sherri said, changing the subject. "Where did they say that truck exploded this afternoon?"

"Ingolstadt."

"Where is it?"

Jim put his finger on the map. "South of here, toward Munich."

"Okay, so where was the first convoy hit, and where do you think the tanks were today when we heard the shooting?"

Jim showed her and watched as she put the edge of a napkin on the map and drew a line along it. "There," she said when she had finished. "The Jagd-panther is moving in a straight line, headed almost due south."

"Wrong," Jim disagreed. "You forgot the hunting lodge. It's a good ten kilometers off the line."

Sherri nodded her head and looked away. When she spoke, the fear in her voice was poorly hidden. "Yeah, I know. It didn't come to the lodge by acci-dent. It came there to kill me. Now it must think I'm dead, so it's going on, on to someplace it has to go."

"You? Why you?"

"I don't know, but I felt it the first time I saw the Jagdpanther; and then, it was in my dreams." Sherri dropped her eyes back onto the map and began following the line she had drawn. "It's going very close to Munich. That's where the monastery records are. I wonder if that could have anything to do with it?" As she talked, she traced the line fur-ther south, roughly paralleling the highway past the Starnberger See and on to Oberammergau, deep in the Alps.

"*Drachenschlaft?*" she asked. "What does that translate to in English?"

"Dragon sleep, or sleeping dragon, maybe. Why?"

"Because, bingo!" she whispered loudly. "That's it. It's the first mountain on the Jagdpanther's route with a name. It fits: *"Where evil hides and dragons sleep"*! That has got to be it. Look right there, just past a village called Eschenlohe."

Jim grunted and took the map. "It is big enough to hide a factory in. Not too far from the main Autobahn and the rail line. Of course, we don't know if they ran the same way in World War II as they do now, but they were probably about the same." Jim shrugged and handed the map back to her. "It's possible, I guess." He looked at his watch and started to get up. "Come on, it's time."

"Time for what?"

He leaned close to her and whispered. "Those GIs went into the whorehouse ten minutes ago. So it's time for us to steal their truck."

"Steal their . . . ?" Sherri started, but Jim's hand touched her lips.

"Right. And then we go find your mountain."

Sherri followed him as they left the cafe. "You can't just walk over there and steal a truck," she said as they reached the street.

"Why not? I stole your car yesterday morning, the half-track last night. It's getting to be a habit."

"Don't they lock them up or take the keys out, or something?"

Jim guided her across the street and stopped long enough for a look in both directions before they ducked into the alley. "If the army made trucks with keys, they'd lose them all before they could get into battle." He grabbed the door handle on the driver's side of the deuce-and-a-half and pulled it open. "Go," he said, and helped Sherri climb up into the cab. He followed her and settled himself into the driver's seat as she crawled over the gear-shift console and into the passenger seat beside him.

"Well, I'll be damned," Sherri said as he flipped a switch and the instrument lights glowed a pale green. The engine turned over a few times and then fired. Jim gunned it once, shifted into gear, and drove out of the alley.

From across the street, Nikoli Malinkov watched them go and then got into a BMW sedan and followed them. They were moving fast, he thought, so fast that they had almost slipped away from him. In fact, it had been by sheer luck that he had caught up with them here.

Last night, he had been on the front porch of the hunting lodge when the Jagdpanther crushed Gnokte and he saw Sherri fall between the treads. He had dropped her clothes, then run back inside and straight out the back door, just as the lodge collapsed around him. He had dived into the snow and stayed hidden then, trying to figure out what was going on. He had still been uncertain when, later, he had walked and found the pieces of Gnokte's body in the snow. But the girl, her clothes, and the half-track were all gone. He had taken stock of his situation. He still had his pistol, his wallet, and identification. He could still be considered "operational," and so he had started walking.

Two hours later, he was still walking when he heard the unmistakable scream of a Sagger missile and then the return fire of a tank gun. With still an hour before sunrise, he had come upon the wreckage of the half-track. Fafner came and rescued the girl, he concluded. But then, what destroyed the half-track? It was beginning to sound like Fafner had not stolen the Jagdpanther. But if not, then who had?

With no more of the puzzle put together, he had found two sets of footprints leading away from the wreckage. Again there was hope, and he followed the trail in the moonlight until dawn.

For a while he had been forced to bury himself in the snow while a platoon of tanks passed by only a few meters away. He had heard the exchange of gunfire sometime later, and by midmorning, he had found the barn. Two people had left obvious signs of spending the night there. He believed they had been gone by the time the tank had stopped there, since there were still the two sets of tracks leading off from the barn.

He had followed the tracks on to Dorfen, where he had made the proper phone call. Within two hours he had new clothes, money, and a car with a somewhat obsolete but totally untraceable MP-40 submachine gun in the trunk. There was also an RPG-7 antitank rocket. The hunt was still on.

The whorehouse had been a stroke of genius on Fafner's part, Malinkov conceded as he followed the truck. The man was obviously smarter than he looked. Now he was keeping the stolen truck off the Autobahn and running instead on back roads as he headed south from Dorfen in the falling snow. To where? Malinkov had no idea, but he would cling to the trail. He held the element of surprise. When the time was right, he would strike.

Chapter Eighteen

⚡

"CAN YOU DRIVE one of these?" Jim asked as the deuce-and-a-half bounced along through the night.

"Yeah, I guess so. Why?" Sherri said.

"Because I want you to drive while I see what we're carrying back there." Jim pointed at the gear shift. "It's easy—all automatic. Just steer it and give it gas."

Sherri nodded, and Jim slipped out from behind the wheel as she wiggled across his lap. "It's big," she commented as she sat perched on the edge of the driver's seat and barely managed to reach the gas pedal.

"Yeah, and it takes a long time to stop."

"I don't have to worry about that. I can't reach the brake pedal."

Jim unlaced the canvas that formed the top of the truck's cab, then reached through and did the same thing to the canvas that covered the bed. He picked up his flashlight and disappeared out the back of the cab.

The cargo bed was nearly full. Jim crawled over a stack of C-ration cases and shone his light on the other contents. Field gear—sleeping bags, canteens, web belts. Some of that may be useful, he thought, and at least we can eat. He picked up two field jackets and passed them forward into the cab. There was a couple of mechanic's tool sets, tracked-vehicle variety, with ordnance tags indicating some pieces were missing. There was one small gasoline stove designed to be carried on a tank. He counted several cases of flat-white and olive-drab paint.

Jim decided he had seen enough for now and

stuck his head back into the cab. "How are you doing?" he asked.

Sherri appeared to be enjoying herself. "Hey, this is kind of fun. Great feeling of power. Volkswagens will do anything to get out of the way."

"We've got to get this thing off the road by sunrise. I know a place outside of Munich where we can hide something this big."

"I think we should keep going," Sherri said, sounding worried.

"Everybody's going to be looking for this truck come morning. We've got a lot better chance of not being spotted at night. Besides, there's some paint back there. When it gets light, we can change the unit numbers."

In the wee hours of the morning, they picked up the Autobahn at Freising and took it only as far as the suburb of Harlachling on the outskirts of Munich. On the south side of Land Strasse Jim swung the truck onto a gravel road that appeared to be swallowed up by a thick forest of tall pines. "Perlacher Forest," he said. "German army has a firing range up here, and past that, there is a whole lot of forest, cut with good roads."

"Then what?" Sherri asked sleepily.

"Then we get some rest. When it's light we'll put some new ID numbers on it and wait for dark."

A mile past the firing range, Jim turned onto a side road and then backed the truck as far into the forest as it would go. He broke off a few branches and laid them across the hood. "They help hide any reflection off the windshield," he said when Sherri asked what he was doing. "There's a dozen sleeping bags in the back. Take one and get some sleep. I'll be there in a minute." He handed her his flashlight and she disappeared into the rear of the truck. Working in the dark, Jim finished his camouflaging and climbed into the back.

Sherri was already asleep in the center of a pile of sleeping bags and field gear. The flashlight was still on and held tightly in her hands. Jim reached for it and felt her ragged breathing on his hand. He brushed a few tangled curls off her cheeks and she moaned, turning her head away but still keeping the flashlight. The thought of kissing her crossed his mind. He wasn't sure why. She was small and girlish, not the sort of woman he would usually consider attractive.

He backed away, lit the small stove, and leaned back on the pile of field gear. In a pocket, he found his pipe and lit it. For a long time, he sat watching her sleep as gray wisps of smoke drifted in the flashlight's yellow halo.

It had frightened him, the rage he had felt when Sherri had been kidnapped. The things he had done to Smythe surprised him. He had tortured the man and would have kept torturing him until he talked or died. There had been a boiling hatred in him when he had picked her stripped and nearly frozen body out of the snow. There had also been a terrible feeling of loss and sadness, as if some important part of him had been torn away. He had felt it only once before—when Kristen left him. No doubt, Jim thought, if the Jagdpanther had not killed the man with Sherri, he certainly would have, and with no less vengeance.

Sherri stirred again. Her breathing was fast and ragged, and her head tossed from one side to the other. Small whimpering noises escaped her.

"Sherri," he said, touching her shoulder. Her eyes popped wide open and she stared up at the canvas top as her breathing began to relax a little. "It's all right. You were just having a bad dream."

Tears were starting to run on her cheeks as she looked up into his eyes. "Damn it, Fafner, I have never, never been so scared in my whole life."

"Yeah, me too." He smiled and reached out for her. His hand touched the back of her neck, combed the blond curls there, and suddenly he was lifting her to him, pressing his lips against hers and feeling her warmth. There was a moment of resistance as her small arms pressed against his chest.

"No, Jim, don't . . ." she said in barely a whisper. And then, there was one tiny cry as she melted beneath him. Her arms encircled his neck, pulling him down and crushing him to her. He wanted, more than anything, to kiss away her pain, to smother her fears in pleasure.

Much later Jim lay exhausted amid the tangle of sleeping bags. Sherri was asleep with her head resting comfortably on his chest and her thumb in her mouth. Her mink jacket covered both of them. Her small breasts moved warmly against his side as she breathed, relaxed and evenly now. As a lover, she had been a complete surprise. With all her talk and money, freedom and travel, he had expected her to be a woman of the world, experienced and confident. Instead, she had been more like a teenager: frightened and uncertain. The approach of her climax had seemed to surprise her, as if it was something that she rarely experienced. When it was over, she had cried and he was not sure why.

On a scale of 1 to 10, Jim thought, she might be rated about a 4 or 5. Yet never, not even with Kristen who he thought had taken all the love he would ever have to give, had he been left with such a strangely wonderful, warm feeling inside. "I love

you, Sherri Vail," he whispered, and closed his
eyes.

The Jagdpanther crested a barren hill and, for a
moment, was silhouetted against the moon. A dangerous position, it noted, and moved on. Pushing
down a wire fence, it crossed a rolling, snow-
covered field where, forty years ago, there had been
a road. It had passed this way once before, on its
way into glorious battle with red dust churning like
brimstone from beneath its treads. Blood-red banners had streamed in the wind and jackboots
stomped as the drumming rhythm of *"Panzer Lied"*
had rung out across the land. It was more than the
destiny of Aryan Germany.

The power went deeper, back eons ago when the
elf Loki, blacksmith to the gods, had shaped *Mirtheil* into the sword of Odin, and the hammer of
Thor. It had grown with mighty Siegfried, second
greatest of the Germanic heroes, overshadowed
only by Hitler himself. Through all time, the power
had grown steadily stronger. The music of Wagner
had spread it like pollen on the magical notes of his
operas of *The Ring*.

It was that music which had called to young
Hitler, awakening him to rise, to take the power,
and to lead. He shaped the power into armies of
rolling steel, armored divisions that crushed the
resistance of all Germany's ancient enemies.

Therein was born the Panzer Spirit. At the moment of crisis, it had lacked only one element: *Mirtheil*. It had come too late, and then it had been held
back by sniveling fools like Linth and Ehrler. The
Jagdpanther had crushed Linth. Ehrler had taken
longer, but in the end, it had killed him too. After
forty years of waiting, of letting the power lie dor-

mant, the Jagdpanther could feel the strength within it growing. With each new kill, it thrived on the power of another vanquished enemy.

The appearance of an elf had been confusing, and even now, the Jagdpanther doubted her death. Something of her spirit prowled on the fringes of its being, recalling other ancient legends from before the time of its beginning. But it would deal with her when the time was right. Now, it must go south, for there was still one other enemy powerful enough to be a threat. It must be destroyed first. And then, the Jagdpanther would hunt and grow stronger and stronger with each new kill until . . . It did not conceive an ending.

For now, it must move quickly, and it must cover its tracks, confusing all pursuers. So far, it had been easy. The art of hunting and being hunted were part of its very being.

Across the field, the Jagdpanther plowed through a narrow ditch and climbed a railroad embankment. It hesitated beside the rails for a moment, then crawled onto them and turned south. With its wide treads centered on top of the rails, it traveled quickly and left no trace of its movement. Even the noise of its passing in the night sounded like nothing more than a train.

The Jagdpanther felt the growing vibration in the rails beneath it ten minutes before it saw the northbound express from Munich. It continued south along the tracks until the headlight of the coming train was a single round bull's-eye of light. The Jagdpanther stopped. The gun tube leveled on the approaching light, and inside, the breech closed behind another 88mm shell. There was no hurry. Let it get close. Let the train see its own death.

The twin diesel locomotives were coupled in

front of six passenger coaches and three mail cars. They were rolling at just over ninety miles per hour when the engineer thought he saw a blue light on the tracks ahead. With reflexes born from years of experience, he hit the emergency airbrakes and locked all of his train's wheels. As his air horns moaned out a warning, he saw the dark form materialize in his headlight. "Panzer?" he said, his last words in this life, just a half second before a shell exploded between the rails, ten yards in front of him. The diesels were still moving well over seventy miles per hour when the front wheels left the broken rails. The engines were propelled into the air and landed on their sides, crashing down the steep embankment to burn in a small creek below. The cars behind them folded like a giant accordion as each one in turn was driven into the others in front of it. Tremendous clouds of snow and smoke covered the train wreck as the debris settled. Only the screams of the dying could be heard above the cold, metallic sounds of settling wreckage as the flames from the engines spread back among the smashed passenger coaches.

The Jagdpanther felt its own strength grow with the train's death. It turned on its treads and left the railroad tracks, picking up speed as it passed into the cover of the nearby forest and continued south.

Little slits of sunlight were peeking through the truck's canvas when Sherri opened one eye and focused it on what was obviously a man's bare chest. She felt the warmth of his skin all the way down her leg and realized that he did not have one stitch of clothing on. "Damn!" she cursed, and pounded her fist on his chest.

When Jim opened his eyes, Sherri was on her knees, looking down at him. "Damn you, Fafner. I trusted you and—and there you are, just lying there with your clothes off and . . . !"

"I believe that makes two of us," Jim answered sleepily. Sherri suddenly realized that she was just as naked as he was. She let out a little scream as she tried to cover herself with her mink.

She was furious and Jim had no idea why. "You've really done it this time!" she snapped.

"I guess that's one way to put it." He reached for her and she crawled away, grabbing up pieces of clothing as she went.

"Stay away from me. Damn, I relax just once around you, and bang, you go and jump on top of me. Who do you think you are, anyway?"

"I thought we made love. By the way, it was wonderful."

Sherri was struggling with her ski pants. "Made love? Crap! We had sex. That's all!" She grabbed her sweater and her mink and crawled out the back of the truck.

"Women," Jim cursed quietly, and got dressed. He shut off the stove, broke open one of the cases of C-rations, and removed a couple of the packages inside. When he climbed out of the truck, Sherri was standing a few yards away looking off into the forest.

"Breakfast," he said as he approached her.

"What is it?" she responded after releasing a long breath.

"Everything: crackers, cheese, candy, and toilet paper, all in the same neat little package."

Sherri took the package without comment and opened it. She sniffed at something that looked like a square cookie and took a bite. "Edible," she commented dryly. "Look, I . . . I made a really big mistake last night, one I don't usually make."

"Is that what it was?"

"Damn right it was."

Jim reached out and touched her cheek. "I'm sorry to hear that, because I was about to say that I think I'm falling in love with you."

"Love? Come off it, Fafner." Sherri threw up her hands. "Look, I was scared, all right? And you? You helped me get through it. So, thanks and all that. Now let's forget it! I'm not right for you and you are most definitely not right for me."

"Knights in shining armor went out of style a few centuries ago. If that's what you're waiting for, you're a couple of dozen lives too late," Jim finished, and turned back toward the truck.

"He is definitely not right!" Sherri repeated under her breath as she watched him walking away. "Is he?"

When Sherri returned to the truck a little later, Jim had opened two cans of paint. "Here," he said. "You're an artist. Paint out the numbers on the bumper and I'll think up some new ones to put on."

"No brush?" Sherri asked.

"Improvise," Jim returned sharply, and climbed up into the truck. By the time he came back out, Sherri had painted out all the bumper numbers. She held up a short stick to which she had tied a small bundle of long, smooth hair.

"Mink," she stated flatly, and showed him a place on the cuff of her coat, where she had removed the hair. "A little expensive, but it makes excellent brushes." She noticed that Jim was carrying a portable radio. "Hey, a ghetto blaster. Where'd you find that?"

"In a duffel bag which belonged to one of the GIs we stole the truck from. Maybe we can get some news." Jim sat the radio down on the bumper and tuned it to the American Forces Network station. They were playing Christmas carols.

"So what do you want on this bumper?" Sherri asked.

Jim thought about that for a while, then gave her a series that would identify a truck belonging to a brigade-headquarters supply unit stationed at Augsburg. "That should confuse 'em," he said.

The radio reported the wreck of the Munich Express almost an hour later. It was noted that the tracks had been blown up and that it was apparently another terrorist attack. Jim located the position on his map.

"It's on the route, isn't it?" Sherri asked, looking over his shoulder.

"Close enough."

"Just north of Munich. I can't believe anything that big could have gotten that far, that fast—and without being seen."

Jim looked thoughtfully at the map. "It must be hiding during the day, just like we are, and moving at night."

"It's already after one o'clock. If we left now, we could get a good lead on it," Sherri suggested.

"It's dangerous to move before dark. We're more apt to be spotted. But you're right—it's the only way. So let's go."

They started south, driving the length of Perlacher Forest and crossing the Isar River at Grünwald. Everything went well for the next twenty-five kilometers south to Wolfratshausen. There they were forced to refuel the truck.

"I don't know how much suspicion we just

aroused," Jim said as they pulled out of the service station. "The army doesn't fuel its trucks at civilian gas stations."

"What do you think they'll do?"

Jim shrugged. "No telling. Let's just hope they were happy to get the business. After all, there aren't many vehicles in Germany that drink gasoline like a deuce-and-a-half."

Nikoli Malinkov watched the truck drive away from the service station at Wolfratshausen and began to realize another problem was developing. The service attendant was hurrying to make a telephone call while watching in which direction they went.

Interesting, Malinkov thought. If they get caught, I lose my only lead to the Jagdpanther. With that unpleasant possibility weighing on his mind, he followed the truck until it was out of town, then passed it and stayed about a mile ahead. He still did not understand what was going on or where the Jagdpanther was. The old man, Gnokte, had rambled on about some factory complex hidden in the Alps. Perhaps they were headed there—for exactly what reason, he could not say. He clung to them now, as his only remaining hope of success.

He checked the truck's position. It was only a small olive-drab dot in his rearview mirror. He accelerated the BMW, ranging further out ahead, looking for some sign of police or army. He hated the thought of helping them, both because they were the enemy and because of the attention it might draw to him. He considered his options and decided he had little available to him that was not likely to draw a great deal of attention. There was also the RPG-7 rocket launcher, which he had requested as an antitank weapon to destroy the Jagdpanther if it could not be stolen. There were several rockets for it, and one of them would probably break up a police pursuit long enough for the truck to get away, one time, for a little while. It would, of course, also bring down the wrath of two nations.

When three military-police cars streaked by him, headed north, Malinkov turned around and followed. Just over the next hill, he caught up with them as they were establishing a roadblock on the southbound side. Fifty yards away, he pulled off the road and into a rest area, and walked casually back and opened the trunk. Being careful not to lift it high enough to be seen, he screwed the two pieces of one of the rockets together and pulled off the safety tag. Then he placed it into the launching tube, flipped on the firing safety, and waited.

Any moment now, he thought, and checked his watch again. It was taking too long; the truck should be in sight by now. There were at least a couple of side roads turning west in the past ten miles or so. Could they have smelled trouble and turned off? Malinkov was almost ready to give up when the truck came over the hill. Two MP cars pulled across the southbound lanes, blocking the way. Malinkov raised the RPG-7 and aimed to hit directly between the two blocking cars. Several MPs were in the middle of the road, waving their arms as the truck approached. The truck, he noticed, was not slowing down. Instead it was coming faster and faster with columns of black smoke boiling from both the exhaust stacks. Across the Autobahn, the MPs were looking worried also. All at once, they began shooting and then running. The truck hit dead center between the two cars, threw them both into the air, and lost a fender in the process. Malinkov set down the launcher and watched as the truck swerved, almost overturned, and then straightened out as it disappeared over the next hill.

Only one of the MP cars had not been hit, and it was now burning rubber in pursuit of the speeding truck. Malinkov laid the RPG on the seat beside him and followed them. He was a few hundred yards behind when he saw the truck make a sliding turn onto a side road with the MPs right behind. Giving his car the gas, he closed the distance quickly as the side road led over another hill and wound down into a narrow valley.

When the truck suddenly left the road, Malinkov thought that the driver had lost control. It jumped a ditch and slid almost sideways down an embankment to a small stream. The pursuing police car tried to stop, spun around, and slid backward into the ditch. By the time six MPs had climbed out and fired off a few useless shots, the truck was driving up the shallow stream, with white water boiling around its wheels and black smoke billowing from the exhaust stacks. The last time they saw it, it was across the stream, driving off over a hill.

Malinkov laughed out loud as he threw the BMW into reverse and turned around. Fafner is no fool, he conceded. First, he rescues the girl, and now this. I may have made a big mistake by not killing him when I had the chance.

Sherri could not stop laughing as the deuce-and-a-half plowed its way upstream like a tugboat. "I didn't know they could do this!" she yelled over the engine's roar.

"Six axles, and all of them drive. The ignition is completely sealed. It'll run as long as it gets air," Jim yelled back as he drove. "Just hope there aren't

any holes out here big enough to swallow us up."
Around the next bend, he spotted a low place on the
bank and turned the truck to climb up and out of
the stream. Five hundred yards farther on, they
pushed down a fence, drove onto a paved road, and
again headed south.

Evening was approaching when they passed
through the town of Mirnau and had to wait for a
herd of cows to cross the road on their way to be
milked. Just ahead, the Bavarian Alps rose like a
jagged wall against the southern sky. The sky was
clear, yet around one peak mist hung like a gray
halo.

"That's the one, isn't it?" Sherri asked, pointing.

Jim took a few seconds to check the map and
then nodded.

"Beneath the misty mountain deep," Sherri said,
her voice distant and low. "I think we found it."

Chapter Nineteen

THE MOUNTAIN ROSE before them like the ruined
walls of some ancient castle. Forests of thick pine
covered the lower slopes up to a line of gray cliffs
on the north face. Above the cliffs, there appeared
to be two rocky pinnacles, shrouded now in a
strange mist. A few wind-sculptured trees clung to
the eastern pinnacle, but to the west was a jagged
point of sheer rock, rising at an odd angle and visible as only a shadow in the mist.

"It does kind of look like a sleeping dragon," Sherri said as they drove toward it.

The eastern face was also cliff-lined, but a curling spur ran out to the west. According to the map, it encircled and apparently concealed a long, high meadow. Only one road up the mountain was shown on the map, and there was but a trace of it remaining.

"Old map," Jim commented as he eased the truck across a narrow bridge. "Probably hasn't been surveyed since World War II. Which, for us, just might be helpful." He pointed at a place in the woods where the trees were smaller. "I think it ran up that way, up toward the meadow." A rail fence stood between them and the old road. To cover their tracks, they carefully disassembled a section of it, drove the truck through, and then reassembled it behind them.

The old roadway wound upward along the western spur. An occasional deer moved in the long shadows of afternoon as they inched along, picking their way carefully on the faint path.

"I think this was railroad track before it was a road," Jim commented.

"What makes you think that? Half the time, I can't even tell it was a road."

"The grades. They're all shallow enough for a train to pull. A road could have been made a lot steeper and shorter."

"Oh," Sherri commented, failing to attach any real significance to the observation.

"If there was a factory complex here, they would need a railroad connection. I think this is the old right-of-way."

"Then it should take us right to the entrance."

"Yeah, the entrance that Ehrler said he sealed."

They arrived at the meadow's edge suddenly as the truck pushed its way through a tangle of branches and into the open. Jim stopped when only the hood and windshield were exposed. The meadow was as the map had indicated, flat and totally concealed. On three sides were mountains, and to the north, two sloping spurs hid it from the valley below. A half-dozen deer looked at them for a moment and then bounded away, into the far trees.

"They could have done a lot of testing out here without being seen," Jim said. In the fading light of evening, they continued on along the old roadbed, which now followed the edge of the meadow. Then it turned abruptly and ended at the base of a ragged cliff. Huge boulders and twisted trees gave evidence that, sometime in the distant past, there had been a landslide here.

Twilight settled around them as they made camp. Using the truck and a couple of boulders as a windbreak, Jim built a small, concealed fire. They dined on C-rations and drank melted snow. The moon rose, nearly full, over the mountain peaks, and although the sky was crystal clear, the mist still clung to the rocky pinnacles above. In the cold moonlight, the mist glowed, and from within were tiny sparkles of light.

"I've been here before," Sherri said unexpectedly as she stood a little way from the fire and looked up at the mountain. Jim only looked at her and so she continued. "Not in this life, of course. I remember the mist around the mountain peaks. There used to be a stone gateway here which led into the caverns. There were runes there which could only be read by moonlight on certain nights of the year. I came to some ceremony here—I think."

"In which comic book was that?" Jim asked sarcastically.

"Knock it off, Fafner. I'm serious."

"Well, I'm sure they crowned you Queen of Ice."

Sherri turned on him. "Will you forget about sex? I told you, I made a mistake. Now just forget it!" She stalked back toward the small campfire. "Do I have to sleep this close to you?"

"You can sleep any place you want. Of course, if you don't want to freeze, you'll sleep by the fire."

"Then make it bigger. I want to sleep over here."

Jim shook his head. "Old American proverb say: 'Indian build small fire, keep close. White man build big fire, keep warm chopping wood.' "

"I hate proverbs."

"One more," Jim insisted. "Dumb broad build big fire, get our asses spotted five miles away."

Sherri groaned as she crawled into a sleeping bag close to the fire and rolled over with her back to him. "You still don't believe in anything you can't see and touch, not even after everything that's happened."

"Actually I try to believe only about half of what I see and touch."

"You saw your missile bounce off the Jagdpanther. And I was right about where the Jagdpanther was headed, wasn't I? How much more convincing do you need?"

Jim did not answer.

"It thinks I'm dead. I can feel it. So there must be some other reason it's coming here—like there's something else here that it's afraid of and has to destroy?"

"From what I can tell, it's doing a pretty good job of destroying just about anything it wants."

"I know. That's why we have to find out what it's afraid of and then use it as a weapon." She rolled over and looked at him. "That makes sense, doesn't it?"

"As much as any other part of this does," Jim conceded. He looked up at the rock cliff above. "Since you've been here before, you shouldn't have any trouble finding the way up the cliffs tomorrow."

"There are steps, carved in the stone, over there somewhere." Sherri's voice was again distant, and she seemed surprised at what she had just said. "At least, I think they are." She shrugged and disappeared into her sleeping bag, head and all.

Jim sat smoking his pipe as the moon moved slowly behind the tapestry of interlaced pine branches above him. Sherri, mysterious, crazy Sherri. Somehow, he felt that the stone steps would be exactly where she said they would be. And if they were, then he was going to have to take most of the rest of what she said much more seriously. Perhaps he had already been doing that for a couple of days now. Perhaps it was only his own inner self who had yet to believe the worst of what was happening.

Ehrler had spoken of the problems of mating magic with technology. That, in his mind, seemed to sum up his relationship with Sherri. He was a practical soldier. Yes, he reminded himself. You are a soldier. You may write your books and play with old tanks for museums, but under it all, you're a soldier, and that's all you'll ever be. Whatever kind of battle was coming, it was still just a battle. Somehow, he would be able to deal with that.

He placed more wood on the fire, crawled into his

sleeping bag, and laid his pistol beside him. Being in love with Sherri? Well, that was going to be a lot more difficult.

He dreamed that night of battles fought. At first it was the tank duel on Golan Heights, and then convoy ambushes in Vietnam. But others followed, a few he recognized only because he had studied them, analyzed them in military science classes; others were completely strange to him, yet he was part of each and every one.

He recognized the trenches and barbed wire at Somme, France, 1917, as the ancient ancestors of modern tanks lumbered across the shell-torn no-man's land of the western front, followed closely by foot soldiers and horse cavalry.

The scene changed. He saw Mexican cavalry riding with guns blazing into a ruined stable yard as a young man died beside him screaming, *"Viva Legion Etrangere!"* Yet, it was not until he saw the white kepi, bloodstained and lying in the dust, that he realized he was fighting with the French Foreign Legion at the battle of Camerone.

Other visions followed in rapid succession. Mounted on a short, stocky horse, he wielded a Scottish claymore and hacked his way into a tightly packed formation of red-coated troops who fought with long pikes.

There were longships with the dragon-shaped bows, beached in a cove. On the rocky shore beyond, he was among huge blond men who butchered each other with swords and axes while the tide ran red with their blood.

Stranger battles followed. One was fought in deep forests against inhuman creatures he had never seen or dreamed of in this life. The head of a dragon rose in front of him; fire belched from its mouth, scorching the ground around him as he dodged right and left, then lunged with his sword, cutting into the monster's neck and spilling green, sparkling blood onto the rocky ground.

Sherri was there—a fleeting, white-robed figure in the forest shadows. Her hair was longer and laced with beads and flowers which glowed and sparkled with all the colors of the rainbow. She was beside him, smiling, touching his face with her hands and kissing him.

"Hey, Fafner, wake up!" Sherri said, shaking him awake. "Come on. It's morning and I found the stairs, just where I said they'd be."

The aroma of fresh coffee aroused him enough to open one eye. It was daylight. The campfire was blazing and Sherri was holding a canteen cup under his nose. It occurred to him that she had looked a lot better in his dream. "I found it in those rations," she said. "And man, you look like you could use it. You sleep like a rock. I thought I'd never get you awake."

The steps were there, just as Sherri had said. They were so old and so well hidden it would have been impossible to find them by accident. Beneath the snow and moss that covered them completely were intricate carvings, unlike anything Jim had ever seen.

"Elf runes, I think," Sherri said excitely as she traced one of the delicate outlines with her finger. "I can't say for sure, because there are no authenticated elf runes anywhere in the world."

"Any idea what they mean?"

"No. I've seen a few runes which are supposed to be related to elfish, but they only vaguely resembled these."

Jim and Sherri started up. So intricately had the

steps been fashioned that, in places, it was almost impossible to tell exactly where the stone had been carved and where it was natural. At one point, Jim reached for a snow-covered rock as a handhold. His hand slipped, knocking off the snow and exposing a stone dragon's head, so realistic it startled him.

"Beautiful," Sherri commented, and continued climbing.

The mist hung along the top of the cliff like a smoky ceiling, and the steps ended on a ledge of flat gray stone. There were caves there, but a few yards inside, each one had been blasted shut and sealed long ago. Above the caves, the ground sloped upward again. The trees here were smaller and thinner than those on the lower slopes, and the ground was rockier.

"A stairway to nowhere," Jim said, looking around.

"All races," Sherri answered, "did not feel the need to destroy their environment like man. Some adapted to it, worshiped it, and enhanced it only when necessary."

For all of that morning, they climbed and crawled through crevices and over boulders, working their way to the east end of the mountain. Always there was the mist, thick and wet and gray. By late evening, they had circumnavigated the entire mountain and were back at the head of the stone stairs.

Sherri was noticeably disappointed. "I thought I could find the way in, just like I found the stairs. Something keeps telling me that the answer is in the mist, but I can't seem to make any sense out of it."

"The mist," Jim repeated thoughtfully. "Maybe that is the answer."

"How?"

"The mist. Why is it here?"

Sherri looked confused. "Because the legend says it is?"

"No," Jim said, "that's the effect, not the cause. Get your mind out of mythology and think about what causes mist."

"Science, how boring. Oh, let me see, mist is—condensation."

"Caused by . . . ?"

"Caused by heat?"

"In this case, I think, escaping heat."

The sun was already up and there was little cover, but still the Jagdpanther rolled steadily southward. Moving in daylight was dangerous. It had learned that years ago, but the sense of urgency was overpowering. It must get to the south, back to the mountain where it was forged, for there, somewhere within the misty peaks, was an enemy that must be dealt with—and dealt with quickly.

Ten miles to the north of the Jagdpanther, an AH-64 Apache attack helicopter flew another leg of its search pattern. In addition to the 12.7mm Gatling cannon in its nose, sixteen laser-guided Hellfire missiles hung from its weapons pods. Each had a range of seven kilometers, and their tandem, shaped-charge warheads were capable of penetrating the heaviest frontal armor of any known tank.

The Apache's pilot spotted the single pair of wide tank tracks, southbound along the edge of a treeline and half-hidden in the shadows. He swung his aircraft in a tight, banking turn to follow, then reduced his speed and dived low, barely keeping his wheels above the treetops. He was certain he was well south of any army training areas, so there was no chance these were the tracks of anything belonging to the military. He supposed there was the vague possibility he was following the tracks of some farmer's bulldozer, but the farther he flew, the more he doubted it. The tracks always avoided the open; they skirted fields and kept to the woodlines, always seeking the morning shadows. Yes, whoever was driving knew his business.

Far ahead, the Jagdpanther felt the helicopter's presence long before it came into sight. This was some new kind of enemy, something it had never faced, and something it had never been taught how to fight. The Apache came in over the trees sooner than the Jagdpanther had expected and swooped low. With its gun barrel elevated at its maximum altitude, the Jagdpanther turned in a tightening circle, tracking the swift machine above it. Impossible, the Jagdpanther decided. The gun could not be elevated high enough, and this enemy moved too quickly and too radically for any chance of a hit.

The Jagdpanther retreated then and searched its accumulated knowledge. Yes, there was a way. Turning away from its enemy, the Jagdpanther headed for the banks of a stream just beyond the nearest trees. The helicopter swooped in again, clinging to the Jagdpanther's tail. A salvo of missiles flashed from the helicopter's stubby wings. Two passed above the Jagdpanther and two more slammed into the rear deck just as it reached the stream bank. The Jagdpanther spun on its treads, sliding sideways down the bank and locking one tread as it went. Its rear deck splashed into the water and its gun pointed suddenly skyward.

As the smoke cleared, the Apache moved in slowly, convinced the missiles had succeeded in turning the Jagdpanther into scrap metal. The pilot brought his craft in ever closer, looking over the strange old armored vehicle he believed he had just destroyed. He marveled at the bright blue light that surrounded it and wondered why no damage was visible. The last thing he noticed was the Jagdpanther's gun barrel moving slightly, tracking him, as the helicopter descended.

There was a brilliant flash of light as the Jagdpanther's 88 fired with only a few meters separating it from the helicopter. The resulting explosion echoed across the hills. Flaming aviation fuel covered the Jagdpanther with burning liquid which flowed in a fiery waterfall down into the stream to rise again as gasping clouds of steam. Through this inferno, the Jagdpanther backed into the stream and moved away, against the current, leaving no trace or trail.

"Escaping heat?" Sherri repeated, looking up at the gray mist hanging along the edge of the cliff. "Escaping heat from what?"

"Escaping from inside the mountain," Jim helped. "Caves usually remain a pretty constant temperature. Outside, it changes every day."

"Yeah, all right. I get it, but where is it escaping?"

Jim was already starting back up the slope. "A factory, built underground where a lot of men were going to work, would need a way to get air to them. Maybe ventilators with air shafts bored through the mountain and camouflaged on the surface."

"Wrong, Fafner," Sherri argued. "The mist was here a long time before the Nazis. The *Eddas* described it centuries ago."

"Very true. Only then, there were caves which let the warm air escape. The Nazis sealed them up to keep people out, but they had to replace them with air shafts."

Sherri thought about that for a moment. "And so the mists stayed," she said finally.

Night overtook them before there was any chance for further exploration. It was near noon of the following day before they found one of the air shafts. It was hidden neatly inside a natural rock chimney. The mist was thickest here, and they could feel the warm air rising to meet them as they climbed down to it. Over the shaft were heavy steel bars, and beneath the bars was a ladder, made of iron rungs, driven into the rock. It led down into the mist below, far past the reach of Jim's flashlight beam. Using a hacksaw from one of the tool kits, they took most of the rest of the day to cut through one of the bars and bend it far enough out of the way to slip through.

"We probably won't be coming out of there for a while," Jim said. "So we better take everything with us that we'll need." They returned to the truck once again and loaded some of the C-rations and a pair of sleeping bags into two of the field packs. Jim removed the batteries from the portable radio and took them to use in the flashlight. Sherri reluctantly exchanged her mink for an army field jacket that had belonged to the truck driver. Then they melted enough snow to fill four of the canteens and decided they were ready.

"Should we go now when it's dark?" Sherri asked, looking up at the moon through the mist.

"Why not? It's going to be dark down there, anyway," he answered. They shouldered their packs and picked their way carefully up the winding stone steps to the bluffs above. The moon was full and pale. Against the mist, it cast eerie light

and ghostly shadows on the rocky crag which concealed the air shaft. They descended silently—first
to the iron bars and then carefully down the ladder
below.

Jim led the way, feeling with his foot in the darkness for each rung and wondering what he would
do if one of them was not there. The descent seemed
to go on for hours. A constant flow of warm air rose
past them in the darkness. At one point, Jim
stepped onto solid ground and found he was standing on a rock ledge. A few feet away, the ladder
continued down into the darkness.

"How far can this go?" Sherri asked as they
peered over the ledge.

"With all this warm air, maybe all the way to
hell."

They continued down, descending step by step
until their arms and legs were numb and aching,
yet still there appeared to be no end. They were no
longer inside a round shaft. Instead, they believed
they were descending some cavern wall, although
the flashlight would not penetrate far enough to
show them anything except the flat stone to which
the ladder was attached.

At last, what Jim feared most happened. He
reached out with his foot for another rung and it
was not there. He stretched as far as he could and
still touched nothing. With one hand, he held on to
the ladder and was reaching for his flashlight when
he looked down.

"Why am I seeing the ground?" he asked, aston-
ished that he could see rocks and scattered debris
below him.

"Because it's getting lighter," Sherri's voice
echoed strangely in the cavern. "It has been, ever
since that ledge."

"That's impossible."

"Elfin magic."

"Bull," Jim countered, but she was right—there was light here, a green glow that came from where, they could not tell. He took another look at the ground below him and wondered how far away it really was. In the strange, unreal glow, it was impossible to judge distance. Still clinging to the ladder with one hand, Jim managed to reach his free hand into his pack and pull out one of the ration packages. He dropped it and heard it hit almost at once.

"Boy, am I glad to hear that." He sighed with relief and dropped to the ground. The distance was just a little greater than he had estimated and he hit hard, stumbling and falling on his face. "It's a pretty good drop," he called to Sherri. "Hang from the last rung and I'll help you." Sherri's body was a greenish shadow as he gripped her legs. She felt warm against him. Her muscles tensed to his touch as he lowered her to the cavern floor.

"Wow," Sherri commented, looking around. "This is really weird."

Jim touched the stone wall with his finger. "Something like fox fire, maybe? Only it's impregnated the walls and everything."

"Could be," Sherri agreed, "in some parts of the world, fox fire is called elf lights or elf fire. The legend could have started with something like this."

All around them, the cavern was filled with a hazy, green half-light. It was not enough to see clearly, but was more like the last traces of twilight on a summer evening. Rock formations appeared as vague dark shapes when only a few feet away. A thin layer of green fog clung to the cavern floor and drifted aimlessly on currents of air as they walked.

Sherri reached out and took Jim's hand. "This is the scariest place I have ever dreamed of," she whispered. "But it's beautiful too. I wonder if I'll ever be able to draw it."

Ahead in the green gloom was a forest of stalagmites, huge and towering to unknown heights in the green void above. Jim and Sherri followed a winding pathway that seemed to have been smoothed and fashioned by some unknown hand. It led at last to an arched doorway of square-cut stones, neatly notched and fitted together. Jim turned on his flashlight and played its beam over the archway. There were runes there also, sparkling with tiny silver stars as the light touched them.

"They're beautiful," Sherri breathed. Still holding Jim's hand, she led the way beneath the arch. A shadow formed in front of them, vague at first. Then, with a sudden terror, they realized that a figure was standing directly in their path.

Sherri screamed and backed into Jim as he tore his hand from her grip and clawed for the automatic stuck in his belt. The figure remained vague and unmoving in the ghostly green light as Jim leveled the pistol, and for a few long moments, no one moved or even breathed. With his other hand, he raised his flashlight and shone it in the face of the shadowy being.

Sherri screamed again and fell against him as the figure's face was exposed in the flashlight's beam. Jim felt his hands shake and the hair on the back of his neck bristle. Before them was Sherri's own face staring back at them out of the green fog.

It was Sherri—there could be no doubt—and yet at the same time, it was not. The eyes were hers,

and the face as well. The hair was a bit longer and
laced with odd flowers and jewels, but the ears
were elflike, long and gracefully pointed. She wore
a short tunic of chain mail with a wide jeweled
belt. Boots, made from the fur of some animal,
covered her lower legs. About her neck was a silver
necklace fashioned of tiny stars. A jeweled crown
was on her head, and her hands rested on a broadsword.

"Welcome home, Princess of Elfland," Jim said.

Chapter Twenty

"A STATUE," Jim said, shocked as he stared at the
likeness of Sherri standing in the stone archway
before them. "It does seem like they know you down
here."

"Unbelievable," Sherri breathed as she reached
out and touched the stone face so much like her
own. "It's me!"

"It's the character you draw."

"My characters come out of myself. I've dreamed
about this one since I was five years old. It's just a
little frightening to meet her face to face, in the
dark."

The statue stood in a tiny grottolike alcove carved
from the cavern wall. Intricate designs of trees and
flowers and stars formed the background while
strange, silver runes bordered the arch. Sooty

smudges and bits of melted wax indicated that once, there had also been candles.

"Is she a princess, a queen, what?" Jim asked.

"She does wear a crown, but from the way she is dressed, I'd guess, none of the above," Sherri said as she traced one of the runes with her finger. "She looks more like a shield maiden—it means warrior."

"Then she must have done something pretty important to have been honored with a statue like this."

Sherri looked strangely at him, as if searching her own mind for whatever it might have been. "Maybe so," she said, and turned again to the runes.

"Can you read those?"

"I don't know if anyone can. Until this very instant, there was no such thing as authenticated elfish runes." Sherri took the flashlight and held it close. "They are similar to some Druid writings I translated once, but these are much more intricate . . . closer in some ways to Sanskrit." She paused and looked closer. "You know, the way these look, it's almost like Druid is an elfish dialect, or lower form, kind of like bad English, I guess. You know? I just might be able to figure these out."

She examined each rune carefully under the flashlight for several minutes and then said, "Okay, I think I've got the gist of it, anyway. It starts like this: *'From out of the mists of time, she rode, on a beast which breathed fire.'* Then, it says something about this all taking place *'Before the dawn of the second age.'* There is no way I can even guess what time period they are actually talking about. But anyway, *'there dwelled beneath this mountain, a darkness'*—no, make that *evil*—'*an evil lord,*' I think. Anyway, '*he corrupted the sacred treasure of Mirtheil and used it for evil. He killed many great warriors who challenged him and scattered their bones on the mountainside for all to see*'; disgusting manners. So, to make a long story short, this is the warrior who finally banished the evil lord. Apparently, she didn't kill him, but only wounded him badly and he went away, somewhere deeper into the mountain." Sherri knelt and pointed at some runes near the floor. "And here, this last part says that for her bravery she was made a princess, but she chose not to rule. Instead, she took a mate and went away, but promised to return again when she is most needed by her race." Sherri backed away from the statue. "Somehow, I really don't like the sound of that last part."

Silently, they left the statue in the mists and continued on. The pathway split and the left-hand path led down at a steep angle. For no particular reason, they chose it. It led them on a twisting course through a labyrinth of natural tunnels where crystals of quartz sparkled everywhere on the walls and overhead. The green half-light brightened as they descended, or perhaps it was that the mist was thinning, or that their night vision was improving. But whatever the reason, they found they could see better and farther as they worked their way deeper into the bowels of the mountain.

The tunnel widened, and suddenly it ended at a round door. It appeared to be made of stone and covered with more carvings, inlaid with silver, which shone brightly in the flashlight beam. There was no visible latch or hinges. "Looks like we took the wrong path," Jim said as he put his weight against the door. "This thing must weigh tons."

As Jim backed away, Sherri touched it with her fingertips, tracing some of the carvings. The door swung open on hidden hinges. "Wow," Sherri said again.

Beyond the door was a narrow ledge, which looked down over a huge, domed cavern. The green light here was pale and the air was clear of mist. Below them on the cavern floor was machinery: stamp mills and drill presses, turret lathes and chain hoists.

"So this was Ehrler's factory. Impressive," Jim said.

"Yeah, now how do we get down to it?" Sherri wondered as she leaned out over the rocky wall. "It must be a hundred feet down there." She pointed to the left. "Look, there used to be stairs, cut into the wall, which led up here; but they're gone now. It looks like they were blasted away."

Jim agreed. "I guess the Nazis didn't want just anybody wandering here."

"Yeah, right. Some of this might be a little hard to explain to your average, middle-class Nazi factory worker."

Just below the ledge they were standing on, and somewhat to their right, one end of a gigantic I-beam was fixed to the cavern wall. It stretched completely across the cavern and two large chain hoists were fixed to it. Across the cavern from where they stood was a catwalk and a ladder leading down from the other end of the I-beam. "Maybe that's our way down?" Jim suggested.

"But we'd have to climb down the first part of this cliff and then walk on top of the beam, all the way over there. Hey, not this girl, no way. I can't do that."

Jim looked at her and smiled in the gloom.

"Sharron Dumbroskie from Pittsburgh might not make it. But a great elfin warrior shouldn't have any trouble."

Sherri took a deep breath. "Somehow, I was afraid you were going to say something like that."

It appeared that the only handhold between the ledge and the end of the I-beam was a crack in the rock, probably caused by blasting to mount the I-beam. "Take your gloves off," Jim ordered. "You'll get a better grip without them." He eased his way off the ledge, found a tiny place that would support his foot, and reached for the crack. With his fingers, he brushed a few grains of sand and broken rock out of the crack and took a grip. Slowly, inch by inch, he worked his way to the end of the beam.

"There," he called to Sherri, "nothing to it. There's footholds all the way, but throw me your pack first. It'll make it easier to climb."

"You just want my food if I fall." Sherri grumbled, but tossed him the pack anyway and climbed off the ledge. For a second, her foot found one of the toeholds, but just as she got both hands into the crack, she lost her footing, leaving her hanging by her fingers. "Damn it, Fafner!" she yelled angrily, "I can't reach the same holds you used; my legs are too short!"

"Then do it all with your hands. Come on, it's not far." He reached out as far as he could across the abyss. "Just another few feet, you can make it."

Sherri groaned and inched her way closer, puffing and panting every inch of the way. His hand gripped her coat sleeve and, with one final effort, she was on the beam beside him.

"Well, we got the easy part done," he said dryly as they looked out across the cavern.

"That beam looked a lot wider from up there," Sherri said. "How far up are we?"

"Far enough to kill us if we fall. Now, don't look down." Jim took her hand as he led the way out, onto the beam and above the abandoned machinery far below. Inch by inch, they worked their way across. The beam was damp and slippery, and each footstep had to be carefully placed. Near the center of the cavern hung one of the chain hoists, and Jim nearly slipped on the electrical wires that ran from the far side and once supplied power to it.

"Watch out for the wires," he warned.

"I would," Sherri said, "but if I look for them, I'll have to look down, and if I look down, I'm going to die, so I'll just have to take my chances, won't I?" Keeping her eyes centered on Jim's back, she felt the wires with the toe of her boot, stepped over them, and kept going.

The I-beam ended at a catwalk which led to a set of ladders for the five-story descent to the factory floor. There, they walked between lines of abandoned machinery squatting like lurking beasts in the gloom. Down the center of the cavern, the way was relatively clear. It looked to Jim like they had been planning an assembly line here, which, had things been only a little different, would have mass-produced monsters like the Jagdpanther that still prowled somewhere outside the mountain.

"Look out!" Sherri warned suddenly, and grabbed at Jim's arm. In front of him was a square hole in the floor, perhaps twenty feet across. He knelt beside it and shone his flashlight down into the darkness below.

"I can't see how deep it is, but there doesn't seem to be any ladder going down." Sherri picked up a large bolt from the floor and dropped it into the pit.

Three long seconds passed in eerie silence, followed by a hollow splash as the bolt hit water, several stories down.

"There sure are a lot of ways to die down here. This is worse than playing Dungeons and Dragons," Sherri said as they eased their way around the pit. "And if you get killed down here, I don't think you get to start over."

With growing confidence, Sherri took the lead. Her night vision, Jim noted, was excellent and seemed to be getting better the longer she stayed down here. Just past the pit, Jim recognized the lower hull mold for a Panther tank. "At Koblenz, I found the requisition form to transfer this here."

They continued on in silence, marveling at the size and complexity of the remains of Project Mirtheil. "I wonder what happened to all of the people who worked here?" Sherri asked after a while.

"Ehrler never said, but as secret as this project was, I have a feeling that either they were never told what they were building, or they're all somewhere like the bottom of that pit."

Near the end of the unfinished assembly line, they came upon two sets of railroad tracks. Several flatcars rested on one of them. Just beyond were towering steel doors. "Maybe we found an easier way out?" Sherri suggested.

"I don't think so," Jim said, looking at them closely. They were bowed slightly inward, as if bent by some giant explosion on the other side. He peeked into the crack between the doors. "A lot of rocks, but you can see a little light here and there. This must be where Ehrler blasted to seal up the factory. I'll bet that the place we camped is just on the other side of a few tons of dirt and rock."

Without a second thought, Sherri headed off in

another direction. "I'm going this way; come on," she said.

"What exactly are we looking for down here?" Jim asked, hurrying to keep up with her.

"I don't know yet. I feel like I'm learning things I forgot hundreds of lives ago."

Yesterday, that was the sort of statement Jim would have laughed at. Now, he said nothing and followed. They passed through another, smaller door and down a long corridor lined with offices and storerooms. One large room was a mess hall where plates with mummified food still sat on long tables.

Stairs led to a lower level. There were sleeping quarters here, large rooms with rows of bunks, still with mattresses and blankets. At the end of the hall was another door. *Entrance forbidden* was printed in German on it but it was not locked and opened easily to Sherri's touch. An iron stairway spiraled down to another part of the natural cavern.

Their footsteps were muffled echoes as they descended the stairs to another, lower level. Before them was a large chamber with wide steps cut into the rock floor which led down to a pair of ancient raised fire pits. The ceiling was a pincushion of stalactites and the walls sparkled with quartz crystals. Above them, hung by rusted iron chains, were ancient, hand-operated bellows. The ceiling was high and blackened with centuries of smoke. Also fashioned of stone were workbenches, and on them, a few hand tools of strange design still lay.

"My God," Sherri gasped, "these are the elfin forges. This proves the legends! This is where Loki forged Thor's hammer. The sword of Siegfried was made here, and maybe even King Arthur's Excalibur.

"The very legends of this place inspired Wagner's music, just like they inspired Tolkien to write *Lord of the Rings*. This is the place he called Moria, and we're standing right here in the middle of it. Wow!" She touched the wooden handle of one of the hammers. It crumbled beneath her fingers, and she pulled away, shocked that she had damaged something so sacred.

"Tolkien had to have researched from the *Eddas* too," Sherri continued, her excitement growing as she spoke. "He wrote about elfin steel, but he called it *mithril*. I don't know for sure, but I suspect he found the word in some old saga and it's actually elfin slang or, maybe, wood-elf dialect for *Mirtheil*."

Jim watched her as she explored the forges like a child at Christmas searching through presents under the tree. She was changing, Jim thought, becoming bolder, yet in some ways more childlike. It was as if she was returning at last to the world where she truly belonged: the warrior princess, coming home to the domain she ruled in another life.

Well, perhaps in her imagination she is, he thought. Then he suddenly reminded himself that there was a tremendous amount of good, solid, scientific evidence right here in front of him that supported almost everything she believed.

Sherri spotted a large passageway leading off from the forge. "I want to follow this one," she announced, and started off down it. It wound its way tightly this way and that for a while, and then ended at another, solid stone door. "I think this leads outside," she said, and touched it with her fingers. Just as before, the walls creaked slightly and the door moved open. Snow swirled in, carried on a stiff, whistling wind. The light hurt their eyes, and they were surprised that the night had passed so quickly. Outside, it was already morning, and it was snowing again. As they looked out, they could see the truck only about fifty yards away. "This sure beats climbing back out that air shaft," she said, and then turned to Jim. "But of course, we can't leave yet; we haven't done what we came to do."

Jim only nodded his head in agreement and Sherri closed the door. "Elves don't really like being underground. They're forest spirits," Sherri said as they walked back up the winding passages to the factory area. "They built the forges here only because they had to keep them secret."

"Secret from whom?"

"Men, mostly. You see what happens when men try to use *Mirtheil*." They walked in silence for a while then, with Sherri leading the way. They passed through the abandoned machinery again, walking generally toward the east end of the mountain. There were more workshop areas here, and storerooms built like cliff dwellings along the sides of the cavern wall.

On the east wall of the cavern, a large square-cut shaft had been bored into the rock and led downward at a steep angle. Narrow-gauge railroad tracks had been laid in the shaft and a couple of small ore cars were overturned nearby. Within the first twenty yards the shaft split.

"These must have been the mine shafts that the Nazis built," Jim said as the green mist became thicker the further they walked.

"They seem like they go on forever," Sherri commented. "I don't think I want to go any deeper—not now, anyway."

They turned and made their way back to the

factory area. For a while, they rooted through a few old storerooms and another area that contained machinery for smelting and refining metal.

They were just coming out of one of the storerooms when Jim stopped suddenly as he saw a large, squatty shadow in the gloom. "A tank," he said. "The Sherman they used to test the *Mirtheil* plates. Ehrler did say that he drove it inside and left it."

It was one of the early M-4A3s, Jim observed as he approached and ran his hand over the tank's hull. It would have the old 75mm gun. There would also be direct-vision ports, which made it hard for the driver to see where he was going, and open ammo storage racks, which were famous for catching fire. The additional armor plates of *Mirtheil* were there, just as Ehrler had described: thin, smooth, and unscarred. It was hard to believe that a platoon of Tiger tanks had ever bounced 88s off it at point-blank range. The work had all been neatly done, and one had to look closely to see the modifications. The shields over the drive sprockets and road wheels were more obvious, but the thin sheath that had been overlaid on the turret was nearly invisible.

On a sudden impulse, Jim climbed up onto the old Sherman. "Michael and I restored a Sherman like this for the museum, years ago," he said, with fond memories showing on his face. "In Israel, there are still a few of these running."

Sherri was standing on the ground looking up at him with a strange expression on her face. She said nothing as Jim stepped onto the turret and opened the commander's hatch, before he remembered that these things were sometimes booby-trapped. His flashlight played on the turret's interior. It was a time capsule from 1944. A few 75mm rounds were still in the ammo racks. Both of the .30 caliber Browning machine guns were in place and loaded with belts of cartridges. The gun breech and firing lock appeared to be all there, as well as the sights and rangefinder. Even the tankers' helmets were still lying on the gunner's seat.

"It all makes sense now," Sherri said. When he looked up, she was standing beside him on the tank.

"What all makes sense?" he asked.

"This is our 'beast which breathed fire.' It's the weapon we need to destroy the Jagdpanther."

Jim's laughter echoed off the cavern walls. "This is scrap metal; it's not going to fight anything."

"But you can fix it," Sherri insisted. "That's what you do, isn't it?"

Jim shook his head and tried to explain. "It's not that easy. This sucker has been sitting here for over forty years. At the very least, the fuel has gone bad and the batteries are useless. There's maybe one chance in ten that the engine would even turn over without a major overhaul."

"But it has to work; otherwise, why would it be here?" Sherri countered. "It was left for us to use."

"You're crazy."

"No, I'm not. This tank shouldn't be here. Ehrler said *Mirtheil* didn't work until it accepted a master, remember? This tank never had a master, and yet they were able to shoot at it with all those other tanks and not hurt it. Something inside this mountain knew we would need it."

"If this was left for us, whoever left it made a real bad choice."

"Why? It's a tank, isn't it? And a tank is what we have to destroy."

Jim thought, This is impossible.

To Sherri, he said, "If this Sherman was rolling straight off the assembly line, a Jagdpanther, even a regular, common, old-type Jagdpanther operated by a crew of nuns, would eat it for breakfast in a one-on-one fight."

Sherri disagreed with a shake of her head. "I don't think so. I think everything works different down here. It's more like a giant game of Dungeons and Dragons. You get extra points for being on the side of good."

"Oh, for Christ's sake . . ." Jim started to object, but she leaned close and touched her finger to his lips. Her eyes were suddenly wide and smiling.

"And maybe for being in love," she added as her hand brushed his unshaven cheek and her arms moved to encircle his neck.

"What . . . ?" Jim started to say, but she suddenly stood on tiptoes and kissed him hard and long.

"I should have recognized you sooner," she whispered as the kiss ended. "When I loved you in another life, you were a knight. You wore armor and rode a horse into battle. It makes perfect sense that now you would fight from a tank; for you have always been a warrior, and I have always loved you—then, now, and forever."

Jim smiled down at her. "You are probably crazy, but I don't have any better explanation, and I do know that I love you."

She smiled and seemed to glow in his arms; then she pulled away and climbed off the tank. "Come with me, my love," she said, and led him silently back to the cavern room where they had found the ancient forge. As Jim watched, she laid out one of the sleeping bags on the floor and then took off her field jacket and rolled it into a pillow. With trembling hands, she pulled off her sweater and fumbled to release her bra. She let the garment drop and held out her arms to him. "Love me," she said, "here, in this sacred place."

Reason and logic took flight on magic wings. They seemed to have no real place here, in this world within the mountain. He reached for her, crushed her to him, and kissed her for a long moment. She melted in his arms as he swept her up and lowered her onto the pallet she had made for them.

"So long," she gasped with ragged breath. "It's been so long, and I've missed you so." Time stopped, the stone walls faded into the mist, and there were only the lovers, finding each other once again after centuries, perhaps millenniums, apart.

Sometime later, Sherri lingered in the warmth of sweet memories, somewhere between sleep and waking. She reached out for her lover and found him gone. Sitting up suddenly, she looked around the strange, stone chamber where curls of phosphorescent mist drifted above the floor, lighted still in the unnatural twilight green.

"Jim?" she called softly. "Jim, where are you?"

Suddenly, she was worried. She collected her scattered bits of clothing and dressed quickly. The stairs and the hallway beyond were deserted. Her footsteps seemed to echo louder, now that she was alone. In the gloom of the main cavern, where the rows of abandoned machines lurked in the half-light, she heard faint hammering sounds, coming from the far end of the cavern. Carefully, she picked her way in that direction. The hammering was louder as she approached the old Sherman tank. "Jim?" she called out nervously, "are you in there?"

"Bring me that crowbar lying on the track," his familiar voice echoed from inside the tank. She wilted with relief and picked up the crowbar. She climbed onto the tank and looked down through the open hatch on top of the turret. Jim was on his knees on the turret floor.

"What are you doing?" she asked, handing him the crowbar.

"Trying to get to the battery compartment," he answered, sounding busy. He immediately began using the crowbar to pry up a metal plate. It came loose with a loud rattle, and he set it aside. "Turn that knob," he ordered without looking up.

"What knob?"

"That one," he answered, finally looking up and pointing. "You've got to climb down in here to reach it."

Sherri climbed inside and turned the knob. She was slightly surprised when the turret rotated a few degrees. "Neat! This must be how you aim the gun."

"Not exactly, but you're on the right track. Now, hold it right there." With his flashlight in one hand, he stared down under the turret floor and mumbled something.

"What are you looking at?" Sherri asked impatiently.

"Batteries. Some of the connectors are gone, but most of the wiring is still here."

"Does that mean you can fix it?"

"No, it just means that the wiring is still here."

"Oh," Sherri nodded. "But, it means you're going to try?"

Jim took a deep breath. "It means I'm trying to figure out if it's possible, that's all. It has a 24-volt electrical system and uses four 6-volt batteries."

"And you think they might still be good?"

"Definitely not. They're totaled. However, four 6-volt batteries could possibly be replaced with two 12-volt batteries and get the same result—for a little while, anyway."

"So, do we have two of those?" Sherri asked, not at all sure what he was talking about.

"Yes, we do—outside on the truck. That's a 24-volt system, too." Jim wiped his hands on a rag and stood up. He kissed her lightly on the lips and climbed out of the turret. On the rear deck of the Sherman, he lifted the heavy, armored doors over the engine bay and looked down at the big Ford V-8 inside. He lowered himself carefully down between the engine block and one of the fuel tanks, felt around for the fuel draincock, and managed to unscrew it. A smelly mixture of water and old gasoline began to dribble out beneath the tank. Before leaving the engine bay, he gave the rest of the engine a quick going-over and failed to find anything major missing. He pulled the oil dipstick and examined a bit of the oil between his thumb and forefinger. As Sherri looked over his shoulder, he gave a noncommittal grunt and replaced the dipstick.

"It looks icky. Is that good?" Sherri asked.

"Could be worse," he mumbled. "Can you do your thing on that doorway again, so we can get out to the truck? Then we are going to have to carry a lot of stuff in here."

"Yeah, sure." Sherri nodded. "So this means you can fix it."

"No. It means I'm going to try."

Outside, at the site of their old camp, they spent the next hour collecting tools, removing batteries from the truck, and draining gasoline into two of the five-gallon cans mounted on the running boards. Jim stopped long enough to take another long look at where he thought the steel doors should be. Then, with two field packs heavily loaded and their arms full, they made several long trips back through the tunnels, past the forge, and into the factory complex.

With considerable difficulty, they lifted out the old batteries from their compartment beneath the turret floor and replaced them with the two new ones from the truck. The battery cables took even longer, and required so much modification that they once again returned to the truck and removed additional wiring before Jim was finally satisfied.

"Aren't you going to check it?" Sherri asked as he climbed out of the turret.

"Later. Next thing is to get some good gasoline in it." Beneath the tank, the old gasoline seemed to have quit draining, so he closed the cock and opened the fuel filler on the rear deck. Into it he emptied both of the five-gallon cans and then returned with Sherri to the truck to refill them.

"There's about twenty gallons in the truck. That won't be enough to run the Sherman for very long."

Sherri looked back nervously over her shoulder as they started back into the tunnels. "How soon will it be ready? The Jagdpanther is close. I feel it."

"It's not a matter of *when;* it's *if.*"

"You can do it. I know you can."

"Good; that makes one of us."

Back at the tank, Jim removed the Sherman's carburetor and disassembled it completely, soaking each part in gasoline and wiping it with a rag. Another hour had passed before he had it reassembled and back on the engine. The distributor came next.

"Points and plugs," he said. "Just like cars used to have before electronic ignitions."

"Oh," Sherri sighed from over his shoulder. "Is that good?"

"In our case, maybe. They are simpler to work on." He touched a screwdriver to the points and was rewarded by a tiny blue spark.

"Neat," Sherri said.

"Neat?" Jim repeated, shrugged, and replaced the distributor cap. He pointed down at something low in the engine bay. "Pump that," he ordered.

"What is it?"

"Fuel pump. If it works and pumps clean fuel up here, then I'm going to finish hooking up the fuel line." From below, there was a faint sucking noise and then fresh fuel squirted out the end of the line Jim was holding. "Okay, that's good."

With Sherri still tagging along behind him, he climbed back into the turret and then crawled forward into the driver's seat. "Cross your fingers," he said, took a deep breath, and threw the master switch. A couple of small red night-vision lights came on in the turret behind him. "So far, so good."

The labels had all worn off the instrument panel, but he thought he remembered the location of almost everything. He found the carburetor primer, pulled it out, and pushed it in twice. The ignition switch was next. He turned it to the On position and watched the instruments light up in front of him. "Here goes nothing," he whispered, and hit the starter.

The engine turned, slowly at first, once, twice, and then picked up a little speed. "Come on, come on, you can do it!" he pleaded with the tank as the old V-8 continued to grind slowly over. He pumped the throttle several times and there was the sound of a small, muffled explosion somewhere in the engine bay.

Sherri let out a startled, short scream just as a second explosion echoed in the cavern, and suddenly the old engine was running. Smoke curled around the driver's hatch as Jim listened to the engine. It was loud. Apparently the mufflers had not been one of the areas protected with *Mirtheil* plates. There was at least one valve stuck, but it might work free. He tapped the voltameter and saw that the batteries were charging.

Sherri's arms were around his neck, and she was yelling in his ear. "I knew it would run. There's some of the magic in it, too. I can feel it. I think it accepts us."

Jim let the engine run at a fast idle for another ten minutes before he tried the gears. He pushed the clutch in and felt for compound-low gear. The gear ground on the first try, but on the next, the transmission seemed to engage. Carefully, he brought up the RPMs and eased out on the clutch. For one uncertain moment, there was a high-pitched whine as the clutch plates fought to stir thirty tons of steel into forward movement. The tank lurched. Treads rattled and road wheels squeaked loudly above the unsteady roar of the engine. With the Sherman moving forward at barely a crawl, Jim tried first a right and then a left turn. To his surprise, both worked and the old tank jerked around in both directions. At last, he eased it to a stop and shut down the engine.

He emerged from the driver's compartment with a wide, boyish grin on his dirty face. Sherri jumped into his arms, kissing him again and again. "You did it! I knew you could do it. I love you," she laughed between kisses.

"Now comes the really hard part." He laughed
back at her. "I've got to teach you to drive it."

Chapter Twenty-one

𝕾

"ME? WHY DO I have to drive it?" Sherri asked as
she looked doubtfully up at the Sherman tank.

"Because one of us has to drive while the other
one loads, aims, and fires the gun. I don't think
you're big enough to carry those 75mm rounds, so
that makes you the driver." He handed her one of
the tankers' helmets. "Here, plug this cord in. It's
an intercom so we can talk over the engine noise."

They found that it took two folded sleeping bags
to raise Sherri high enough to see out the vision
port, and another bag behind her to push her far
enough forward to reach the controls.

"The steering is easy," he insisted, pointing over
her shoulder. "The lever on the right turns the tank
to the right; the one on the left turns it left."

"Why don't they use a steering wheel? It would
be a lot simpler."

"No, this is simpler and less apt to break down.
Each lever is like a clutch. It locks up one tread
while the other one keeps going and turns the tank.
Simple, right?"

When they finally restarted the engine and Sherri
had a chance to practice driving, she had less trouble than Jim had expected. Having driven sports
cars, she understood the gearshifts. Her biggest

problem was that she needed both hands and all her strength to pull either of the steering levers. Pushing the brake pedal was just as hard.

"I can do it," she insisted as she backed the tank away from the twisted remains of a huge drill press she had just run into. Jim told her to shut off the engine, and added that she had gotten all the practice they could risk with the small amount of fuel aboard.

With the engine shut down and Sherri exhausted, Jim turned his attention to the Sherman's 75mm gun. He worked the breech a few times, opening and closing it stiffly. If he could find some grease, he might be able to loosen it up some. He removed the firing lock from the rear of the breech, disassembled it, and cleaned all the parts before putting it back together.

One of the lenses on the gunner's sight was cracked but still usable. He tried the switch that turned the turret electrically, found it didn't work, and spent over an hour repairing it.

"Do we really need that?" Sherri asked as he worked.

"Without it, I'd have to turn the turret with that little knob on the hand crank. It's too slow."

Once the switch was working again, he looked at the six 75mm rounds lying in the storage rack in the rear of the turret. "We better hope these babies work, because they're all we've got." He removed one from the rack and loaded it into the gun. The breech closed behind it with a cold, metallic ring. Jim wiped his hands on his pants and decided the tank was about as ready as they could make it.

"Now, just one more little project: We've got to break out of here."

*   *   *

It was almost an hour after sunrise when Nikoli Malinkov stopped his car at a rest area on the southbound side of the Autobahn. With his binoculars in his hand, he walked a hundred meters or so up to a small hilltop where he could see far to the south. Spread out before him for several kilometers were open fields, broken only by small scattered areas of forest. He looked for tank tracks in the snow. He was learning that the Jagdpanther moved mostly at night, following the railroads and occasionally hiding its tracks in the waters of shallow streams. He had also realized that it was headed doggedly south.

He scanned the woodlines, looking for any telltale signs of its passage, for the Jagdpanther had shown that it was smart enough not to cross open ground unless absolutely necessary. One small village—Malinkov thought it was called Eschenlohe on the map—was nestled among the gently rolling meadows. Just to the east of it, he spotted the tracks. They were, as he had expected, beside a line of trees and not more than a few yards from a stream. On the streambank were the clear, black scars where a tracked vehicle had crawled out and headed immediately into the trees. A hundred yards farther south, he saw the tracks again, at the base of mountain with twin peaks, shrouded in mist.

Interesting, he thought. Gnokte had talked of a factory complex hidden beneath a mountain, somewhere in Bavaria. A perfect place to hide . . . and maybe repair a Jagdpanther? He considered it a likely possibility. Running his binoculars over the mountain slopes, he failed to see anything out of the ordinary until he looked closely at the base of the cliffs. There, he thought he picked out the well-camouflaged outline of a truck, but he was not sure.

He lowered the binoculars for a moment to rest his eyes, took a deep breath, and raised them again. There was some movement in the trees along the mountain's lower slope. A dark, square shadow was moving upward, leaving a trail in the snow.

A smile crossed his pockmarked face. "Jagd-panther!" he whispered. "You are getting careless, moving in the daylight. A fatal mistake this time, I believe." He stayed on the hilltop just long enough to pinpoint his position on the map and then ran to his car. The beast was flushed; at last the hunt was nearing its end. Again there was hope of success. He gunned his car out onto the Autobahn and took the next exit.

The Sherman clattered its way slowly down between the empty flatcars. Jim walked in front, using his flashlight as a guide as he carefully picked the route. It irked him somewhat to have Sherri driving. He could have done this easier by himself. But when the battle came, he could not drive and shoot also, so he had resolved that Sherri should get all of the driving practice possible.

He waved the flashlight to the right and the Sherman followed as he approached the high steel doors. Steadily, he guided it forward until its bow was almost touching the center of the doors, then he signaled for a stop and heard the engine drop roughly back to a high idle. He climbed up into the turret and put on his helmet. "I'm going to swing the turret to the rear to protect the gun tube," he said into the helmet microphone. The electric motor whined and the turret swung quickly to the rear. He closed the hatch above him. "Close your hatch," he said.

"I can't see anything with that closed," Sherri's voice crackled over the intercom.

"Close it and use the vision port, or you'll get a pile of rocks on your head."

There was a moment of relative silence before Sherri said, "It's closed. So okay, here goes." The Sherman lurched forward and the shrill screech of steel grating against steel rang above the engine's roar. The treads slipped for a moment on the cavern's tarmac floor and then dug in. The whole cavern seemed to scream as the Sherman inched its way forward, bending the doors before it. Steel beams dropped onto the turret, rattling everything inside as if Thor's hammer were banging on the hatches. Through his periscope, Jim saw a sliver of light. It grew steadily as they inched forward, pushing past the doors and breaking one of them off its hinges. Boulders half its size slid in front of the Sherman. A brown cloud of rocks and dirt showered down from the cliffs above as they broke free into the early, golden light of dawn.

On the other end of the intercom, Sherri was cheering as the Sherman reared up and climbed over another boulder.

"Slow it down," Jim called as he fought to open his hatch and look out. "Okay, that's better. Now, left turn and let's find ourselves a good ambush hole."

They moved carefully beside the cliffs for about fifty yards to where a shallow ravine ran east and west. With Jim guiding, they eased the Sherman down into it until only the gun tube and the top of the turret were visible. Jim swung the turret a few degrees in both directions, deciding he had an acceptable field of fire, and told Sherri to kill the engine.

A strange silence followed the big V-8's last sputter. Sherri climbed out of the driver's hatch and stood with Jim on the bow of the tank. "Good spot, I hope," she said, looking around.

"The Jagdpanther has to come up from somewhere out that way, because there isn't anything but cliffs behind us. With a little luck, we might get the first shot at his flank or rear." They left the tank and cut some limbs to camouflage the exposed turret. They stuck a few pine boughs into the ground near the gun muzzle and Jim smeared snow along the entire length of the tube. When they were finished, they checked their work from several yards in front of the position and decided it looked good.

"Now, we wait." Jim sighed, and with his arm around Sherri's shoulder, they walked back to the tank.

Ahead was the mountain, high and dark. The twin peaks stood shrouded in a slow swirl of mist. Drachenschlaft, "where the dragon sleeps"—there could be no mistaking it. The Jagdpanther skirted a small pasture behind a farmhouse just before dawn. Dogs had barked in the distance and cattle stirred nervously, but the Jagdpanther ignored them and continued on, moving carefully and quietly. When the sun rose, it was near the lower slopes and was tempted to use the road in order to move faster.

Patience—it had learned the importance of patience long, long ago. Patience was a critical element in warfare. An advantage always went to he who could choose the time and place for battle. And so the Jagdpanther approached the mountain using all the available cover, following the stream and then staying as far inside the woods as possible. It neared the old railroad bed and kept to the far side, using the embankment to help cover its approach. Just beyond the trees was the meadow where it had first trained with the others of its kind. They, of course, were all gone now, but that mattered not. They were inferior, and had they survived, it would have had to destroy them also, just as it must destroy that one last inferior hulk still rotting away inside the mountain. Yet, it sensed the presence of a powerful enemy, one more dangerous than a discarded Sherman sheathed in *Mirtheil* but without a master and without the knowledge of experience. No, there was something more. The elf girl had escaped, it sensed gradually, and so had the man who had so foolishly attacked it with his puny missile. They were here, somewhere on the mountain.

The Jagdpanther poked its long gun barrel cautiously from behind the trees. Before it stretched the Alpine meadow and, beyond that, the doors into the mountain. The doors were open. The enemy was out and battle was near. The Jagdpanther felt its power swell within it. Battle—glorious battle, it thrived on battle, grew stronger with each new kill. Battle—for battle it was built, for battle it lived and grew. It glowed blue. Black smoke belched from the exhaust pipes and the treads spun, kicking up snow and dirt as the Jagdpanther roared out across the open meadow.

Ten minutes earlier, Sherri had noticed faint blue sparks dancing on the Sherman's turret. Another two minutes passed before Jim spotted the Jagdpanther's shadow creeping slowly onto the lower slopes. "Target, eleven o'clock, a thousand meters out," he announced instinctively.

"Yeah, I see him," Sherri whispered as if she might be heard that far away. As quickly as the shadow appeared, it faded into the shadows again, and they waited. The seconds dragged like minutes, and minutes like hours.

"I hate this waiting," Sherri commented quietly.

"That's good," Jim answered without lowering his binoculars. "I'd be really worried about you if you were having fun."

"Yeah, well, maybe this was all a dumb idea. I mean, it all seemed to make a lot more sense down there inside the mountain."

"Dumb idea? What about us, was that a dumb idea, too?"

"No, not that. I mean about using this tank to fight that tank and—"

"You're right, it's a real dumb idea. Now, have you got a better one?"

"No, I don't. You know I don't."

Jim lowered his field glasses at last and pointed toward the treeline, just across the south corner of the meadow. "Then, we go with the only plan we've got."

Sherri took a nervous breath, held it for a second, and then released it noisily. "Oh, all right, let's do it. But, damn it, Fafner, kiss me or something, will you?"

Jim smiled and dropped into the turret. Beside him, Sherri did the same thing, and in a second's time she was against him with her arms locked tightly around his neck, and her lips hot and trembling against his own. She pulled away and gave him a weak smile. "Oh boy," she said, and started to crawl into the driver's seat. "This is the dumbest thing I ever did."

Jim watched her go, and then pulled on his helmet and slid into the commander's seat. He blinked his eyes to focus them through the periscope as he silently tracked the Jagdpanther's advance. It came on fast, heading straight for the open doors. As the range closed to within a hundred yards, Jim left the periscope and moved to the gunner's position. One red light glowed above the gun switch, indicating the gun was loaded and ready. He pressed his eyes against the telescopic sight and his hand found the turret traverse switch. He began tracking his target, turning the turret fast enough to place the cross hairs out in front of the charging vehicle.

The Jagdpanther moved with the grace of a running cat, its heavy suspension pumping like iron muscles in rhythm with the uneven ground beneath it. Clouds of snow boiled from beneath the spinning treads and blended with the coal-black diesel exhaust. It's beautiful, Jim thought. Like a single, painted work of art on some division commander's wall, it embodied all the fast, sweeping power of tank warfare—all of the Panzer Spirit.

The Jagdpanther was close now, very close, and still coming fast. In another few seconds it would pass directly in front of the Sherman's gun at a range of less than fifty meters. Jim's hand sweated on the trigger as he forced himself to hold his fire for another precious second.

"Now," he whispered, and squeezed the trigger. The old Sherman rocked back sharply on its suspension. A tiny stream of hydraulic oil squirted from a leaking line on the turret ceiling as the recoil system was suddenly and abruptly exercised after forty years of neglect. The muzzle blast blew down most of their pine-bough camouflage and shook the snow from the gun tube.

Through a mist of flying snow and smoke, they saw the Jagdpanther stumble under the 75's impact. Instantly, it locked one tread and slid side-

ways in the snow, its long gun tube swinging
quickly toward the Sherman's position.

"Go!" Jim yelled into the intercom. "Reverse, get
us out of here!" At that moment, he knew it had
been a mistake to shut off the engine. He had
weighed the possibility of it taking too long to re-
start against the danger of the exhaust fumes being
spotted.

If she floods it, we're dead, he thought as the
engine cranked over a bit slowly. The Jagdpanther
was still turning, but it had seen them, he knew. Its
gun was elevating, and in another second it would
be aimed directly at him. Still, the old V-8 cranked
steadily over and he could hear Sherri talking to it.

"Come on, engine, be a good engine; start for me,
right now!"

The engine fired, and Sherri found reverse on the
first try. Fifty yards away, the Jagdpanther was
stationary, its gun tube level, and Jim felt like he
could see all the way down it. The Sherman lurched
backward just as the Jagdpanther fired. Inside the
turret, it sounded as though someone was ringing a
bell, a very large bell. The impact almost knocked
Jim off his seat as the Sherman's engine roared
behind him, and he knew that somehow it was still
moving.

"Ouch, that hurt," Sherri said. Running in reverse, the Sherman crashed its way through a half-
dozen trees before Sherri brought it to a stop, as
Jim struggled to ram another round into the 75.

"Where is he?" Jim called as he closed the breech
and moved to the periscope on the hatch.

"I can't see him. He's behind the hill somewhere."

"Okay, left turn and move out slow. We'll try to
keep him guessing." Jim raised his eyes just above

the hatch and swung the turret around in the direction where they had last seen the Jagdpanther. This was a bad way to run a tank, he decided. He needed three more arms and another pair of legs to cover the jobs of commander, loader, and gunner all at the same time. It was, however, a little late to make any changes.

Thirty seconds passed before Jim ordered another right turn. This time, the steering clutch stuck for a second or two and the Sherman climbed partway up a tree trunk before its sheer weight bent the three-foot-thick pine down to the ground and trampled it beneath the treads. "Leave a few of those standing, if you can," Jim remarked dryly. "We might need the cover later."

"Stuff it. I'm doing the best I can," Sherri countered, and despite everything, Jim smiled and almost laughed. He was relaxing, concentrating on nothing but the problems of the battle at hand. It was always this way. The waiting was the worst part, and now that was over. The first round had been fired and from then on it was a game—a deadly one with no second prize, but a game nonetheless—and one had only to play it.

"Right turn and bring up your speed." He swung the turret around to the front.

"You don't want to go that way. The Jagdpanther's back there!"

"In front of us, I hope. If I guessed right, we'll be close enough to put our muzzle right up his exhaust pipe." Even as he spoke, the Jagdpanther's sloping side appeared through the trees, less than thirty yards to their front and moving. Jim jumped for the gunner's seat, pressed his eyes against the sights, and swung the turret. Diesel smoke was blowing across the turret as they passed behind the Jagdpanther a few feet away from its exhaust pipes. Jim squeezed the trigger just as the Jagdpanther climbed on the rough ground. Its bow rose and the rear deck dropped. The round went a few inches high, skimming over the Jagdpanther's engine bay and exploding beside the escape hatch. In a blinding flash of light, screaming shrapnel showered against the Sherman's hull.

"Don't slow down!" Jim warned as they pulled away. He risked a quick look over the rim of the hatch and saw the Jagdpanther turning fast. With its engine roaring, the Sherman plowed through a patch of dense thicket as Jim looked desperately for some kind of cover. Long before he found any, an 88 screamed over his head and shattered a tree trunk in front of them. Jim dropped to the turret floor and hurriedly reloaded. By the time he stuck his head out of the hatch again, the Jagdpanther was not in sight. "Turn her around, slow left."

"Where is he?"

"I don't know."

With the turn completed, Sherri stopped the tank and let the engine idle down. They were in an area of thick underbrush, where the trees were smaller and the visibility only a few yards. Jim looked nervously around, craning his neck above the turret. The Jagdpanther was out there, somewhere close— but where?

In the driver's compartment, Sherri also had her head above the hatch. "I can't see much from down here," she said. Even with the noisy idle of their own engine, they felt surrounded by ominous silence. The sun was almost above the mountain peaks and soft, pale light filtered through the trees to play in little dancing pools on the snowy forest floor.

"Maybe we got him," Jim said without really believing it.

"No way. He's out there, I can feel him—and he can feel me."

The seconds ticked by, slowly stretching into one minute and then another. Jim kept turning around in the turret, trying to look in all directions at once. The Sherman glowed with a pulsating blue, brighter and brighter. They felt the sound before they heard it. At first it was something halfway between ragged breathing and the rough idle of an engine.

"Listen," Sherri whispered, pulling off one of her earphones. "It's close, real close."

"Where, damn it?"

Trees to their right moved; a thirty-foot pine snapped at ground level and fell across the turret as Jim ducked for cover. "Reverse, fast!" he ordered, and started to swing the turret. The Jagdpanther was on them, long before the turret could swing through even a few degrees of arc. It charged out of the brush like an enraged bull elephant.

Gears ground on the Sherman as Sherri missed reverse, then found it. They lurched backward, just as the Jagdpanther's muzzle passed inches above Sherri's head. The Sherman was knocked sideways by the impact of the collision. It clipped another tree and only its own momentum kept it moving. Jim was knocked to the turret floor as the two tanks ground against each other. Amid a blizzard of falling branches, the two tanks broke away and again lost sight of each other in the heavy brush.

With Jim guiding her from the open hatch, Sherri continued to back the Sherman through the heavy forest. He saw the ravine too late to avoid it. "Halt," he yelled a split second before the Sherman's bow rose skyward and they dropped over the steep bank.

They slid backward, down into a tangle of vines
and dead trees, with Jim clinging to the hatch and
barely managing not to be thrown completely out.
The rear of the Sherman found a tiny stream at the
ravine's bottom and came to rest there, with its
bow still pointing up the bank.

"Sherri, you all right?"

"Oh sure, just great." She sounded almost in
tears. "I hurt everywhere. I miss my Ferrari. I miss
my mink and I want to go home and draw pictures.
Oh yeah, I'm just great. So, what do we do now?"

"It's pretty steep behind us, but let's try to back
up the other side. Take it slow and try to get it right
the first time."

"Got it," Sherri breathed nervously over the intercom, and carefully shifted into reverse. She
eased back slowly, giving the treads a chance to dig
in. The Sherman began to climb steadily for the
first yards and then slid back to the bottom. "The
way we came in is not as steep. I think we can crawl
out that way."

"No," Jim objected. "Too dangerous. If the Jagdpanther is waiting and catches us 'belly up' as we
come out, he'll put an 88 through us for sure. Remember, there isn't any *Mirtheil* on the bottom of
our hull."

"So what do we do?"

Jim took another deep breath and wished for a
better idea. When he did not get one, he said, "We
sit and we wait until he sticks his bow over the top
of this ravine and then we give him one in his
bottom."

"Is this idea going to work any better than your
last ones?"

Before there was time for any answer, the muzzle
of the Jagdpanther's 88 poked its way into view

above them. Jim scrambled for the gunner's position and pressed his eyes hard against the sights. The 88's muzzle moved slowly forward, extending further and further out over the ravine. Jim had begun to realize that the Jagdpanther did suffer from at least some of the inherent problems of other German-built tank destroyers. It had an extremely narrow field of vision and, being turretless, it sometimes took too long to bring its gun to bear on targets to its side and rear. These two facts alone seemed to be all that was keeping the Sherman alive.

Above them on the top of the ravine, the Jagdpanther's bow was now inching its way into view. Despite the winter cold, sweat was running freely down Jim's forehead as he held his sights on the Jagdpanther's lower hull and waited. One, two more seconds passed. The cross hairs centered between the Jagdpanther's treads.

Jim fired and yelled, *"Go,"* without waiting to see the results of his shot. The Sherman began trying to fight its way up the bank, slipping and sliding, throwing rocks and dirt as it went. Through his sight, Jim could no longer see any sign of the Jagdpanther, so he climbed quickly to the hatch and raised his head cautiously. Ten yards remained between the Sherman and the top of the ravine. Their momentum was good and it looked as if they would make it easily. Five yards . . . Jim raised himself higher, and there it was. The Jagdpanther was waiting for them just beyond the edge.

"Reverse, fast!" The order was beginning to sound very familiar. The Jagdpanther fired. Dirt and rocks and shrapnel blasted into the Sherman's left fender as they started sliding back down into the ravine.

"Now, what?" Sherri was yelling in his ear.

"Try to turn her down the ravine. We'll run downhill as far as we can!"

"Why not?" Sherri grunted as she locked the left tread and fought to find a forward gear. As she did, Jim stumbled to the ammo rack and loaded another round. "Two more in the rack," he noted grimly. "We better start doing some damage real soon."

The Sherman picked up speed quickly as it ran downhill, crashing along the brush-choked stream and pushing its way past boulders and fallen trees. A hundred or so yards later, they broke out onto the old railroad bed within sight of the cavern entrance. They crossed the roadbed quickly and turned their back to the mountain, keeping the raised roadbed between them and where the Jagdpanther must still be.

They moved cautiously now in a giant game of cat-and-mouse. The trees formed an archway ahead, where the roadbed started across the meadow beyond. There they saw the Jagdpanther suddenly roll up into sight.

"Halt," Jim ordered, and scrambled for the gunner's seat. Again, his cross hairs found their mark; again he squeezed the trigger and the Sherman rocked on its stiff suspension, rolling heavily with the weight of the blast. He saw the round hit—a clean, textbook shot on the gun mantlet, inches below the gun tube. The Jagdpanther shuddered, just as before.

"How much can it take?" Jim cursed, and hurried to reload. Sherri already had the Sherman moving in reverse, trying to back out of the line of fire, when they were hit. Over the intercom, he heard Sherri scream as the Sherman spun sideways and seemed to go out of control. Jim fell, still cradling the precious heavy round in his arms. His shoulder hit hard against the breech, sending pains shooting down his arm and up to his neck. Above the sights, he saw one of the switch boxes hanging loose, and several storage racks had been ripped from the turret wall.

For a moment he stared at the steel warhead cradled now against his chest and, while still on his knees, forced it into the gun. He staggered painfully to his feet and almost tripped over the expended shell casings which were rolling around on the turret floor. With his arms still hurting badly, he managed to close the breech.

"Sherri?" he called into the intercom.

"I got a fire up here, but now it's a lot easier to see out, there's a big hole where that little window used to be!"

Fire—the one most horrifying of all possible deaths for a tanker. Without slowing down, Jim grabbed one of the fire extinguishers he had taken off the truck and moved to the left side of the turret. Reaching forward, he sprayed white powder over Sherri's shoulder until she looked as if she had been fighting with sacks of flour. The fire died to a thick haze of gray smoke. It appeared to have started in the electrical system and ignited some of the leaking hydraulic oil. Jim noted the engine was still running.

"Try to keep us moving. Anything is better than taking another hit like that." He patted her shoulder and started back into the turret wondering how much power loss they had suffered.

He raised his head above the hatch, just far enough to see that they were backing down the roadbed. He ordered a slight turn to get them back under cover. In front of them, the Jagdpanther was

coming fast, grinding its way down the roadbed as
the Sherman tried to retreat. Jim gripped the turret
traverse lever and tried to swing his gun back on
target.

Nothing happened.

"No turret power," he cursed, and reached instead for the manual hand crank. It would be slow,
but there was no other way.

"He's close!" Sherri's voice pleaded in his ears.
"Can't you shoot?"

Jim ignored her; after all, there was really no real
appropriate reply.

He had one idea left. There is, he had once been
told by a drunk man in a bar, one Achilles' heel on
every tank ever built. One tiny place where thickness
of armor offers no protection. One place where a
round should, in theory at least, be guaranteed fatal.
That place is directly down the gun tube. A round
there should explode the round that was already
loaded, blowing off the breech inside the turret, and
bingo—instant brew-up. He'd always figured it was
bull, but now he was about to give it a try.

Chapter Twenty-two

As the Jagdpanther charged down at them along
the old railroad bed, Jim pressed his sweating face
against the sights and aimed the Sherman's gun.
He struggled to lay the cross hairs exactly on the
large, oval-shaped flash-hider mounted on the end

of the Jagdpanther's 88. It appeared to be an impossible shot, even at this range, but the Jagdpanther was running on the smooth surface of the railroad bed. The range was closing fast, too fast. At any second, the Jagdpanther might put another 88 into them. He could wait no longer; the cross hairs were on, the gun switch was on. Sweat ran in a steady stream down his face and into his eyes. This was insane, he thought, and fired.

The effect of the round was not immediately apparent. It exploded against the Jagdpanther's slanting, frontal armor and Jim thought at first that he had missed completely. But a split second before the Jagdpanther returned fire, he saw that the flash-hider was bent slightly sideways and a piece of it was missing. The 88 fired before he could see anything else. He instinctively braced for the impact of the round and feared it would be fatal.

But the impact never came. Instead the round whined off at a crazy angle and exploded against the cliffs—two hundred yards away.

"What happened?" Sherri asked.

"He just blew the end of his own gun tube off."

The Jagdpanther rolled to a stop, glowing a brilliant, pulsating blue, and for one fleeting moment, they thought it was going to burn in the blue flame Ehrler had mentioned.

It did not. Instead it seemed to shake itself, and once again started toward them.

"I think you just made it real mad," Sherri said.

From the Sherman's hatch, Jim looked desperately for some place to retreat. The Jagdpanther was ahead, blocking any chance of breaking out across the meadow. To his left was the rocky, brush-choked ravine down which they had recently retreated, and to his right, the forest was too open and descended off toward the stream. Behind him was the mountain, with its rock cliffs fifty yards away. The steel cavern doors hung open and crooked on their broken hinges—a gaping mouth, hungry to swallow up anything that dared to venture within its reach.

"Let's go for the tunnels!" Sherri's voice crackled suddenly over the intercom. He shuddered at the thought of trying to move a tank through that deadly maze of abandoned machinery and flooded shafts, but at the same time, he also knew it was their only chance of prolonging this hopeless fight.

"Okay, left turn," he ordered, and the Sherman lurched tiredly into motion with more smoke than normal pouring from her exhausts. They were losing the engine, he was sure. Engines usually did not last long when you fired up one that had been sitting for years. Even if the rings and bearings remained good, the oil or water pump usually failed pretty soon.

Sherri completed the turn, and they headed for the gaping doorway back into the mountain. "What does the oil pressure gauge read?" Jim asked.

"Which one is that?"

"Small and round, on the panel in front of you, reads zero to sixty pounds pressure."

"I don't think it's working."

"Tap on it."

There was a short pause as they roared on toward the black hole in the mountainside. "Okay, that's better," Sherri called. "It says about twenty now."

"Damn."

Darkness swallowed them as they rumbled in through the broken doors. The flatcars were shadowy forms as they passed down between the railroad sidings and the loading ramps. "Where's that first elevator shaft, the one you almost fell in?"

Sherri asked as she rode as high as she could in the damaged driver's compartment.

"Should be straight ahead. I can't see it—wait, there it is. Turn right, quick!" The black square was in front of them, getting closer with each clank of the Sherman's treads. Inches separated them from its deadly abyss when the steering clutch finally engaged. The Sherman jerked around into a right turn and smashed its way over a couple of drill presses. Jim held his breath. One piece of metal, if caught just right in the drive sprocket, could take off a tread in a matter of seconds, crippling the Sherman and leaving it unable to move.

He gave a slight sigh of relief as they at last freed themselves from the twisted mass of machinery and got the Sherman back on clear ground. "Straight ahead now, and real slow," he said into the intercom.

Behind them, the natural light of day was only a pinpoint—a single large star in a hellish night sky. Ahead, the phosphorous green subterranean glow outlined the square mine shaft in the cavern wall. Sherri eased the Sherman a little to the left as they entered and started down. Again, there was the mist, green and swirling in the eerie light.

"I don't remember it being this thick down in here before," Sherri noticed as they passed one of the side shafts. She was silent for another moment and then said, "Jim, this isn't working, is it? It's beating us."

"We've hit it every place that should stop it and, at best, I think maybe we've done some minor damage to its gunnery."

"There's gotta be some other way, something we're doing wrong."

Jim did not answer as they crawled slowly down

the mine shaft, moving ever deeper into the bowels
of the mountain. They felt the distant rumble within
the mountain more than they actually heard it
above the engine's ragged idle. The Sherman rocked
slightly with an uneven vibration. Dirt and a few
small pebbles dropped from above and rattled off
Jim's helmet. "Damn," Sherri breathed nervously.
"I think the whole mountain is pissed off now."

The rumbling died away and the tunnel divided
in front of them. Sherri said that they should go to
the right. "Go," Jim answered, having no idea why
it should matter, and then added, "Slow down.
There's something on the left."

They passed a vertical shaft bored down from the
side of the tunnel. The hoist and buckets for lifting
ore up from some lower level were still hanging in
the gloom. Ahead, the tunnel split once again, and
this time they went left. Around the next corner,
several small ore cars blocked the passage. "Push
them out of the way," Jim ordered, and the Sherman moved ahead, pushing the cars for a few yards
before one of them derailed and the others followed,
overturning in the shaft. The Sherman flattened
them and continued on.

There were more divisions in the tunnel, and
places where other tunnels crossed, and they began
to wonder if they were simply running in circles.
The Sherman's blue glow, which had faded when
they first entered the cavern, began to return.
Slowly at first, and then growing steadily brighter,
it bathed the tunnel around them in its eerie light.

"It's followed us," Sherri said. "And it's not far
away."

Jim dropped into the turret and rammed another
shell into the main gun. "Just one more after this
one," he said, and closed the breech. They neared

an intersection where two tunnels crossed. The Sherman's blue glow remained constant as they inched their way forward and hesitated for a moment at the junction.

"No sign of anything," Jim said, and they moved on, but a few yards down the tunnel the Sherman's glow began to pulsate rapidly. Jim shot a worried glance over his shoulder at the crossroads behind them. There was a faint blue aura there, also. "He's behind us!"

Sherri jammed her accelerator pedal to the floor and Jim started cranking the turret around by hand. Halfway around, the gun tube struck rock. "The tunnel's too narrow, I can't swing the damned gun!"

"Great. So what do I do?"

"Keep going. Look for a corner, any corner." He saw the Jagdpanther roll into the center of the junction behind them. For a moment it hesitated and then started turning. Its own gun tube struck the wall, and the Jagdpanther seemed to jerk angrily as it backed into the wall behind it and was forced to make three separate moves to complete its turn.

"Hold on, he's going to fire any second now," Jim said none too calmly into the intercom, and then ducked into the turret. Above him was a blinding flash of light. Rocks rained onto the turret like hail on a tin roof.

"He missed!" Sherri cheered.

"Not by much he didn't," Jim growled back, and peeked out the hatch. "Looks like a corner up ahead to the right."

"I see it. No sweat."

"No sweat, your ass. You got about five seconds before he fires again."

The corner came clearly into view. The Sherman scraped the walls as Sherri turned sharply. The Jagdpanther's next round exploded on the corner of the wall directly over the engine bay and gave them another shower of rocks. On they ran, blindly for a while, taking right and left turns on nothing but intuition. The Sherman's glow faded slightly as the minutes dragged by without any apparent end to the maze.

"Can you still see your fuel gauge?" Jim asked.

"Yeah, but I don't want to look at it. It was on empty when we came in here. You got any new ideas?"

"Yeah, one." Jim tried to project some note of confidence in his voice. "The next place the tunnel splits, we'll turn around, back down one of the shafts just far enough to cover the junction, shut it down, and wait."

"I really was hoping for a better idea than that."

"So was I."

It was several more minutes before they approached another split in the tunnel. "Do you smell something?" Jim asked, and strained his eyes to see into the misty gloom.

"Yeah," Sherri returned quickly, "like smoke. We on fire again?"

Jim spun around to look at the engine bay, expecting to see smoke or flames. "Engine's okay," he reported, seeing nothing unusual, and stuck his head back into the turret. Once again, everything looked unchanged.

"I think it's coming from up ahead," Sherri called.

The Sherman's bow was just passing what had looked like another tunnel division when Jim stuck his head back out of the turret. "Halt!" he yelled.

"Shut it down, quick." A giant jagged crack in the mountain was directly in front of them. Beyond its edge was nothing but air and rising smoke, silhouetted against a dull red glow. The end of the Sherman's gun tube was out over the edge when the treads squeaked in protest and then locked. The tank bowed forward and, from his dizzying position on the turret, Jim could see tongues of orange flame leaping from a smoldering sea of molten rock hundreds of feet below. The Sherman halted, teetering on the brink.

"I don't think I want to see this," Sherri said.

"You don't," Jim assured her, in almost a whisper. "Just put it in reverse, but hold your brakes while you do it. One more inch forward is too much."

With all her strength, Sherri held one foot on the brake pedal and pushed in the clutch with the other. She moved the shift lever slowly and found what seemed to be reverse just as the brake pedal began to feel spongy under her pressure. For one sickening half-second, the Sherman leaned forward. Treads spun, kicking rocks and gravel off into the inferno below. The left tread caught first, kicking the rear around, and they backed away at an angle.

From a wide spot at the end of the shaft, a narrow ledge ran along the edge of the abyss in both directions. It was wide enough for the Sherman to move on but not to turn around. Resolving that this was as far as they could go, they inched backward a few more yards along the right-hand ledge, turned the Sherman's frontal armor in the direction of the shaft, and shut off the engine.

"Do you know where we are?" Sherri asked as she pulled off her helmet and leaned over the gun tube for a better view of the pit below them where crimson hues of molten rock bubbled in the mist.

"Yeah," Jim answered as he climbed out of the hatch. "The end of the trail, for us."

"Worse than that." Sherri sighed. "This could be just where the Jagdpanther wanted us."

He sat down tiredly on the front of the turret. "What are you talking about?"

Sherri gave him an embarrassed look. "There's one other little part of the legend. Ehrler mentioned it, but I forgot. *Mirtheil* can also be destroyed by returning it to the fires from which it was forged." She pointed over the edge, at the boiling caldron below. "And right down there, I'm afraid, are the fires in question."

Jim grunted thoughtfully. "That would work both ways, right?"

"Huh?"

"If the *Mirtheil* that went into both of these tanks was forged here, then a fall from this cliff is just as fatal to the Jagdpanther as it is to us."

"Yeah, I think so."

Jim smiled grimly. "Well then, that's the best odds we've had all day."

"Gee, you're an optimist for once. There may be some hope for you yet." She kissed him then, lightly at first, with her hands cupping his dirty face and holding it preciously in front of her. And then, his arms were around her tightly, crushing her to him, holding her in an embrace that they well knew might be their last. As the kiss ended, she lowered her head to his shoulder and her fingers combed through the hair on the back of his neck. "I hope I don't lose you again today. I just spent a very long lifetime trying to find you."

"So did I." The Sherman began to glow beneath them. Jim sighed. "It's time."

Sherri looked down at the blue aura rising around them. "Take care, my love," she whispered, then pulled away from him and took a deep breath. "Okay, let's get this over with."

Jim watched as she climbed gracefully through the tiny hatch over the driver's compartment and began pulling on her helmet. He donned his own helmet and lowered himself into the turret. This time he pulled the hatch closed behind him and eased himself into the gunner's seat. "Can you hear me?" he asked after he plugged in his intercom.

"Just like you're whispering in my ear." Sherri's voice was steady.

"Don't try to start her yet. Let's play dead for as long as we can."

Sherri answered in a voice totally devoid of humor. "That was a terrible choice of words."

From within the mine-shaft entrance came the familiar electric blue glow. It brightened slowly as the Jagdpanther approached. It was moving very slowly, Jim thought. Perhaps for the first time it was aware that it faced the possibility of failure.

The muzzle with its broken flash-hider appeared first, inching forward into view. Jim made a slight adjustment on his sight and gripped the trigger. The Jagdpanther's bow was in view now as, bathed in the blue light, it inched out onto the ledge. Its long gun tube extended far out over the abyss before it halted and began to turn slowly toward the Sherman. Wide treads clawed at the rock, chipping and grinding as they turned the massive war machine. The gun tube rose slightly and leveled at the Sherman's turret.

"I think he's going to shoot," Sherri whispered through the intercom.

"No. He needs to push us off into the fire—make the destruction complete. Start engine!" Two seconds passed as Sherri pushed the primer and then turned on the ignition switch. The big V-8 rolled slowly over, picked up a few RPMs, and then slowed again.

"It won't go!" Sherri's voice bordered on desperation.

"It's flooded! Hold the accelerator down for a couple of seconds and try it again."

"Have we got a couple of seconds?" Sherri asked as the Jagdpanther moved toward them, confident now of an easy kill. It stopped suddenly and glowed brighter. The wide, clawlike treads spun in reverse as the Jagdpanther hurried to back onto the wide place and swing its bow toward the shaft entrance. Something moved there.

"What the hell. . . ?" Jim whispered, and moved his sights for a better look. "We got more company. There's somebody standing there with some kind of a rocket launcher."

"It's Graff," Sherri said, "or Malinkov, or whatever his name is. How in hell did he get here?"

The Jagdpanther jerked uneasily back and forth, swinging its gun first toward Malinkov and then toward the Sherman, but never getting far enough to aim at either.

"This is crazy," Jim said, "but it looks like it can't make up its mind who to attack."

"Since when is it afraid of a little old rocket launcher?" Sherri said.

The answer hit Jim like a sledgehammer. "Try the engine, now! It's going to attack Malinkov first."

"Why the hell would it do a stupid thing like that?" Sherri sounded very confused as she hit the starter and the engine ground over one more time.

"Good solid Nazi logic, taught to it by—"

The Jagdpanther rolled toward Malinkov, and he fired the RPG-7. The rocket bounced off the Jagd-panther's sloping frontal armor like a harmless rock and whined away over the abyss. Malinkov took a few staggering steps back against the tunnel wall. The damaged flash-hider came at him like a swift sword with many blades. He reached for it stupidly, grabbed it with his bare hands, and tried to force it away from his body. Points of jagged steel tore his hands to the bone, but still he held on. The elf face on the fender laughed at him as his bloody hands slid along the gun tube and the jagged edges of the muzzle brake ripped into his chest, nailing him against the tunnel wall.

Blood ran in a steady stream down onto the tunnel floor as the Jagdpanther backed away with Malinkov impaled on the gun tube. At the same instant the Sherman's engine caught and roared unsteadily to life. Sherri dropped the transmission into high-range first gear and they lurched forward. "Try to hit him as far forward as you can!"

The Jagdpanther was turning toward them. It was a brilliant electric blue now with squiggling snakes of blue fire dancing all over it. The Sher-man's speed increased quickly. The old V-8 was screaming madly behind them. The Jagdpanther backed another few inches until its rear road wheel hung just on the edge of the abyss. "Another mistake," Jim whispered, and sighted the Sher-man's gun at the ground in front of that road wheel. "Firing main gun," he announced calmly, and squeezed the trigger.

Rocks flew out from the edge of the abyss. The Jagdpanther staggered for a moment, as if losing its balance. The bow rose slightly and then the treads again dug in, and it started forward just as the Sherman smashed into its right front fender. The Maybach diesel screamed at a fever pitch as the two steel monsters locked together in mortal combat against a hellish backdrop of smoke and molten rock. *Mirtheil* met *Mirtheil*, crushing, ripping, and smashing. The Jagdpanther began to slowly inch forward, pushing the Sherman in front of it. The wide treads caught on the Sherman's hull at the transmission housing and climbed instantly up onto the left fender. The Jagdpanther tilted suddenly, losing traction as the Sherman lunged forward, pushing its way almost beneath it.

Sherri glimpsed Malinkov's body dancing puppetlike with the flash-hider protruding out of the middle of his back. The Jagdpanther's treads began clawing their way up the bow and toward the broken hatch inches above her head. Again the sneering face on the fender glared at her, but this time, it did not seem to be laughing. There was fear in those eyes—and recognition. She knew then, in that one microsecond of time immemorial, that she had fought here, on this same ledge, once before in some distant, past life.

Then suddenly, all she could see were the treads, spinning above her and tearing themselves apart. Things were breaking all around her; glass was shattering, wiring was coming off the wall, and gauges were popping to pieces.

"Get out of there!" she heard Jim yell at her, and then the intercom went dead and she could hear only the scream of the engines. Leaving, she knew, was out of the question. Without her, the engine would stop. She ducked as low as she could in the driver's compartment. Her leg was numb against the accelerator. How long could it all go on? she wondered. How long could the engines continue to scream? Above her, she saw the bottom of the Jagd-panther's hull for an instant and then it was gone. There was smoke in the driver's compartment, thick and hot and choking, but she no longer cared. The Jagdpanther was falling, falling down, down into the molten caldron below—back into the fires from which it was forged. Nothing else really mattered. There was a final scream of tortured steel behind her and the Sherman's engine stopped.

Someone was pulling on her, dragging her back out of the driver's compartment and into the turret, pushing and pulling her up, telling her to climb and to hurry. She saw the hatch above and reached for it. She was outside the tank. Jim was there, lifting her down off the hull and carrying her in his arms.

From the ledge, they saw the Jagdpanther founder on the molten sea below. Then a flaming star of brilliant blue engulfed it, hung there for a few unreal seconds, and then dissolved into nothing.

Sherri turned to see the Sherman for one last time, perched precariously on the edge of the abyss. One tread was off and the drive sprocket had been sheared away. The gun tube hung at a sad angle and smoke poured out of the engine bay.

"It's dying, isn't it?" she said weakly, and then the rocks gave way beneath it. It toppled forward and followed the Jagdpanther down into the fiery abyss. For a moment, it also was a star of blue, and then it was gone.

Chapter Twenty-three

"I DON'T understand it," Sherri said as she stared off over the restless sea of molten lava bubbling in the abyss below them. "Why did it attack Malinkov? He was no threat to it."

"We'll never know." Jim shook his head and took her arm as they walked back along the rock ledge.

"You knew," she insisted. "You told me it would attack him first."

"It was just an educated guess, based on history."

"Yeah?"

"The Germanic mind has always considered Russia its greatest threat. That's probably why Hitler invaded Russia so early in World War II and then ended up fighting on two fronts."

"It doesn't sound very smart."

"No, but that's also why German soldiers fought like hell against Russians, just to stay alive long enough so they could surrender to Americans. In their case, it was damned good thinking. The Russians worked their prisoners to death in slave-labor camps, while the Americans sent their prisoners home and financed the rebuilding of Germany."

Sherri nodded. "And everything the Jagdpanther knew, it learned from Von Norden, who was a German officer and a Nazi. That instinct would have been in his mind, subconsciously perhaps, but definitely there."

"If Von Norden knew it, the Jagdpanther probably learned it," Jim concluded, and then shrugged. "Well, it's a theory, anyway."

With one last look behind them, they started walking up the sloping mine shaft, back toward

the main cavern. The mountain rumbled again—
louder this time—and the ground shook beneath
them.

"What's happening?" Sherri asked, looking
around.

"I don't know, but I don't like it." The rumbling
continued and they hurried on. It was not until
they reached the factory area that they saw what
had happened. At the far end of the factory area,
there should have been sunlight coming through
the open doors. There was none.

"Landslide," Jim cursed.

"The mountain is hiding its secrets," Sherri said
in a faraway voice.

"Come on," Jim said, taking her arm. "We'll use
the door near the old forges."

"We can try," Sherri said, "but I think it's been
blocked too." The mountain remained silent now
as they made their way back through the abandoned living quarters and down to the ancient
forges. When they reached the door, it opened to
Sherri's touch but beyond it were only rocks and
darkness. She looked up at the ceiling for a moment
and then said, "It's all right. We'll have to go out
the same way we came in, back up through the air
shaft. It's been left open for us."

"That means you'll have to walk back across that
beam and climb the cliff again," Jim reminded her.

"No sweat." She shrugged.

They lingered for a while at the ancient forges
and Sherri seemed reluctant to leave. She ran her
hand lovingly over the stones. "They're all gone,"
she said with a tear in her eye. "The elves—they
were my people, and now, it's like I'm the only one
left." She looked strangely at Jim. "Maybe I'm not
supposed to leave, this time."

"Yes, you are." Jim's voice was gentle. "You've kept them alive with your pictures. You can't stop doing that."

Sherri looked into his eyes for a long time and finally nodded. "I'm ready," she said. "Let's go."

They made the long climb back up the catwalk and across the beam to the crack in the cliff. Sherri climbed easily and opened the door back into the maze of stalagmites and crystal-covered walls. The green mist thickened again as they walked, climbing slowly higher up inside the mountain.

The shadowy statue materialized before them once again. "I want to see it one last time," Sherri said, and walked close to it. She stood silently in front of it for a long moment and then a small sound escaped her. "Jim, look!"

He took a few steps and looked over her shoulder. The statue was different now. It was still Sherri. The jeweled crown was on her head and flowers still laced her hair. But now she wore a tight sweater, ski pants, and boots. A familiar mink jacket was draped over her shoulders, and in one hand was a tanker's helmet.

"They changed it," she blurted out. "The elves— they're still here somewhere, hiding in the mists." She turned quickly several times, looking in different directions. "I can feel them, but I just can't quite see them." She turned suddenly back to the runes and read them all once again.

A look of confusion had spread across her face when she looked up at Jim and said, "They still say the same thing. That means it's not over. The evil is still here, and someday, in some other life, you and I, my love, must fight it again."

"*From out of the mists of time she rode, on a beast*

that breathed fire," Jim whispered, and took her hand as they left the statue behind and started the long climb up, out of the mountain.

Epilogue

⚡⚡

ANSBACH, WEST GERMANY. The United States Army Headquarters, Europe, announced today that they had successfully shut down a major terrorist ring, which had been responsible for several recent attacks on both military and civilian personnel. General Gerard Walker, overall commander for the operation, would say only that all details of the operation must remain classified, in order to protect future antiterrorist operations.

General Walker growled thoughtfully as he tossed the copy of *Stars and Stripes* onto his desk. He turned his attention to an official-looking U.S. Government form: *Permanent appointment to position of museum curator, U.S. Army Tank Museum, Ansbach.* He scanned it quickly. *Mr. James Fafner is hereby appointed to the position of . . .* The rest he already knew, so he scribbled his name at the bottom and tossed it into a basket on his desk marked Outgoing.

Beneath it was a pay voucher, authorizing the payment of a consultant's fee to Sherri Vail, Inc. in San Francisco, California. He looked at the amount, coughed, and then signed it.

"Hold my calls," he said, touching his intercom button. "I'm in conference." He reached for a cigar and lit it. A smile slowly crossed his hard face as he propped his feet up on his desk. From a drawer, he pulled out a comic book and smiled at the title: *Princess of Elfland, #27*.

"Sooner or later," he said to himself, "if I read enough of these damned things, I'm going to figure out what the hell those two really did."